"BAD DOG!"

The brute transform[ed] ... writhing spider of a ... a quick shake. Bones popped and the brute went limp.

Its mate overcame her surprise and lunged for Remo's ankle—but the ankle vanished at the last possible instant. Her teeth slammed shut on empty air, then Remo's leather shoe squished her head like a bug.

The other rebel dogs had a target for their blood mania—and their better-behaved pack members joined in. The pack closed in for the kill. The compact, muscular bodies flew into Remo Williams and tried to latch on to his arms and legs, clothing, neck, anything they could get their fangs into.

"Sit," Remo said, flinging a big beast to the carpet, with such momentum the thing's ribs shattered and pierced its fur.

Remo swatted another animal against the wall.

"Stay."

CREATED BY WARREN MURPHY & RICHARD SAPIR

THE DESTROYER™

BAD DOG

A GOLD EAGLE BOOK FROM

WORLDWIDE®

TORONTO • NEW YORK • LONDON
AMSTERDAM • PARIS • SYDNEY • HAMBURG
STOCKHOLM • ATHENS • TOKYO • MILAN
MADRID • WARSAW • BUDAPEST • AUCKLAND

First edition April 2006

ISBN 0-373-63258-4

Special thanks and acknowledgment to
Tim Somheil for his contribution to this work.

BAD DOG

Printed in U.S.A.

And for the Glorious House of Sinanju,
at www.warrenmurphy.com

1

Johnson Jonas accepted a titanium driver and eyeballed the shaft, then addressed the tee, took his stance and scrutinized the length of the fairway a yard at a time. He examined the sand traps and the trickle of a creek that lurked in the rough, and studied the green for blemishes. Not a blade of grass was out of place.

Jonas allowed his face to feel the speed of the breeze. The wind was from the northeast, gentle. Not that he enjoyed the breeze—it was a factor working against him. He judged it was not much of a factor so long as he timed his strokes carefully during the frequent doldrums.

Johnson Jonas rehearsed his swing on an imaginary ball, mentally walking himself through perfect posture and controlled movement. He made a practice swing, judged it to be satisfactory, then addressed his actual ball.

It was a custom-made ball. The per-ball price was exorbitant by some standards, but Johnson Jonas wouldn't sacrifice even one iota of performance to substandard equipment.

He knew perfectly well that the most expensive golf

clubs and golf balls wouldn't make a good golfer out of
a poor golfer. But he also knew that a less-than-perfect
club would hit with imperfect precision. He knew that
a golf ball without precise balance could drift off course,
and even a fraction of deviance could grow to a big slice
over a hundred yards. He refused to allow shoddy equipment to affect his playing. Jonas was a man who liked
to control his environment. By equipping himself with
only the best tools—be they clubs, balls, lawyers,
market analysts or wives—he increased his likelihood
of success in life. Life, to Jonas, meant business, and all
the accoutrements that made a man successful in business.

Only once in a great while did he take the time to be
by himself long enough to relax. He relaxed on the golf
course—but there was no reason not to make the most
effective use of his time even then. So he used his re-
laxation time to sharpen his skills. Since business was
conducted on the golf course frequently, one must be
good enough to win—or good enough to take a dive
without looking as if you were losing deliberately.

Something smelled bad, forcing Jonas to step away
from the ball. He wrinkled his nose at the sky and traced
the direction of the smell. It was surprising that he
smelled anything at all. The Connecticut Heights Country Club went to great lengths to keep out anything foul-
smelling.

Good God. Droppings, right on the green.

"Phone," he demanded.

His phone landed in his hand.

"Wayne."

The phone dialed Wayne Baum, director of the club.

"Good morning, Mr. Jonas."

"Not so good. You've got droppings on the greens."

"Animal droppings?" Baum asked.

"I certainly hope they're not human."

Jonas thrust away the phone and waited impatiently for the arrival of the groundskeeping staff. Jeremy Doleenz arrived on the scene in minutes and didn't get out a "good morning" before he was directed to the offending droppings.

"Deer, I imagine," Doleenz concluded after cocooning the mess in several layers of plastic wrap and tucking it away, then spritzing the sod with odor neutralizer. "Can't keep them out, what with the public land and all."

Groundskeeper Doleenz went away.

"Phone!" Jonas snapped.

Nothing.

"Phone," he said in a more reasonable tone of voice.

The phone emerged. Jonas irritably told it to call the office. Then he controlled his voice and told it again. It complied.

"Give me Avino," he said to whatever human or machine answered.

"Paul Avino."

"I want this problem with the country club to go away."

"Which problem, sir?"

"The public-lands problem. We've got animals shit-ting all over the place because we can't put up a fence because we've got a few acres of public land in the mid-dle of the rough on the fourteenth hole. What are you going to do about it?"

"Retain a lawyer who specializes in property law?" Avino suggested. "My expertise is corporate finance."

"Whatever. Just get it handled. While you're at it, what's with the field trippers? There must be a hundred old grandmas and grandpas on my golf course this morning. They're not even members, but we had to let them come and see our course."

"I don't know anything about it, sir."

"Connecticut Heights Convalescence Home, they call it."

"Oh. My mother is there. It's for the elderly and in-firm. I guess this is their monthly outing."

"I see," Jonas snarled. "And is your mother a mem-ber of the Connecticut Heights Country Club?"

"No, sir."

"Then why is she here?"

"Another concession to public-use lands, I imagine."

"More reason to take care of the public-use-lands problem, I think you'll agree."

"Yes, sir."

Jonas flipped off the phone and pushed it away. "Take it," Jonas snapped needlessly.

"Yes, sir."

Jonas was startled by the sound of a human voice. "Who're you?"

"Your caddy, sir."

Jonas cocked his head and slit his eyes. "You are a stinking liar."

"No, sir, I'm really your caddy."

"*That* is my caddy!" Jonas thrust his hand at the Caddy-Droid X9000. It was as big as a lawn tractor and steered itself around the course using a global positioning system, a digital map of the course geography and proximity sensors to keep it from hitting a human or landscape feature. Slots in the droid were powered by small pneumatic fingers to accept and deliver various items such as golf clubs, balls, cell phone, beverages and cigars. Every bit of it was voice-activated.

"It's not working properly, sir. Remember, I was sent along this morning to attend to it?"

Jonas now recalled all of this. He had been particularly annoyed that the C-Droid was creating trouble again. For a quarter million bucks, the thing should be perfect. But it dropped items, especially cell phones. Sometimes commercial air traffic messed up its guidance and it wandered into the sand.

"Fine. Whatever. Keep your mouth shut."

"Yes, sir."

"I said, keep your mouth shut."

The human caddy—actually, he was just a mobile mechanic—nodded.

Finally, after what seemed like hours of delay, Jonas

prepared to hit the ball. He pulled back on the wood—
and froze at the apex of the swing when something
growled at him from the rough.

"Oh, now what?" He spotted something looking at
him from the low vegetation.

It was a dog.

"Oh, that's beautiful. We don't have deer, we have
a damn stray roaming around the place."

Another head appeared in the rough. And another.

"It's a pack," Jonas said.

The pack growled. They trotted out of the rough and
formed a tight circle around Johnson Jonas. Powerful-
looking creatures, with dense white and brown and
black coats. They had brilliant dark brown eyes, and
Jonas thought he could actually see the muscles flex
around their jaws. Whatever breed they were, they were
all the same. Even the markings looked similar, as if
they came from the same lineage. They were sniffing
the air around Johnson Jonas, and low growls rumbled
deep in their chests.

"One of those show-dog kennels left its damn gate
open and the inventory got out," he announced. He
didn't feel as brave as he sounded.

"Phone!"

Nothing happened.

"Phone," he said, trying to modulate for the speech-
recognition system.

The phone emerged from its storage cell on the
Caddy-Droid X9000 and extended to Jonas on alumi-

num fingers. Jonas would have to reach over the dogs to take it.

"You!" Jonas snapped. "Call for help."

The scared-looking human driver wasn't as stupid as he looked. He slithered out of the driver's seat of the Caddie-Droid and onto the roof, a protective canopy of hard plastic, then reached down to take the cell phone. He opened it and poked the buttons, then held it up to Jonas, shaking his head wildly.

"What the hell's the matter with you?"

The driver shook his head and pointed at the phone.

"You a goddamn mime?"

"You told me not to speak, sir."

"What are you talking about? Don't answer that. Just call for help."

"The phone won't work."

"'Course not. It's my phone. I don't want other people using it. Hold it up."

The driver held out the phone and Jonas shouted, "Phone Wayne!" The phone remained lifeless. "Phone Wayne. *Wayne. Wayne*! Wayne."

The dogs were distracted by the strange modulation of his voice as he tried to communicate with the phone, but their distraction didn't last and they were growling again.

"Toss it to me," Jonas said.

The driver gave it a neat, underhand toss and the cell phone sailed three feet over the tips of Jonas's fingers.

"Idiot! Miserable fucking idiot! You don't know how

to throw a damn cell phone?" Jonas helplessly watched it bounce on the green a few feet away, still open and awaiting his orders.

The shouting agitated the dogs. The growls became snarling and barking.

"Okay, it's all okay," Jonas said, calming his voice and lowering his hands, but the dogs couldn't be appeased. They tightened the circle, then lunged at his legs. Two of the brutes got a good, strong grip and crushed the flesh of his ankles. Their jaws were more powerful than they even looked.

Jonas collapsed. He kicked, but then the other dogs clamped down on his feet. Another animal set its jaws into Jonas's neck. A pair of mutts ripped through his trousers and tore into the flesh of his upper thigh.

Jonas made a horrid sound, a suffering, dying-animal sound.

The display on his phone came to life, but no one saw the message that said "Dialing Mom." It rang and someone picked up on the other end.

"Hello, dear. Johnson? Are you there?"

Only the dogs heard old Mrs. Jonas on the phone, and they didn't care.

Johnson Jonas himself was going through catastrophic shutdown of bodily functions. His eyes fixed on the empty sky and his breath came out in a long, ugly rattle.

The Caddie-Droid seemed to think that meant something and handed the corpse a sandwedge.

THE HUMAN CADDY was already gone, legs pumping him up and down the rolling hillocks alongside the green. He felt as if he were riding a roller coaster. He craned his neck over his shoulder, expecting to see the dogs closing in on him, but they weren't there.

He should have been looking where he was going. He ran into a hillock and tripped on his face. His nose gushed blood and he did a pushup that brought him back to his feet and running again. He was sure the delay gave the dogs time to catch up to him, but he didn't dare look back again. He had to get to the safety of the golf center.

When he topped the next rise, he saw that the golf center was not a safe place to be after all.

There were more dogs. Many more dogs, sturdy white and brown and black beasts—and they were slaughtering the visitors from the Connecticut Heights Convalescence Home. Picnickers, day-trippers, as well as serious golfers, were being attacked everywhere the caddy looked.

A group of bridge players was being torn to pieces on the red-and-white-checked tablecloth they had spread under a big, leafy tree. Their pitcher of lemonade spilled and mixed with their flowing blood.

A trio of severe women with the look of just-retired schoolmarms had been laid out on the first tee, and two of them were having their flesh torn open. Wayne Baum, the club director, was making a valiant attempt at running away, but he was brought down by a pair of animals that growled at him, nuzzled him, then tore into his soft tissues savagely.

Somewhere deep inside his mind the caddy noticed that some were being slaughtered while others were ignored. There seemed to be some deliberation to the selection. But he didn't really think of this until later on. Right now all he was worried about was saving his own skin.

It wasn't as if there was anyone he could help here. There were more dogs than there were people. He wasn't about to start trying to drive them off. The caddy looked for a way out. The first tee, the patio cocktail bar and the landscaped grounds were all turned to killing fields. For a moment he entertained the idea of making a mad dash through the slaughter and getting inside the building, then he saw more dogs on the inside. Behind the glass of the French doors were frantic movements of human beings being slaughtered in the formal lounge.

The caddy could only go back the way he had come—across the course. Back he went, running fast, veering away from the pack of dogs that had attacked Mr. Jonas. He couldn't avoid them, though, and they came into view and closed in on the caddy. Effortlessly, they loped along with him.

With their alert faces and perked ears, they didn't look like savage animals. If the caddy met one of them on the street he might have tried to make friends with it. They actually looked like sociable creatures. They encircled him, and when he ran faster, they simply trotted along. One of them came close and gave him a big sniff. The caddy didn't know what to do. Should he push the thing away, or let it do what it wanted? The animal came in front of him and put on the brakes. The caddy got the message and stopped running. The dog held him there with threatening snarls.

The other dogs closed in and sniffed at him. It wasn't a hungry sniff, just an attentive sniff, as if the caddy had been rolling around in something interesting. For the first time, the driver noticed the leather collars around the necks of all the dogs. The collars all matched and were affixed with irregular shapes, black or metallic. Why in the world, the caddy wondered briefly, would a pack of strays all wear the same, expensive-looking collars?

Then, an even more surprising thing happened.

The dogs stopped sniffing the caddy and trotted away without giving him a backward glance.

2

His name was Remo and he didn't see a need for karate lessons.

"Are you satisfied with the man you are now?" the dojo owner asked.

"Sure," Remo said. "Why not?"

Dojo owner, Xavier Force, arched his eyebrows and made a sad sort of a smile. "I'll tell you why not, Remo. You're a mess. You're out of shape, your posture is poor and your skin is sallow. You do not demonstrate self-confidence, my friend. I can help you gain back your confidence—and reclaim your manhood."

"In karate class?"

"Yes. What you need to understand is that karate is much more than just fighting skills. Karate is a way of looking at the world. It's a way of living. It will give you back the spark that is missing from your life. Don't you want that?"

Remo scratched his chin. "I feel okay the way I am."

"I got news for you," X. Force said. "You're not okay. You're tepid. You're passive, buddy."

Remo said, "No, I'm not, really. In my company, you have to be aggressive to be the biggest order-taker in the East Coast district. They call me Ram-Rod Remo."

"To your face. But what do they call you behind your back?" X. Force asked.

Remo shifted in his seat across the dojo owner's desk. "Well, once, one of the other regional guys said I was spineless."

"Yes?" X. Force nodded.

"I broke his legs."

"Oh, really?"

Remo shifted again, as if making an embarrassing confession. "Yeah. Really."

"I don't believe you."

"I didn't mean to. I got a little carried away."

"With what? A sledgehammer?"

"No. Just my hands."

The dojo owner made an unpleasant sound, like air leaking out of the tight, spitty orifice of a rubber balloon.

"You don't believe me?" Remo asked.

"No way, Jose."

"It's Remo. Now, I was telling you about one hundred percent silk Koh-Mo-Nos, the newest trend in martial-arts wear."

"Remo, why in the world do you think I'd want to buy these ugly ass robes for my students? From the guy who doesn't even practice martial arts."

"Oh, I do practice martial arts, just not karate," Remo

said. "How do you think I broke that guy's legs? The guy was a tae kwon do black belt."

"So, you're trying to tell me that you practice some other kind of martial arts, and you use these robes, and now you want me to buy them, too."

"They're the biggest new trend in martial-arts wear."

"You said that already."

"Sorry."

"You sure don't have much of a sales pitch," the dojo owner continued. "In fact, I think you are full of shit. I don't think you are even a martial-arts-uniform company salesmen at all. In fact, I have never heard of the Koh-Mo-Nos company. I haven't heard about a new trend in martial-arts wear. In fact, I have never seen anything so ugly in my life."

He grabbed the wad of silk off his desk and held it up as if it were very dirty laundry. It was a silk robe in a mishmash of colors. There were lavenders and earth browns. There were honey maple and gleaming oranges. It all clashed.

"Okay," Remo said. "Sorry to waste your time." He stood up, with his cardboard box of Koh-Mo-Nos under one arm, and caught the sample robe that dojo owner X. Force flung at him.

At the door of the small dojo office, Remo stopped and seemed to have something more to say. X. Force looked up from some correspondence and said, "What now?"

"I bet that you would take my Koh-Mo-Nos a little

more seriously if you took me, personally, more seriously," Remo said.

"Yeah? You got that right."

"Well, how about a demonstration?"

"Dude, be careful what you ask for. Are you challenging me?"

"If you're not too busy."

"You have got to be kidding," X. Force said. He shook his head at the papers on his desk. "Okay. You know what? I *never* turn down a combat challenge. Not because I'm full of myself, you understand. It's my reputation. I got this school, and I can't afford to ever give anybody the idea that I might be a coward, or it would affect my enrollment. I really don't wanna fight you, Remo. I really don't want to wipe your ass all over the floor of my dojo. But now I'm going to. This is just my way of apologizing in advance."

"Oh," Remo said. "Okay. Thank you for being upfront."

X. Force stomped out into the one large room that made up the classroom of the X. Force Karate Academy. It was wall-to-wall mats. X. Force stepped out of his sneakers and turned on Remo.

"Okay, let's do this."

Remo shifted from foot to foot. His eyes flitted over the gathering of teenagers in brown belts being led through their warm-up routines.

"With a class in session? With them watching?"

"This dojo is busy morning, noon and night. There

ain't no time to do it when there ain't nobody watching. You want this competition, it is going to be a real competition and it's going to be now. Put up or shut up."

"Hey, I have no problem with that," Remo said. "But I do want to put on my one hundred percent silk Koh-Mo-No first."

"Fine. Just do it."

Remo ducked into the changing room and emerged wearing a long tea-green-and-banana yellow Koh-Mo-No. He twisted his hands, and for the first time X. Force noticed the man had extraordinarily thick wrists.

"I don't know if that thing is fair in a fight," X. Force said. "It's the strangest damn getup I've ever seen. I may be laughing too hard to defend myself."

But Remo stepped forward and adopted some sort of a readiness stance. X. Force had never seen anything quite like it. But he put up his fists and prepared to engage his competitor.

The brown-belt class came to a halt and the students moved in to watch. They spread out along the edges of the mats, giving Remo and X. Force room to engage. X. Force bounced on his feet, moved in close and delivered a pair of strikes to the head of the Koh-Mo-No robe salesmen. It was a lightning-fast attack that never quite seemed to connect. X. Force couldn't breathe suddenly, and he wondered why. He wondered why he was looking at his own ceiling. He came to his senses, only to discover he was stretched out on his back with the wind knocked out of him.

He rose to his feet, arms held up in a defensive position. He bounced on the balls of his feet and glared at Remo. The brown belts were hissing among themselves. The instructor of the brown-belt class was wide-eyed with alarm.

"You okay?" Remo asked. "Sorry about that."

"You're faster than I gave you credit for," X. Force said. "I guess I ought to really have put some effort into this fight."

And with that, X. Force moved in tight on Remo the Koh-Mo-No salesman. He delivered a blow to his stomach and a kick with the bottom of his own bare foot. He sensed rather than saw Remo evading the gut-crunching blow, and X. Force compensated the strike zone with well-honed reflexes. Still, he couldn't zero in on his target—Remo had vanished.

When the momentum of the strike was dissipated Remo reappeared, delivering an up-front and personal body blow that happened so fast that the karate instructor couldn't even see the technique. X. Force felt himself going in circles, then he toppled onto his back on the mat. Again.

He tried to spring back to his feet, but his feet wouldn't work. It took him a full minute to get some sort of control over his body—and it was the longest, most humiliating minute of his life.

The brown-belt class made sounds of enthusiastic awe.

"What was that?" X. Force barked. "That was no karate move, friend."

"Oh, sorry, I don't know karate. I told you that. I know this other sort of martial art. It's kind of better than karate."

"Wow, you're not kidding," said a teenage punk with a buzz top. "Did you see Sensei X. go in circles like that?"

"Did you see him go down like that?" added one of his classmates.

"What is your martial art called?" the buzz-cut brown-belt demanded.

"Uh, well, I'm kind of glad you asked. It's an old school of fighting that has never been seen in this country before."

"How come you know it, then?" Buzz Cut asked.

"My sensei immigrated to the U.S. He taught me everything I know."

X. Force came off the mat and lashed out at Remo when Remo was turned away. This was a dishonorable attack. It was not proper karate. The blow was also too vicious to be called strictly sportsmanlike—it was meant to injure him, maybe badly. One flat, hard hand speared into Remo's throat, while the palm of the other hand thrust into Remo's upper lip.

But neither blow connected and X. Force's forward momentum wasn't checked before someone grabbed his arm and used it for leverage. X. Force found himself the unwilling participant in a pirouette. He tried to plant his feet on the ground, but he was nudged in the shoulder, and the rotating continued. He spun around three times, four times, five times, and he let his body go limp, hoping he would simply collapse in a heap. A heap was slightly less humiliating than a spin. There were shouts of excitement from the young brown belts, and they weren't encouraging their beloved sensei. The kids were into the show-off named Remo.

X. Force stopped with such force it was like hitting a wall, and X. Force's inner ear simply stopped trying to cope. He wobbled, his eyes rolled to the side and he flopped onto the mat with his head rolling from side to side as if he were seriously drunk.

There was a surge of cheering and gasps of amazement and juvenile utterances of appreciation.

"That was the coolest thing I have ever seen."

"Whoa!"

"Wow!"

"Oh man!"

"Dude, you have *got* to teach us how to do that!"

"But what *is* it? Come on, man, tell us."

Remo seemed to be thinking it over. Then he said in a low voice, "Who knows *t'ai shou jiao ch'uan*?"

"Tie Shoe Joe Chin?"

"Good. It means Ultimate Fast Wrestling Fist, and like I said, it's been sort of a private fraternity up until now. It's been practiced in a secret monastery in China since it was invented in the 1920s, but the monks finally got fed up with all the other martial arts getting all the glory. Obviously, they've got the best martial art of all. Some of these monks came to the U.S. to recruit students, which is what I am. Now we're going around spreading the word. Now that you've seen the demonstration, I hope you'll be interested in learning about it."

The buzz-cut kid had a head that looked like it was flattened during birth but never popped back into shape. His brains worked, however. "You trying to sell something? You want us to join a different dojo?"

"Not at all," Remo said, holding his hands up in a sincere-looking oath-taking salute. "This is the only dojo in the city that's authorized to teach *t'ai shou jiao ch'uan*."

"It is?" asked Buzz Cut.

"It is?" X. Force groaned.

"Why do you think Sensei Xavier let me toss his ass around the place?"

"I did?"

"He's one of the first martial arts professionals in this country to get trained in *t'ai shou jiao ch'uan*." Remo turned and brought the bruised-looking X. Force to his feet. Hidden from other eyes, he displayed a pamphlet entitled *T'ai Shou Jiao Ch'uan: Secrets of the Ultimate Martial Art*. Remo winked and tucked it into the front of X. Force's robe. X. Force blearily nodded.

"Really, Sensei X?" Buzz Cut asked.

"Really," X. Force agreed.

"You saw what it can do," Remo said. "You wanna kick ass—you study karate. You want to *really* kick serious ass, then you study the way of the Ultimate Fast Wrestling Fist. Up to you. But I have to tell you, not many people get the chance to be a martial-arts pioneer."

The kids were vibrating with excitement.

"Can we join up, Sensei X?"

"When are you starting classes, Sensei X?"

"Wait," the buzz-cut kid said. "What about the *gi?*"

Remo looked down at his robe. "Wearing a Koh-Mo-No is a part of being a *t'ai shou jiao ch'uan* student."

"It looks really fruity. Do we have to wear it?"

"Yeah," Remo said. "Only, you know what? If you ever see a guy wearing one of these things, and you tell him it's fruity, you're as good as dead. Because the guys who wear these things know how to do what I just did."

"How do we get 'em?"

"You said they were fruity."

"They are fruity, but it's worth it to learn to tie shoe."

"Wait a second," Buzz Cut said loudly, and the tide of the excitement halted. "How much?"

"Free with your *t'ai shou jiao ch'uan* tuition," Remo said.

The buzz-cut wedge-head kid made a grunt of delight. "Where do I sign, man?"

REMO LEFT X. Force's academy feeling better than he had in weeks. For once, everything was working out for him. His little scheme was working out better than he ever imagined.

For months he had been burdened with truckloads of Koh-Mo-Nos—silk robes in a bizarre assortment of incompatible earth tones and pastels. Going into business selling the things was not his idea. He hadn't even been consulted. Still, he had an obligation to get them in the hands of the American people.

But even Americans had enough taste to see the Koh-Mo-No as an ugly hybrid of uncomplimentary styles. The only retail success had come from selling them to homemakers for disassembling and reuse as slipcovers for throw pillows and end tables. That didn't help. The Koh-Mo-Nos had to be *worn*. That was their purpose.

Finally, Remo found a way to make it happen. It started a few weeks before, when he was stopped at a red light, with a bunch of kids crossing to a grammar school. One of the kids was in a white robe and a black belt.

"Hey, what's with the outfit?" Remo asked him.

"It's a *gi*. I take karate. You got a problem with that?"

"I just didn't know you could wear them to school."

"My *gi* is a badge of pride," the kid announced defiantly. "Besides, if some *fat-ass jock faggot* gets to wear his football jersey to school, I should be able to wear my *gi*. Right? I said, am I right?"

Another kid crossing the street was a hulk of an eighth-grader in a football jersey, who was quick to speak up. "Yeah, right, of course, Tony. No argument from me." The big hulk hurried away.

The black-belt kid grinned and gave Remo a thumbs-up.

A minute later, he spotted another kid in a *gi*, and then another.

One *gi* was a novelty. Three *gi* were a trend.

Remo found a bookstore. It did have some books. They were in a narrow space behind the coffee shop, beyond the wall of displays for music and video. With the help of the attendant at the information desk, he even located a few books on martial arts. He bought *What You Need to Know to Succeed At Tae Kwon Do* and *The Way of the Happy Sun Fist Warrior—the Wise Path to Enlightenment Using the World's Most Effective Martial Arts Practices*.

He took them to the Kinkie Kopies and slapped them on the counter. The clerk was startled when he took his brand-new books out of the bookstore shopping bag and began ripping their pages out.

"I need some books printed. Take this stuff, put it together like it's all from the same book. Name it *Mysterious Secrets of the Ultimate Martial Art* or something like that.

"This is copyrighted material," the clerk said. "I can't copy it."

Remo said. "Oh. I'm not going to sell it or anything. Just give it away."

"It's still illegal. You need public-domain material."

"Ah, crap. Where do you get that kind of stuff?"

"Well, you could research old books with expired copyrights." The clerk was a young, full-bodied, bright-looking woman. Her name tag said she was Daphne.

"Sounds like a lot of work," Remo complained.

"Web sites might have the material in electronic format already."

"Me and computers don't get along."

"I could do the research for you and just charge you by the hour."

"Great, Daphne," Remo said. "How long would it take?"

"Depends on what you want and how easily I find the material."

Remo nodded. "I'm not picky. I just need a martial-arts manual of some kind. It's got to look sort of real. Then I'll want some copies."

"Ten? Ten thousand?"

"Are those my only choices?"

"You can get as many or as few as you want, but the bigger the quantity, the less it costs per copy."

Costs were not something Remo worried about. He was, theoretically, rich as Midas. "Let's go with ten thousand copies. Can I pick it up tomorrow?"

Daphne was alarmed. "I was going to suggest a couple of weeks."

"But can I pick it up tomorrow?"

"To rush it through, it will cost more. And I'll have to pull an all-nighter putting the content together. I don't even know what you want to include."

"Daphne, I trust you implicitly. You have total creative freedom." Remo handed her a credit card. She began adding up charges and bit her lip when she handed him the charge slip, printed with an outrageous total. He signed it without looking and pulled out his sack of Koh-Mo-Nos. "Here's the real trick. Can you make it look like the people in the pictures are wearing these things?"

Daphne didn't know quite what to make of the odd colors, but she was enjoying the feel of the silk as she rubbed it between her fingers. "I'll use Photo Shop to work them in. Can I call you if I have questions?" Daphne asked, sliding the credit card to him.

"No questions. Just do it. Keep this in case you need it." He slid the credit card to her again. "And these." He dropped the sack of Koh-Mo-Nos on her counter.

"Fill this out please," she said, and handed him a client contact form.

Remo twisted his neck to read the last name on his credit card, then wrote Remo Suavay on the info form. Under Address he penned in the word "hotel."

"Which hotel?" Daphne asked, tucking her lip under her teeth again. It was a cute habit, and Daphne was a cute Kinkie Kopies clerk, but Remo had other things on his mind at the moment. He dodged the hotel question, even when Daphne insisted that it was company policy that all clients provide their address and marital status.

"Why would you care about my marital status?" Remo asked.

"To be honest, I don't care one way or another," cute Daphne said, leaning over the counter in such a way that strained the integrity of her blouse buttons.

"Well, I'm married," Remo lied.

"Will she be there later tonight? I might need to come over and consult with you about your pamphlet design."

"I told you, I trust your decisions. No consultation needed. Besides, what do I know about martial arts?"

Daphne was still trying to wheedle the name of his hotel out of him as Remo backed out the door, promising to return the following day.

The truth was, he was tempted to accept Daphne's bold come-on, but he was in a big hurry to get his pamphlets. The Koh-Mo-No monkey had been perched on his back for months, and he was eager to see if his crazy scheme worked for him. Daphne didn't have time to dally if she was going to have his instruction manual done tomorrow.

Turning down an eager young Kinkie clerk was easier than it looked. Remo Williams got bold come-ons from women all the time. It was a side effect of his training.

Interestingly, his training was in martial arts—and he really did know the mysterious secrets of the ultimate martial art. The ultimate martial art was Sinanju, and Remo was a Master of Sinanju.

Compared to Sinanju, other martial arts were slap-fights. It had been born in the village that was also called Sinanju, where the fishing was poor and the people seemed to have no agricultural skills besides fishing. This was as true today as it was thousands of years ago, when the village was founded and the people found for the first time that they did not have enough to eat.

Desperate for a way to get food into the hungry mouths of their starving children, the Sinanju men began to hire themselves out as assassins. Killing other human beings they could do.

And they were good at it.

Their skills improved, and new skills, according to the legends, were bestowed on the Sinanju assassins by the gods themselves. The tradition developed until there was just one assassin from the village at any given time. This Master of Sinanju was the absolute ruler of the village and controller of the income that came from his employment—and that income expanded as the reputation of the Sinanju Masters spread around the world. The Masters could now command fees that only kings could pay, and it became their custom to accept employment only from the rulers of nations.

The knowledge of the Masters was jealously guarded. A Sinanju Master had capabilities that no other humans had—even if they were simply extensions of normal human abilities. A Sinanju Master could see a weapon flying at him and then could move himself fast enough to dodge it—a slung rock, an arrow shaft or a bullet, it made no difference. A Master could sense the pressure threshold of the surface of a pond and adjust his stride so perfectly that he would seem to be walking on water.

A Sinanju Master controlled his body, producing

heat or conserving it like no one else could. This made it possible for him to stay comfortable in freezing temperatures or desert heat.

There was more—great skills and strange side effects. One side effect was the odd attraction that a Sinanju Master inspired in the opposite sex. It had to do with pheromones or fluctuating neurons or something. Remo didn't understand it, and he was always striving to control it. And he could control it, when he really tried. The problem was, he had to keep working at it, every day, or the aromatic neurons sprang to life again and he started getting hit on by Kinkie Kopies clerks.

He was tired of the unwanted attention. It was pretty easy to say no, especially when there was an end in sight to the Koh-Mo-No fiasco.

Twenty-four hours later and the pamphlets were ready as promised. Daphne had a copy for him to examine on the counter. She was wearing a Koh-Mo-No—pumpkin-orange and lime-green. Daphne was not a skinny girl, and she wore a Koh-Mo-No that was several sizes too small. When she leaned over from the other side of the counter, the pamphlet disappeared beneath her cute, mostly exposed bosom.

"You're supposed to wear something underneath those, you know," Remo pointed out.

"Does this meet with your approval?" She nodded down at her front. She might have been referring to the brochure, except the brochure was buried under Daphne's décolletage.

"Yes, very nice," Remo said politely.

"Well, how do you know when you haven't seen it all, silly! Here, I'll show you." Daphne teasingly withdrew the Koh-Mo-No belt, but Remo snatched the brochure out from under her like a magician yanking a tablecloth from beneath a couple of overfilled punch bowls.

"Daphne, this is great." Remo had the brochure just inches from his face, so there would be no doubt what it was he was praising. "Where'd you come up with this name, *t'ai shou jiao ch'uan*? I love it. And you have Koh-Mo-Nos in every picture. Wonderful. What's this?" He waved the page-four illustration of a man in a Koh-Mo-No spinning his opponent in a full circle, like he was spinning a top. "The Spin Strike of Disorientation?" Remo read happily.

"It's the signature move of the *t'ai shou jiao ch'uan* warrior," Daphne explained. "You send your opponent flying in a circle."

"I can do that. Perfect."

"When you spin strike somebody, it leaves them breathless and vulnerable."

"You really have a lot to teach me about martial arts," Remo said. "But time's a-wastin'. Thanks so much."

Daphne was frustrated beyond belief when Remo Williams departed with his boxes of brochures.

Remo Williams's loss was Tom Burrows's gain. When Burrows strolled into the shop to get his MBA thesis copied, he found himself face-to-face with a cute young clerk spilling out of a strange, silky robe and sexually frustrated to the point of madness. She didn't even ask for his name before dragging him into the back room.

Meanwhile, Remo began visiting dojos up and down the East Coast, jump-starting the bold new martial art called Ultimate Fast Wrestling Fist.

3

The Foreman was the best at what he did, and he did whatever needed doing.

He wasn't a hit man precisely, although he had been the instrument of more murders than he bothered to count. He was really a jack-of-all-trades. Whatever you wanted done, no matter how illegal it was, the Foreman got it done. He was the ultimate amoral handyman.

His methods were unorthodox, especially in high-risk endeavors. Sometimes his progress was slow. Often he would approach a specific task from one angle, perform much planning and allocating of resources, then abandon the plan without warning. For no good reason, other than to explain that he had discovered inherent risks in the plan, and another avenue of attack was needed. This made some of his prospective employers extremely suspicious—but there was no questioning his success rate. He would only do the job his way, but he always got the job done.

A couple of months back, Jackie Mack had called the Foreman a "fuggin' flake."

"They say he's a flake but they say he gets the job done, no matter what kind of a job," said his second-in-command.

Jack McIntyre glowered. "I know what they say. They say he's not shy about spending money and then throwing it away when the job's half done."

"But he always finishes the job."

"Aye. They say that, too."

"He never gets caught."

"Aye. But his people do. Sometimes."

"But there's no comebacks, Jackie," said Jackie Mack's second-in-command, touching him lightly on the nape of the neck.

"I know."

"That's what we need now, Jack. Somebody who will do the job right, t'hell with how much it costs us."

Jackie Mack didn't like the very idea of the Foreman. The man was too mysterious and strange, and it meant he had something to hide. The fingers stroking his neck were softening him up, and he jerked away angrily. "We can't go throwing away so much cash."

"We can't afford not to, Jack." Maureen McIntyre lowered her voice, although they were alone on the littered New York beach, where they sometimes came to discuss matters of grave security.

"Maur, listen, lass, he wants five hundred grand, plus expenses."

"We have it."

"It's too much!"

"No amount is too much if it gives us the Tommy Johns district." Maureen folded her arms defiantly, pressing up her bosom. The peasant blouse with the scooped collar was overfilled before—now the contents bulged out the top.

Jackie tried to keep his mind on the subject at hand. "It's a waste of money. The Foreman's a known dingbat."

"And you're known as a cheap-ass tightwad who won't spend five bucks for a knife when there's a rope 'round your throat."

"Maur, it's too much money, and that settles it. Aye?"

With that, Jackie McIntyre walked back up the beach to their waiting car. The discussion was at a close. He wouldn't tolerate her bringing it up again.

Maureen McIntyre followed after him, feeling sad but determined. She knew what she had to do.

She got up in the deep of the night, just as she always did, and headed for the washroom, but on her way she lifted Jack's mobile phone from the pocket of the pants she'd flung over a chair back earlier in the evening.

It had been an enjoyable farewell romp.

She entered the washroom, turned on water and found the number in Jackie's call history. She dialed it and was mildly surprised to hear a man answer, saying, "Foreman."

"This is Maureen McIntyre."

"I see."

"My cousin has decided your services are too expensive."

"Fine with me. I've taken another job, anyway. Did Jackie Mack have you call to haggle me down?"

"No. I know you're not a negotiator. As I said, it's Jackie who thinks you're too expensive. Not me. I am willing to pay you the asking price for the job."

"You'll hire me. Working independent of Jackie Mack?"

"Yeah. And there's another job, too. I understand you offer discount rates for multiple jobs. I hope you can spare the time from your other job?"

"Maybe."

"Will you work for me, then?"

"Let's meet to discuss it," the Foreman said.

4

The Foreman felt an itch of excitement when he hung up the phone. Something about the conversation had intrigued him in a way he couldn't explain.

He really shouldn't be taking side jobs right now, but it wasn't that he was busy. He spent most days sitting around watching the clock tick, then going out for a few hours each night for a quick job in the New York metropolitan area. He planned on being here for days, still. Why not take a few hours to enjoy the company of the intriguing Ms. Maureen McIntyre? He would meet her, just to hear what she had in mind.

The Foreman steered his rented pleasure boat out into the Atlantic Ocean, miles off the Maine coast, keeping his boat alongside the Swedish shipping vessel. It was an unimpressive cargo chip that was just finishing its crossing from Stockholm—but this boat wouldn't be docking in America anytime soon.

It had been a long night already, and the captain of the Swedish ship was irritated about all the hours spent cruising back and forth in international waters. The captain didn't understand why his contact in the little boat was leading him around like this—it wasn't as if the coast guard was on their tail.

But the Foreman wasn't about to let the ship dock. Not yet. Every time he directed the Swede to steer his ship into the mainland, he sensed danger. He had headed them in to Walker's Point, Portland, Cape Small, a couple of smaller port towns, and there was always a silent alarm going off in the Foreman's head.

The captain could stew all he wanted, but the Foreman wasn't going to drive his precious cargo into a risky landing. The cargo was too important, and the captain was paid to follow instructions.

The Foreman had lived his entire life with people who couldn't understand what he was doing or why he was doing it, and the Foreman never explained his actions to anyone. He was always right—that was good enough for him.

He was right this time, too.

He was assuring the safety of the ship by being with the ship. If the ship steered into a port where there was danger, then the Foreman was in the same danger and the warning went off. None of the warnings were especially keen, so the risk might be small but it was a true risk. The Foreman *never* took risks.

Finally he directed the captain to steer into port at a small fishing village called Fleet. "Better be a go this time. I'm sick of playing games," the captain growled, but the Foreman ignored him.

The landing was turning out to be a safe one. No warning instincts came to life in the Foreman's head, even when they were slowing down to tie up at the wobbly dock at Fleet. The wharf structure should have worried the Foreman. It looked like a stiff breeze would collapse it. But he sensed no danger. The Fleet wharf would hold itself together at least until he was done using it. The Foreman raced ahead of the Swedish ship to make the necessary arrangements.

No danger alert came from the sea-worn fisherman who manned the tiny house on the end of the pier. He hobbled out to greet the Foreman with paperwork on a clipboard.

The harbormaster had stale-beer breath and he had a mobile phone with a credit card scanner.

"Two ships?" He looked up from the paperwork.

"The other ship will be here shortly." The Foreman poked a thumb over his shoulder. "Charge all talking fees to my card, please."

The Scandinavian shipping vessel had just come through the mouth of the harbor and slowed as if afraid to approach the dock.

The harbormaster shook his head. "We don't have no cargo equipment here," he said. "Just a crane for fishing nets. You want me to wake up Alfie? Alfie runs the crane."

"We don't need equipment," the Foreman said. "We don't have much cargo, and you have been extremely helpful. We would appreciate it very much if you allowed us to go about our business without interference."

While talking, the Foreman pulled out a tight wad of folded bills and tucked it into the threadbare pocket of the harbormaster's flannel shirt. The master craned his neck to see the wad. He couldn't see how much it was exactly, but it was more than enough.

"Will do," he said, and returned to his little shack, where the window lit up with the glow of a television screen. The Foreman wondered what the old harbormaster was watching.

The Swedish ship slowed and made contact with the wharf with a feather touch—and still the structure swayed gently on soft pilings.

The Foreman had already called for his trucks. They, too, had spent hours wandering along the Maine shore waiting for the ship to come in. They arrived in Fleet in minutes and backed up to the end of the dock, but none of the drivers dared to venture farther.

The loading bay on the side of the Swedish ship swung open. The rear panels of the trucks were raised. The Foreman tested the winds and knew that there was no danger at this moment. It was time to off-load the cargo.

The dogs emerged from the ship's bay in ordered rows, and there wasn't a yip or a whine. They padded down the ramp, across the wharf and into the trucks, ninety animals making the transition in a matter of two minutes. The trucks drove away.

The Swedish captain nudged his ship from the wharf just as carefully as he had approached it. The pier had leaned into the ship, and there was a real chance the structure would collapse without the ship's support. The dock groaned and leaned.

The Foreman motored away from Fleet and, the last time he looked, the wharf was swaying gently. The harbormaster in his little hut must have felt the movement underfoot, but he never left the television.

The Foreman would have enjoyed a few hours of TV time, too, but as soon as he got home he would need to check on operations out west.

Utah should be going to the dogs right about now.

5

The commies were taking over Utah. Karl Cherbourg knew all along somebody was going to take over Utah, but he expected it to be foreigners of particular Oriental persuasion.

See, Utah was stationed in close proximity to the treacherous enemy nation of Canada, where they were letting the slant-eyes take over. Utah was also close to the West Coast, where the anti-American city of Seattle was overrun with slant-eyes. So it made sense to Karl that it would be the slant-eyes who moved in on Utah.

Or maybe the darkies. Or maybe the towel-heads. Hell, they all hated true white people, and they were all proved to be violent by nature.

Especially the redskins. Of all the non-Americans who ever came and dirtied up *his* country, it was the Indians he hated most at this time in his life. It was the dirt-squatting Tontos who took Karl Cherbourg's wages on a regular basis. Them and their Ho-Chunk-No Casino, with their sleazy blackjack dealers and rigged-up quarter slots. Not a month went by when Karl didn't have his money stolen from him by the Indians.

With all the lesser races slinking around looking for trouble, who'd have thought the Red Menace would come crawling back, too? It was unexpected, but it shouldn't have been. The Communists had never actually gone away. They just went undercover as legitimate businessmen and set their sights on wager-earners like Karl Cherbourg and Utah Sheet Metal Specialists, Inc.

Utah Sheet Metal surrendered to the commies without so much as a struggle; they changed the company health insurance over to a Health Maintenance Organization.

"See how they suck you in?" he said. "They don't give us no choice. They just sign us up against our will. Now we're in bed with Stalin."

Janice at the coil cutter said, "Well, I like the HMO better. And it costs less than the old plan."

"You been brainwashed, Janice. You been tricked and now you're a part of the socialist system."

"Well, I like it," Janice said.

Karl nodded, satisfied. Janice didn't argue because she knew she couldn't win. Karl was a well-read man, and he was a man with strong beliefs that carried him through each and every day. You couldn't argue with a man like him because he knew what he stood for and he knew why he stood for it.

Janice was a cog in the wheel. Karl liked to think he had educated her a little during the months they worked side by side, her cutting off pieces of metal, him stamping them in the big press. Janice always let him talk. She nodded a lot. She didn't argue with him much. He was sure she was becoming a smarter human being from their association.

But then sometimes she'd come up with a zinger. Yesterday she'd said, "Personally, I don't mind black people. Seems to me they're just as many good ones and bad ones as there is white people or Mexicans or what have you."

Karl was floored. "I thought we settled this months ago, Janice."

Karl explained everything again. Janice didn't debate him, but was she really listening? If she was really listening, how could she still have such asinine opinions? How could she let herself stay blind to the truth about, as she called them, "black people"?

Maybe it was because she didn't give him enough respect. If she knew his full story then she would know he wasn't just a thinker, but a true doer. Karl had done some mighty important things in his day, and they were things he rarely talked about. But it was time to tell Janice. She was special. He looked down on her like his own daughter.

At the very least, he knew he could trust her. Janice was a woman who didn't blab to no one.

"Janice," he began, timing his words around the regular clunk of the five-hundred-pound metal press. "It's time you ought to know a thing about me."

Janice gave him a funny look. "What?"

"Something personal from my past."

"Why you want to tell me something like that?"

"I just do.

Janice could at least have shown some appreciation. Wasn't every day that a man unburdened himself. But she just fed off another few feet of steel from the coil and pressed the button to slit it.

The fresh-cut square of steel traveled on rollers to the cradle at Karl's feet like some sort of a silent acknowledgment. Karl lifted the sheet in his greasy leather gloves and popped it into the press plate. He palmed the activate switch and the press dropped with a heavy crunch and lifted again.

Karl removed the formed steel pieces that would be assembled up the line and leave the factory as a Crafty Jack Tool Organizer.

"You know I come from Alabama, right, Janice? I ever tell you that?"

Janice didn't answer. She was making a noisy slit in the sheet metal. Karl didn't wait because he knew he had told her a hundred times.

"Folks in Alabama are different from folks here in Utah. Down in Alabama, we get things done, instead of sitting on our butts all day. Know what I mean?"

"No," Janice said.

"Don't take no offense now, but the folks in Utah don't notice the world going on around them. They don't pay attention to what's going wrong with the world and they sure don't do anything about it. Down in Alabama, we're a little better. You see?"

"No."

Karl was getting a mite irritated with Janice's attitude. She wasn't exactly attending to him as well as she should have, and here he was telling her the most important thing ever.

"Me and some friends of mine in Alabama, we paid attention and we saw what was wrong and we took steps sometimes to right them wrongs."

Janice stared at him. "Karl, I hope you're not telling me about something illegal. Because I don't want to hear it."

"I'm telling you about something patriotic, and I think it's important that you hear it."

"Why?" Janice had her hands on her hips and she looked defiant.

"Because I care about you, Janice."

Janice didn't bat an eye. "You're as old as my daddy."

Karl raised his hand. "I'm not making a pass at you, girl, I'm saying I care about you some and I want to tell you something I think is important."

Janice turned back to her coil of steel and slit another square.

"You're right about me being old. I'm fifty-nine and I keep thinking I'm going to get the cancer. See, my daddy died of pancreatic cancer and his daddy, too. Both at my age."

Janice put her own greasy-gloved hand to her mouth. "You had the new physical, didn't you!" she exclaimed. "Karl, are you sick?"

"Nah. Passed with flying colors. But I almost wish I *would* get the cancer already, 'cause as soon as I know I'm dying, I can tell the whole world the truth. But right now, I'm just telling you alone."

Janice's eyes were blazing. Now she seemed mad about something. Who knew what these women were thinking of half the time?

"I used to be a part of a group of local boys in Alabama, see, and we fought for the freedom of the white man."

Janice hit the slitter button. "I don't want to hear it, Karl."

"It's important, and I know you won't tell no one. See, there were some blacks in the town who got to feeling too comfortable living among white folks. They didn't know their places."

Janice said nothing. She didn't look at him.

"So, we strung 'em up."

Now she looked at him. "My God. You killed them?"

"Killed 'em dead. Seven black boys, all told. Seems like every two, three years the darkies would get b'lligerent, trying to poke their heads up, you know? Not staying down where they belong? Then me and my boys, we'd do our deed for keeping the civil order, so to speak, and then everything would be back to normal again for a while. When you think about it, we was really saving lives. You know, them darkies start feeling free to move around town and do whatever they please, they get all wild and running gangs and putting their whores on the street corners and selling dope to the white kids, and next they start killing each other. So as I look at it, we kept down the murder rate in our little town."

Janice hadn't slit any metal in a while.

"That's the kind of man I am, Janice. Now you know."

"I think I'm going to be sick."

"Are you on your monthly, girl?"

"I'm going to call the police." Janice took off her gloves. "I guess I better make it the FBI."

Karl was stunned. "I told you this in confidence, girl."

"I never said I'd keep my mouth shut about anything, Karl. I didn't even want you to tell me."

"You wouldn't cause me no trouble. I'll deny saying anything."

Janice was thinking it over. "I guess everybody knows you moved up here for a reason, and all the talk is that you must be on the run from the law. So I guess the law would want to know. Anyway, I can't say nothing. I just can't and I just won't." She stepped from the control cockpit.

"You gonna betray me when I told you this out of caring for you, Janice?"

"I guess you made lots of bad decisions in your life, Karl. I don't even like you. I hate everything you stand for. And even if I didn't before, I do now."

She walked up the aisle between the banging machines and assembly stations. Karl Cherbourg caught up to her and put his greasy glove on her shoulder.

"Don't touch me!"

"Keep your voice down! Ain't you got no sense?"

"Get him away from me!"

At that moment Douglas Morgan stepped between Karl and Janice.

Douglas Morgan was the worst man Karl ever knew in his whole life. He was a black man—extra-black. Black like coal. He had big black hair that must have stuck out of his head more than an inch, and it was perfectly trimmed like a billiard ball. He had big African lips, a wide African nose. What made him worst of all was how he talked, which was like a white man. He was studying to be a lawyer, using scholarship dollars stolen from white kids.

It had to be this darkie who put his nose into Karl's private business.

"Leave her alone, Karl."

"This is between Janice and me. I just want to talk to her."

Douglas looked over his shoulder to where Janice was. Karl couldn't even see her.

"Janice?" Douglas asked.

"Keep him away from me!"

"Karl, why don't you go sit and cool off while Janice makes a phone call."

"This ain't your business, nigger."

Douglas nodded. "And I hope to keep it that way."

"You asked for it." Karl Cherbourg put his fist right up the darkie's gut. He'd flattened many a blackboy with his famous sucker punch. Right to the kidney. Sometimes it put them in the hospital.

Douglas wasn't phased by either the N-word or sucker punch.

"You just gonna stand there and take that, Dougie?" asked Jerry Ander. He was a known friend to darkies—especially to Douglas Morgan.

"What should I do?" Douglas asked Ander.

"Hit him back."

"His smell might get on me, Jer."

Oh, God, a darkie and a darkie-lover were funning with him, at the very moment he was being stabbed in the back by someone he thought he could trust.

"I need some police over at Utah Sheet Metal," Janice was saying somewhere close.

Karl lashed out with his knee, right into the darkie's crotch. Then he put his fist into the boy's face, then his ribs. Somebody grabbed Karl from behind and sat him on the floor—it was the nigger-lover Jerry.

"Don't hurt him," Douglas said.

"The cops are coming," Janice announced.

"Bitch!" Karl said. "Fucking bitch!"

Now he had attracted a crowd. Work came to a halt. Machines grew quiet.

"She's a back-stabbing bitch!" Karl bellowed. He wanted everybody to hear the truth.

They gathered around her, protecting her in a huddle. She was in a chair, being comforted as she related her story. There were exclamations, and then all the people came together to share the story. In minutes the gossip had spread to the entire third shift. Thirty-six sheet metal benders, stampers and assemblers knew the deep, dark secret of Karl Cherbourg—everybody but Douglas Morgan. He had planted himself in the aisle between Karl and Janice and it didn't look as if he was ever going to move.

"Jesus, man, whatever you did to that nice lady, it must have been heinous."

"They're staring at you, nigger," Karl said miserably.

Amelia Grounds, the shift supervisor, came up to Karl, shaking her head sadly. She was a diminutive grandmother of eight, months away from retirement. "Is it true, Karl? Did you do this horrible thing? I'll believe you if you tell me it is not true."

"It's true. I did it. I'm proud of it. Everybody hear me? I did it and I'm glad I did it."

He had waited a long time to go public. It should have been a moment of real good feelings and pride, but all there was around him was people who thought he was trash, and they showed it on their faces.

"I feel sorry for you, Karl," Amelia said. "Your judgment will be harsh. The hand of hell will reach out to accept you."

Normally the ambient noise of the machinery would have drowned out the sound of gunshots. With machines powered down, they all heard the crack of a gun. The receiving doors pushed open and Gittleman came through. He was the night-shift security guard, and he fell against the door, pushing it closed. His revolver hung loose from one hand. The other hand was held against his chest in a mass of blood.

"They're coming! They killed Bates!"

It was all too surreal. Utah Sheet Metal had carried on for a thousand night shifts without any big interruption, and now all this was happening.

"Who's coming?" Amelia demanded.

"The darkies!" Karl announced. "They're taking over! I knew it was coming someday."

"Who's out there?" Amelia demanded.

Gittleman couldn't talk. His blood was pumping out and his eyes rolled up into his head as a forklift driver bound his mangled hand with torn rags.

"Call the police!" someone shouted.

"The police are already coming," Janice announced dumbly.

Something hit the door. It sounded like a body. Somebody screamed. The door nudged open against the prone form of the security guard, who gathered his consciousness enough to go wide-eyed and kick at the door.

Something yelped.

There was something stuck in the door.

It was a paw.

Then there was a snout, and the dog pushed through, followed by another. Then they came streaming in, one after another, with hard, compact bodies and black, white and brown coats. They made for Gittleman.

"Get them off!"

The forklift driver threw a fist at a dog, but it snarled and grabbed his sleeve and dragged him out of the way. The dog pack swarmed onto the guard. One of them clamped its jaws hard on his wrist, and the hand sprang open, releasing the revolver. Others locked on to his arms and legs, while the pack leader went for the throat. He sank his fangs into Gittleman's neck and tore it open.

There were screams. There was panic. The dogs scattered left and right except for four animals that stood over the body of the security guard. They snarled savagely at a group of sheet-metal benders who were going on the offensive.

The benders had armed themselves with metal tools, and they began swinging at dog skulls.

The dogs recoiled or fell flat on the floor, but when the clubs whistled past them they sprang at the attackers. They sank their fangs into human flesh and held on until the attackers were rolling on the floor, trying to flatten the dogs under their own bodies. Then the dogs released them and backed away.

There were screams from the other end of the plant. A band of plant workers had discovered the rear exits blocked by other dogs.

"They got us trapped in here," said one of the assemblers.

"Let's charge them all at once!" Amelia ordered. "Let's force our way out."

The overnight shift charged the doors en masse, and the dogs came to meet them in a frenzy. They struck at ankles and legs and brought their victims crashing down. Two human beings managed to get through the doors. The others retreated. It was chaos.

The dogs kept snapping until the humans clambered up maintenance ladders and crawled onto stacks of steel sheet. Anywhere a dog couldn't climb, the people sought safety.

Karl found a safe place high up on his own stamper. The greasy press plate was eight feet off the ground. No dog was going to get him here.

It was a strange thing to be up here and look across the plant at all the other people perched in high places. There was some crying, but mostly they were too shocked to make a sound.

Not everyone could get to high ground. Some folks were wounded on the concrete floor.

"Oh, God, they're good as dead," Janice said. She had sought the safety of the steel coil she was slitting. In its cradle, it was well off the ground and she straddled it, making her almost as high up as Karl.

Two of the dogs took up guard duty at the exit doors and stood watching the interior of the plant, while their companions sniffed among the fallen wounded.

Alan Ansel was the first to catch their interest, and

he backed away from them on his hands, dragging one stiff, bloodied leg behind him.

"Help me!"

"Up here." It was Douglas Morgan, lying on his chest on an empty pallet that was high up in the arms of a forklift. He reached down. Al Ansel propelled himself faster on his hands, biting back the pain of his leg. The dogs hurried from side to side, sniffing the air around Al.

"Now, man," Douglas urged.

Ansel pushed off the floor and got himself up on his good leg. Douglas grabbed Ansel's wrists in midair— and then the dogs got mad. One leaped into the air with amazing agility and locked his jaws on Douglas Morgan's forearm. The second dog clamped his jowls on the wound that half severed Ansel's ankle.

"Oh, Jesus," Ansel cried.

"Shut up," Morgan said.

Then there was the weirdest picture Karl had ever laid eyes on. It was so freakishly quiet. Morgan didn't move a muscle, just hung over the side holding on to Ansel. Ansel was breathing rapid-fire but not making a sound. Everybody in the whole damn plant just held their breath.

All you could hear was the sniffing of the dogs. The one that held Morgan was making loud snuffling sounds from his mouth and nose, and the one that held Ansel breathed in and out through his mouthful of torn flesh.

Then they let go, almost at the same moment.

Morgan pulled Ansel right off the floor and onto the pallet, grunting from the strain. Ansel looked as if he wanted to scream from pain but he managed to stay quiet, too.

The dogs had lost all interest in them anyway.

They sniffed Swartoff, the tubby guy who ran the assembly line. Swartoff rolled his eyes until the dogs went away.

They nosed around Mohorne, a new assembly-line worker and fresh high-school dropout. She just stared at them until they went away.

They smelled up McGee, the skinny man who had never said a word to anybody in two decades of working the line. The dogs found something different about McGee. They sniffed. One barked. The other one barked. They sniffed and snarled.

McGee remained perfectly still.

The dogs tore into his neck and inner leg. McGee mooed like a cow, and when the mooing stopped, McGee was spurting blood from two open arteries.

The dogs ran through the aisles, leaping up at the shift workers. They sniffed their victims. They didn't try to get too close. They simply sniffed them until they were satisfied, then moved on. When they came for Janice, she panicked. She got to her feet and leaped for the dangling hook of a coil crane. It was way out of her reach. She was never going to make it. She landed on the coil again, her arms windmilling. The dogs put their paws on the side of the coil and sniffed the air around her.

Janice sprang into the air. It was an amazing thing to see her soar directly into the air and close her hands on the crane hook. If the situation hadn't been life-and-death, there would have been applause.

The dogs snuffled loudly and barked. Janice craned her head. The dogs yelped and leaped and barked.

Janice slipped.

She tried to adjust her grip, but there was grease on the hook. She made a whimper and then she lost her grip. She landed on her feet on the coil, her legs flew apart and she came down hard, right back where she had been—straddling the coil of rolled steel.

The dogs howled and reared up on either side of the coil—and they sniffed her.

Then they left her alone.

They stood under Karl Cherbourg and barked. Karl was out of their reach. He wasn't going to let them mutts get anywhere near him.

He was way smarter than the others on the overnight shift at Utah Sheet Metal Specialists, Inc., and especially smarter than some hungry dog. The animals circled the stamper with growing excitement.

One of them turned back to Janice, ran and leaped onto the coil. She was face-to-face with the creature until the dog leaped off again. It sailed onto a steel grate that formed the top of the scrap-steel bin.

It was taking the stairs to get to Karl Cherbourg.

Karl retreated to the other side of the plate press, but he couldn't go far. He clung to the hydraulic cylinder, his clothes and hands smeared with black grease.

The dog on the grate leaned far out, pointing his bloody muzzle at Karl, and sniffed the air.

The dog whined, pranced from one foot to the other, then leaned out again. Farther. Closer to Karl. Its eyes widened. It growled. It snarled. It barked at Karl. It pranced excitedly on the grate and snarled like a big predator cat. The dogs below took up the behavior. Two more canines trotted out of the rear of the plant with bloody muzzles, and they joined the frenzy below.

"Get away from me!" Karl shouted.

The dog on the scrap bin was acting rabid—pacing, whining, turning circles. It stepped to the edge of the metal grate and tried to reach its long muzzle out to Karl.

Karl kicked it in the muzzle and guffawed. The dog yelped and cowered.

"Stop it, Karl. He'll bite you."

It was Morgan. Telling him what to do. A coal-black, white-talking darkie giving him advice.

"Go to hell, nigger. I ain't scared of no dog."

"That dog ain't scared of you, either, Karl," Douglas shouted.

What the hell was the stupid darkie talking about? The stupid dog was trying to reach all the way over to the press plate, and Karl delivered another kick in his direction. The dog retreated, ears flat. When the animal reached across the next time, Karl was ready for him.

"Don't!" Douglas said.

But Karl knew better. He stood on the edge of the press plate, and when that stupid dog came close enough, Karl kicked him right in the jaw.

The dog opened his mouth, and Karl's foot landed in it.

Oh. Morgan was right. The dog wasn't afraid of Karl. He had been play-acting for Karl's benefit. Karl was outsmarted by a dog.

All this went through his mind during the horrible moment when the dog sank its teeth through his shoes and through his foot and then dragged Karl off the press plate.

When he hit the floor, the dogs came at him from every direction. He felt his neck blossom. He felt the cold of the outside air caress the exposed muscles of his inner thigh.

It was only in that very last fleeting second of his life that he admitted he had never believed any of his own rhetoric. He always knew he was a coward who was always looking for somebody to blame. He had always known in his most private thought that he'd need to get himself some serious church-sanctioned forgiveness before his end came.

He hadn't done that. Now he was dyin' with some horrid sins on his soul.

So what would come next?

It terrified him, and then he felt icy death take his hand.

6

Harold W. Smith shuffled his foot to the left, then right, then he removed his hands from the keyboard to look under the desk.

The absence of his fingertip pressure on the hidden keyboard caused the screen, mounted beneath the glass desktop, to go instantly dark.

Smith was irritated with himself, unable to see anything in the dark under the desk. He finally felt the tiny switch under his heel, and when he tapped his sole the screen illuminated itself again.

It was the latest upgrade Mark Howard made to Smith's computer terminal. His arthritis was making his knuckles twinge more frequently and it was harder for him to keep his hands always on the keyboard while he worked.

But the keyboard needed an auto shutoff feature for security reasons. Smith's elderly secretary, Eileen Mikulka, could enter the office at any time. The woman had been with Smith for years without ever learning that a clandestine federal agency was operating behind the scenes. She must never discover the secret.

People who learned the secret, no matter how innocent, were assassinated. In most cases.

Mrs. Mikulka was slower than she once was and she became addled now and again, but most of the time she was still the efficient secretary who had kept the Folcroft machine running smoothly for decades.

Which meant security could not be relaxed, even in the face of Harold Smith's worsening arthritis. Keeping his hands on the keyboard for hours at a time was painful, if he happened to be paying attention to such things as bodily discomfort. Mark Howard had eased the problem with the tiny thumbtack switch on the floor. When Smith was working, he could move his foot onto the switch and keep his screen illuminated—if he had logged into a special security routine, and if he engaged the sensor within five seconds of removing his fingers from the keys.

But he never seemed to be able to find the switch. Mark had adjusted its position three times and he still had to fumble for it.

But when he finally got it going, Smith could rest his hands in his lap and read his open windows.

It took time to get used to absorbing information in this way. He would read from several open screens covering entirely different information sources, then he would use his hands to scroll further down all the screens and continue reading each of them. It was an interesting exercise in mental discipline to keep four concurrent information inputs organized in his mind.

Smith, just like his secretary, was suffering the ravages of age. Unlike Mrs. Mikulka, he was still as mentally sharp as he had ever been. It was his intelligence, along with his perfect reputation for incorruptibility, that had earned him his role as the director of the U.S. government agency called CURE, as well as the top position at Folcroft Sanitarium in Rye, New York.

Folcroft was a real, working private hospital, but it was also a front for the agency known, to a very few, as CURE. The name wasn't an acronym. The agency was named by the young, idealistic U.S. President who conceived of the agency as the cure for a sick nation.

The President could see disaster looming in the future of his beloved country. The law-enforcement agencies were unable to control crime, largely because they were hamstrung by the limits set by the U.S. Constitution. Respecting the rights of all citizens meant providing built-in loopholes for criminals. The criminals and killers had too many shields in place to keep them from being caught, and too many opportunities for escaping punishment when they were caught.

CURE was established to adjust the balance—to fight back against the criminal menace by ignoring the most sacred law of the land. CURE would protect Americans' rights by violating those rights—the right to privacy, protection from unreasonable search and seizure, and guarantees of due process.

Nothing in the makeup of the government gave the President the right to take measures so extreme, and it was a political risk for the young president to associate himself with CURE. If anybody ever found out about it, CURE would look like a power grab. The potential for abuse was massive. The President knew that a man in his position could never and should never be entrusted with that kind of power.

What was needed was an independent commander for CURE, a man with proved incorruptibility and unquestioned loyalty to his country—and strong devotion to ethics. Clearly, when the time came to wield extreme power under questionable circumstances, a sense of right and wrong would be a better guide than the country's goals and ambitions.

The young President searched the ranks of patriots who had served the nation and proved their mettle. The ideal candidate emerged from the ranks of the CIA. He was an intelligence expert with a rock-solid reputation for being extremely intelligent and incisive. He was known to be an unquestioned patriot—and all agreed he was the last guy you would invite to a dinner party.

Harold W. Smith, along with his meager charisma, lacked a sense of imagination But his other personality traits made him perfect for the job.

There was one problem—Smith was retiring from the

CIA and planning on taking a professorial position. He might have no interest in another government assignment.

The President asked Smith to come to the White House for a meeting.

Another problem emerged during the interview. Harold W. Smith clearly had his doubts about CURE—would it really help? Would it help enough to justify violating the Constitution?

Despite his doubts, Smith didn't hesitate to accept the position of CURE director. Smith was, after all, a die-hard patriot. He could never turn down an important assignment from the President of the United States, even if it meant taking his personal life completely off course.

Smith, along with a close friend from the CIA, Conrad MacCleary, brought CURE into existence. Hidden behind the disguise of Folcroft Sanitarium in Rye, New York, CURE was invisible. Even the staff of intelligence experts who were hired to collect data for CURE didn't know they worked for a secret government agency. Only Smith, MacCleary and the President knew.

Then came the assassin, gunning down the idealistic young President as he waved to his people from the back of a car.

A president could suggest assignments, but could only issue one direct order to CURE, and it was the order to shut the agency down. Smith thought that the new president would take this step without hesitation, but, in fact, CURE continued.

Smith and his network of operatives continued to reveal illegal activities that the FBI and CIA and other law-enforcement agencies would never have known about. Smith passed along the intelligence, prodding the other agencies to act on them. His results were mixed. Even Smith admitted at last that CURE was not living up to its potential. CURE had to evolve. CURE needed an enforcement arm of its own.

Remo Williams, a cop in New Jersey. Raised by nuns in an orphanage, and trained to kill by the military. MacCleary had witnessed the man in action. He was a skillful taker of human lives.

Remo wasn't asked to join. He was hijacked. A carefully staged operation turned Remo the beat cop into Remo the death row inmate. There was the matter of a murdered man in an alley, and all the evidence at the crime scene indicated Remo was the murderer. In one of the shortest death-sentence trials in state history, Remo was convicted, and soon enough found himself strapped in the electric chair. Remo fried and Remo died and that was the end of the story, as far as the State of New Jersey was concerned. Anybody who ever knew Remo thought he was dead and buried.

But the execution had been rigged by CURE, just like the murder and the trial. Remo woke to find he was a prisoner of CURE, and CURE presented him with just two options: join the agency as its assassin—or be assassinated. Remo took the first option, and trained with various experts brought in by MacCleary. There were hard-ass commandos and firearms experts, but the strangest instructor was a tiny, annoying Korean senior citizen who dressed in kimonos and called himself Chiun, Master of Sinanju.

Chiun was another choice made by Conrad MacCleary. He had heard rumors about the Masters of Sinanju, and how they were the premiere assassins in the world. Harold W. Smith had his doubts.

So did Remo—for all of ten minutes, until the little old Korean man dodged Remo's bullets and beat the tar out of him.

Remo learned to respect the old man, who began to train him in what Remo thought of, at first, as Korean karate.

Remo learned Sinanju well. So well that even Master Chiun was surprised, and intrigued, by the skills of the American war veteran. It seemed that Remo was advancing into realms of Sinanju learning that had never been taught to adults, or non-Koreans. Only the children chosen to be groomed as future Masters of Sinanju learned what Remo was learning.

Chiun was, in fact, fulfilling a Sinanju prophesy in coming to America. Legend said there would be a Master who would come from across the sea, far from the village of Sinanju, and was destined to be the greatest of all Sinanju Masters. Remo fit the bill. Chiun dedicated himself to giving Remo the full course of training and ushered him along the ritualistic progression to the rank of Master, finally installing him into the position of Reigning Master.

Chiun wasn't a part of Smith's plans for CURE, but Chiun wasn't going anywhere. Remo and Chiun became a team of assassins for CURE. Chiun proved himself to be invaluable—and Smith found himself paying higher and higher retainer fees. Chiun insisted on payment in gold, and his contract stipulated that the gold must be delivered to Sinanju itself—a village inside the enemy state of North Korea.

Over the years, Remo Williams earned the title of Master of Sinanju, and recently became Reigning Master of Sinanju. As Reigning Master, Remo was, on paper anyway, the decision-maker of the Sinanju dynasty. He controlled Sinanju's enormous wealth. He dictated the terms of Sinanju's employment.

The reality was much different. Remo didn't care about the wealth—he hadn't cared about money when he was an underpaid cop or when he was Chiun's protégé and he didn't care about it today. He had as much cash as he needed.

As far as dictating employment—well, Remo wasn't inclined to take the services of the Sinanju Masters to other employers. He couldn't see working for some other country. After all, as Conrad MacCleary knew perfectly well from the start, Remo Williams was a U.S. patriot.

HAROLD W. SMITH witnessed the change in Remo Williams's status over the years, often with trepidation.

When Remo was first brought under the control of CURE, there was every reason to think he might betray the agency. Why not? He had been framed for murder, kidnapped, his entire life upset.

Remo proved himself, but for years the young man was clearly a CURE employee, and he acted like one. Smith told him what to do; Remo complained to high heaven, then he did it.

Even Remo wasn't aware of his growing power, but Smith saw the change. And Smith learned more about the nature of the Sinanju legacy and the scope of Sinanju abilities. The Masters fighting skills were not just better than other combat disciplines; they were on an entirely different level.

Then came a day when Smith realized that Remo Williams, now Master of Sinanju, was more powerful than Smith had ever dreamed a human being could be. Being a Sinanju Master, Remo could make things happen. He could expose CURE should he ever choose to do so. He could bring down the government. None of this seemed likely, but he could if he wanted to.

Or Remo could disappear completely, leaving Smith powerless. In fact, Remo had come close more than once.

Now Remo was Reigning Master. Even with Chiun still running the Masters' day-to-day duties, Remo was more inclined to make his own decisions. He insisted on having some official input into his CURE assignments—even forcing Smith to agree to a contract renegotiation that said Remo Williams had a voice in CURE assignment priorities. Of course, the language of the contract had been almost incomprehensible when Remo presented his first draft. Remo was not a word man.

Lately, there were new revelations for Harold Smith. He discovered the blood link between Remo and Chiun—Remo was actually descended from Sinanju. What had shocked Smith was the improbability of Chiun and Remo finding each other, hundreds of years and thousands of miles away from Sinanju. It had happened years before they themselves became aware of the bloodline link. It was too improbable to have happened by chance, but what could have engineered the chain of events? Specifically, what had manipulated CURE into bringing it about?

Questions that Smith found deeply disturbing, and questions he knew would never be answered.

There was the discovery, by Smith, of the existence of Remo's more immediate family—his biological father, his adult son and daughter. There was a native American tribe in Arizona, all of them, likewise, descendants of Sinanju.

And with these revelations, and the huge security problems they opened up for Smith and CURE, there came a new and even more unsettling revelation: Smith discovered that he was virtually powerless to deal with these threats. His power, and CURE's power, was dwarfed by that of the Masters.

Smith did try to meddle in the affairs of Remo's Sun On Jo family in Arizona, and it was the first time that the sometimes sophomoric Remo showed Smith that he did, in fact, understand how much power he wielded. Remo engineered the downfall of CURE and, rather clear-headedly, Smith had to admit, gave Smith a choice. It was much like the choice Smith had given Remo when he woke up following his execution, which was no real choice at all. Smith must keep his hands off the Sun On Jo and even put in place mechanisms to ensure the tribe wasn't harassed by anyone. The alternative was that Remo would expose everything, ending CURE, directly resulting in the death of Smith, and sending the federal government into a turmoil of scandal.

Smith—like Remo, years before—took the first option.

Then there was the matter of Sarah Slate. She was a lovely and intelligent girl, but she was an imposition upon Smith. She knew the Masters of Sinanju for what they were, and when she was staying at Folcroft and nursing Mark Howard, her inquisitive mind quickly unraveled the secrets of the U.S.'s most secret government agency.

Harold W. Smith had without hesitation ordered the assassination of innocent people who got a glimpse behind CURE's black curtain. He would have sent Sarah

Slate to her grave, as well, but his hands were shackled. Sarah Slate had saved the life of Remo Williams in some way that Smith still did not understand. She had become a favorite to Chiun, of all people. He had presented her with a small pendant showing the symbol of the House of Sinanju—and it was gold, the substance most precious in the Sinanju tradition.

There would be no touching Sarah Slate. If Smith harmed her, Chiun would undoubtedly learn he was responsible and the consequences were unimaginable.

There had been numerous other threats to CURE over the years. Every new president who came to office had the potential to shut the agency down. But CURE continued, and Remo and Chiun continued. And the work they did, to this very day, would have met with the approval of the idealistic young President who first sought to cure his sick country.

Right now, he was in a waiting mode, with his attention focused on the investigation in Utah. The attack at a steel parts plant had been the second such dog-pack attack within a few hours. In both cases, the death toll was staggering.

What was disturbing was the possibility that the attacks were planned and staged by human trainers. In both cases, the animals had been described as wearing unusual, broad leather collars that may have carried with some sort of electronic devices.

But what was worse, the attacks happened thousands of miles away from each other. The Connecticut golf course was hit in the late morning and the Utah factory was hit in the middle of the night shift, some thirteen hours later. It would have been feasible for the same pack of animals to be moved from the East Coast to the Western states in that much time.

But other attacks were just coming to light. Dozens of them, across the country, and they were nearly always fatal. The scale started small and quickly built up. Clearly, there were packs in Utah, on the East Coast, and in perhaps three other parts of the country.

Murdering people by the hundreds.

But why?

Smith disliked the waiting part of the job, when a crisis was brewing but there was no more information for him to gather, no action he could take. That was when he was at the mercy of the perpetrators, and all he could do was watch and wait for something to happen.

But when it happened, he would be watching.

7

These days the facility was known as Woods Cross Hermitage. "Hermitage" sounded so much nicer than "Sanitarium," which had been dropped from the original name.

Woods Cross was home and hospital to a few hundred people from the wealthiest families in Utah. They came to Woods Cross when they became too ill to be cared for at home. They came when they grew demented, or comatose. They came when they became addicted. They came when they were calling too much attention to themselves.

None of them were prisoners, strictly speaking, but many of them were in this place because they had no real choice. Go to Woods Cross or get cut off from the family money.

For a black-sheep cousin who had never had to live without an income, Woods Cross's Addiction and Recovery Retreat was a much better option than homelessness.

The hermitage was run with all the amenities of a fine resort. It even boasted a boating lake and an eighteen-hole course. The rooms were well-appointed, with daily maid service. Meals were prepared under the direction of an excellent chef. Medical facilities were first rate.

Not all the patients of Woods Cross Hermitage were from wealthy families. For tax reasons, about half the patients were folks with insurance paying their way. Still, they were screened selectively to be sure that the working-class patients who got in were not *objectionable* working-class patients.

Segregating the cash-payers and the insurance-billed was not good public relations.

What almost no one realized was that careful segregation did take place at Woods Cross every day. The wealthy, cash-paying patients were given preferential treatment in all kinds of special ways—and the method of segregation was so simple it was invisible to almost every resident and visitor. It was just a matter of evens and odds. The even-numbered rooms were for the cash-paying, well-to-do patients. The odd-numbered rooms were for those patients whose bills were paid by health insurance at negotiated, discounted rates.

The management knew the system, but even most of the staff didn't understand the full scope of the segregation. They knew only that meals were served to the rooms on one side of the hall before they were served on the other side of the hall, and the meals on the other side of the hall were sometimes not as hot, never as fresh, or from a different menu entirely. The shift nurses' schedules always seemed to give just a little more time to one side of the hallway than the other. Calls were answered a little more quickly. Sheets might get changed a little more often. The view was certainly nicer on that side of the building.

But the differences were subtle, hard to pinpoint. You couldn't prove anything. Not that anyone really wanted to. Even the patients who came to Woods Cross Hermitage on the insurance company's buck felt lucky to get in, since the hermitage was taking a loss on them. Being second class at a classy resort-style hotel was way better than being in a state-run facility.

Still, the richest patients at Woods Cross could suffer from their illnesses just as much as the others. All the money in the world couldn't buy a cure for cancer.

Marcus Hillman, for one, was praying for death. He begged for it every night, beseeching his Maker to reach down and snatch his soul from his body.

It gave him pain, and humiliating debilitations, but Marcus knew this was nothing compared to what would come. Ravaging pain. His stomach would be removed. He would descend into a drugged fog to stifle the pain, but the drugs would lose their efficacy and the pain would be so intense it came anyway. Marcus would know only delirium and agony for weeks before he finally died.

But that was months away, his doctors promised. "You've got a good half a year left, Marcus," the cancer specialist assured him, as if it was good news. It wasn't good news at all. He wanted his life to end now, before he reached that state of endless suffering. And so, seeing the moon come through his window, full and pale and bright, he was moved to again pray to his Maker for deliverance from life.

But this time his Maker answered him and dispatched the agents of death to take him. Marcus saw the night creatures coming for him, loping across the grounds of the hermitage, dark and silent as shadows. They were the Wolves of Thanatos. The Hounds of Hell. One of them looked up at him from the silent grounds of the hospital and for a moment the ghastly moonlight changed the creature's eyes to demon-red.

"God," Marcus prayed hurriedly, "I think I've changed my mind."

Marcus glanced out the window. The creatures were gone. No sign of movement. There was nowhere they could have gone—they just vanished. God did quick work, Marcus thought.

He felt like slapping his forehead. If God was really that responsive to his prayers, why had he been praying for death in the first place.

"What I'd really like, God, is if you could get rid of the cancer altogether. That would solve about all my problems. I'd really appreciate it."

Marcus finished praying and sat in his easy chair, trying to sense his body for changes. How would he know if God had whisked away the destructive mass of intestinal tumors? Would he have to wait for his next round of tests? He couldn't just watch them vanish the way the creatures had vanished from the courtyard.

BUT THEY HAD NOT vanished. They had a way in. It was a basement storage room window, and for years the laundry staff had been told to keep it closed. People had been fired because they'd refused to keep that window closed. Finally, one of the laundry staff, as she was being terminated, pointed out that the laundry room routinely reached temperatures that were above the standards of the occupational services health codes. The laundry worker pointed out that firing her for reporting a health-code violation fell under whistleblower statutes, and she would be entitled to triple damages plus back pay.

"Plus, you'll have to solve the problem with a new air-conditioner for the laundry room. Bet that would cost a lot of money."

The management team conceded the point. It would cost thousands for an upgrade to the cooling system.

"All you have to do is let us keep the silly window open for ventilation," she said reasonably. "And all I want to do is keep my job."

The management saw the light. They unfired the laundry worker and studiously ignored the open window for years afterward. After all, how much of a security risk was one small basement window, really?

The hounds nudged the window open a little farther, then clawed the narrow screen until it tore. The damp, hot air from the industrial linen dryers tickled their nostrils, and one of them scratched his nose with its paw as it waited its turn—then it joined the stream of dogs that slipped soundlessly through the torn screen.

It landed on its front paws in a cartful of hot, dry linens and bounded to the floor. The machines were churning noisily, but the room was deserted. The overnight laundress was on her cigarette break on the opposite side of the building—in fact, when she stepped out of the service door and lit up, it had been the signal the dog handler had been waiting for. The handler saw the glow of the cigarette from his spotting scope hundreds of yards away, which prompted him to give the signal to the dogs to move out.

Now the dogs rushed to the ground level inside the building, and the pack leader paused momentarily outside the door that would let the pack out of the stairwell.

"Up," came the command from the handler, and the pack leader ascended another level. The pack followed. There wasn't a yip or a bark, only some light panting and a few snuffles. At the second floor landing, the leader waited for the entire pack to gather around, and then the next order came.

"Inside."

Two designated door dogs gripped the door lever handle in their teeth and pulled down until they felt the mechanism release, then dragged it back. Several of the other dogs inserted their noses into the gap and wedged it open. The door dogs muscled their way into position and held it open with their bodies as the top dog and the rest of the pack entered the residence hall.

"Scatter," came the handler's command from their radio receivers. Each animal had a small speaker affixed to its collar, with the speaker on the underside of the leather. The sound issued directly into their bodies. They felt, as much as heard, the low-volume commands.

The dogs obeyed the order, spreading out up and down the dark hallway. The floor was carpeted with a rich art deco pattern. The rooms were numbered with tiny brass plates. It looked like a hotel more than a hospital, at least on the second floor. There wasn't even a nurse's desk on this floor. None of these patients needed that kind of care.

A dark-eyed male dog and its stocky female companion followed their command. They scattered, which they understood to mean they should spread out from the rest of the pack within the confines of the place they had been directed to. They came to the end of the hall and sat facing a numbered door, then awaited their next command. The rest of the pack was taking up stations in the hall by the doors.

"Wrong."

The command came only through the speakers of the two dogs, not the whole pack.

The big male and the stocky female looked for another door. There was another one almost directly across the hall. They crossed to it, sat and waited.

"Stay."

The door must have been okay, because they were told to hold their position and await further commands. Along the length of the hall, other dog pairs were being ordered from the one side of the hall to the other side. The big male had no understanding of the purpose to all this, but it didn't need to understand. It was simply performing its duty, doing what it was trained to do. The big male would have had absolutely no understanding of the concept of even-numbered rooms and odd-numbered rooms.

"Strike. Strike. Strike." The command came through the collar speakers of the big male and its stocky female, and strike they did, pulling open their door and slipping inside the room, raising their heads and inhaling the first heady breath. The air in an enclosed space was always potent with information. The big male caught a scent it recognized. The bitch snuffled excitedly. This was a ripe target.

They closed in on the source of the smell—the figure on the bed. The dogs came close and sniffed the body. The smell emanated from the sleeping man on the bed. It was faint. Just a trickle of aromatics leaking from the pores of the sleeping man. The dogs knew the smell. It was one of their triggers.

"What's that?" The man on the bed was alerted to the presence of something in his room. He started to sit up, but the male dog bounded onto the bed astride the man.

"Hey!"

The man never said another word. The male clamped its teeth into the soft, fleshy part of his throat.

The sleeping man fought back. He thrashed his legs and punched the male with his arms. The female sank its fangs into his forearm and tried to hold it, but the man on the bed was too strong. The man rolled to one side, then the other. The big male dog bore down harder, keeping the pressure on the man's neck.

The strength seeped from the man's limbs, then his body, and finally he slumped in the bed. Then the male tore up his throat. The female had by then dragged over the bedclothes and chomped through the flimsy flannel of his pajama bottoms and ripped the flesh open. The man in the bed was still alive, for the moment, and the blood spurted out of his open arteries.

The dogs left him to spill his lifeblood, jumping to the floor and trotting into the hall again. They came to another closed door.

"Wrong," came the command through their collar.

The dogs patiently went to another door.

"Strike. Strike."

They yanked the latch and went inside. There was an old woman in the bed, with her hearing aids on the bedside table. She never heard the pair of canine assassins enter her domicile. They came to her bedside and evaluated her—inhaling her odor.

The dogs learned everything there was to know about the old woman. Her blood was tainted with too much salt and the lingering poisons of regular nips of alcohol, and her pores still exuded the ashy smell of toxins from a cigarette habit that ended years ago.

Despite all this pollution, the big male dog didn't sense the smell of sickness, not even the obscure tinge of a sickness that had not yet begun to spread inside her body.

The dogs had olfactory senses that were attuned to the smell of human illness better than most other creatures on the planet. He could smell a dormant cancer years before it began to grow, or an infection that was months away from beating the domination of the body's white blood cells.

Despite the abuses of her body, this woman had the genetic makeup to keep most cancers at bay. She would almost certainly not get sick anytime in the next several years—not with one of the lingering illnesses that could be battled by modern medicine. Not by one of the illnesses that the dogs knew how to sense.

The old woman sat up, but the big male dog was turning away from her. She was not a target.

The bitch didn't quite have the male's keen nose. The bitch was not yet satisfied that the old woman was not a target, and it held its stance as the old woman began a low, moaning wail of terror. The bitch snarled menacingly.

The male called its companion away, and the bitch obeyed, as she had been trained to obey, but with reluctance, and the male felt a flash of irritation.

As the female left the room, the male nipped her flank. The bitch yelped and sprang ahead, then responded with a menacing growl, which the male ignored. For now. The female was the more savage of the pair, and that made it the better killer, but it was too eager to kill. The bitch had a taste for human blood. The male's strongest impulse was to obey its commands.

They came to the next room as sounds of alarm came from farther up and down the hall. The humans were growing aware of the army of assassins in their midst. Soon the alert would spread, and then their commander would give them the order to vacate the premises.

They came to another door. "Wrong," said their handler through the collar speaker. And another door. "Wrong."

The female snuffled with impatience. They crossed to the other side of the hall. The male had a vague notion that all the attacks being carried out were on this side of the hall, none on the other. He got the expected signal. "Strike. Strike."

The male dragged on the door latch, opened the door and slipped inside with the female.

MARCUS HILLMAN heard one cry. Then others. He went to the door, trembling, and peered through the keyhole. Low shapes were lurking in the hallway.

His creatures of death had not been called back to the nether realm. Of course, Hillman told himself, it was common sense that supernatural entities could be summoned with the will of the mind but never so easily banished. Marcus brought them into the mortal plane with the promise of a soul for the harvesting, his own, but reneged. The creatures of death would not be denied.

Marcus Hillman opened his own door. Up and down the hall the doors stood open. He saw a pair of demon dogs emerge, then drag open another door, their wolfen fangs scraping against the brushed-steel handle. They rushed into the room and then Hillman heard a cry of terror. There was a rustle of movement. A thump. Human gagging. And the dogs came out again with fresh blood smeared on their muzzles.

They went to their next door, examined it, then let themselves in.

"No," Hillman whispered.

The dogs were gone.

Another pair of animals appeared from a room up the hall and came his way. There was a tall male canine with the clear-eyed intelligence of a well-trained animal. Its companion was a female. The bitch truly looked like a hell-hound, with a blood-soaked face and bloodlust glittering in eyes.

"Here I am," Marcus Hillman announced.

The female trotted to him eagerly, but the male narrowed its eyes.

The bitch stopped in front of him and snuffled his bare shins. Marcus knew dogs. Thirty years ago he had raised a few litters of greyhounds. This wasn't a breed he recognized, but he could see that the excited bitch was lactating—which made her more repellant.

The male cocked its head in front of Marcus. It

sniffed, but it waited. And then, it seemed, a word was spoken.

"Wrong."

It had not come from the dog. But there was no one else who could have spoken it. The male stepped away.

The female was agitated. The male snuffed, ordering the female to get away.

"No. I'm the one you want," Marcus insisted. "I'm the one who brought you here."

The male ignored Marcus. The female bared its teeth and growled at him, on the verge of attacking him.

"Yes," Marcus whispered. "Take me. Leave the others."

The male dog snapped, and it was as good as saying no. The bitch backed off, still growling. It wanted to spill his blood. Why wouldn't the male let it?

"You don't understand—I'm the one you came for." He went to her, hands open at his sides, making an offering of himself.

Other dogs were lingering nearby, but came no closer. The bitch snarled, but the male dog growled menacingly and came behind her. She looked over her shoulder at him, disdainfully, then turned back to Marcus.

"Come on!" Marcus challenged.

The female snarled and lunged, but before Marcus even closed his eyes to accept this fate the male dog pounced, bearing the female dog to the carpet with its front paws, rolling the bitch on her back. The bitch wriggled and came to its feet in a fury, turning on the big male with gnashing teeth. The male waited then stepped aside at the last moment. The female's fangs clacked together on the male's throat, but only combed through dense fur without finding flesh. The male was quicker and stronger, and it chomped into the female's powerful neck, then took it yelping to the floor. The male held the female on its back and bore down. The bitch pawed frantically at the air but couldn't reach the male. The female's eyes rolled white and terror-struck, until it went limp in submission. The male released the female and it came to its feet gasping and holding its head down by its paws.

The male padded to the door across the hall.

"No," Marcus protested, but the other dogs closed in to keep him where he was.

The male stood in front of the other door, the humbled female sulking behind, as if waiting for a signal. The male must have decided it was a door worth opening, because it took the handle in its teeth, only to have the handle twist open on its own.

"No," Marcus said. "Piney, don't open it!"

The door was already opening. "What?" Piney asked sleepily.

"Close it and keep it closed!" Marcus cried.

Stu Piney saw the dogs and he closed the door fast. The slinking female yanked its snout back just in time.

"Leave him alone. Take me." Marcus waded through the gathering pack. Canines shoved into him, knocking him on his back, half inside his own room, as more dogs thronged on Piney's door. The chastened female was sniffing the cracks under the door, excitement growing, and then the door big male dragged the latch down and the weight of the dogs pushed it open. They flooded into Piney's room, there was a strangled cry and Marcus heard the sound of rending flesh.

The attack was blessedly brief, and Marcus tried all the while to push himself to his feet, in vain, against the powerful brutes that pinned him down.

Then the brutes fell back, and the attackers in Piney's room streamed out again, and all of them hurried down the hall to the stairs. Something had summoned them away.

In seconds they were gone.

Hillman hurried into Piney's room, hoping against hope that the pack had been pulled away before they could finish the deed—hoping that somehow Piney had been spared.

Piney, of course, had not been spared.

8

On the floor of the main room of the little apartment in
the private wing of Folcroft Sanitarium, there were two
short reed mats. They were meditating mats, not sleeping
mats. Two mats was an extravagance, when one could just
as easily use a single mat for sleeping and meditating.

But when you had a dungeon full of gold bars back at
the family home, you could afford to buy an extra reed
mat.

Being the middle of the night, no one was meditating at the moment. The mats were empty. Between them
were two simple cut flower stems, each with a cluster
of small, brilliant red chrysanthemums. The flowers
would have excited a botanist, had he realized they
were from a genetically pure strain, descended from the
first chrysanthemums ever cultivated by human hands.

Between the flowers lay a newspaper clipping from
the *Baltimore Sun*.

The phone rang, but it didn't seem to disturb the
snoring that reverberated from one of the adjoining
bedrooms. It rang again. Remo Williams emerged from

the second bedroom, still wearing the self-satisfied look he'd had plastered on his face for days.

His eyes fell on the newspaper clipping, and he wandered to it, then descended into a cross-legged position on his sitting mat. The newspaper clipping faced away from him, but he read it again anyway. He was pretty proud of himself.

When he finished the article, he noticed that the phone was still ringing. The snoring from the bedroom was keeping time with it.

Remo rose and answered the phone. "MOS central, your full-service assassination experts. My name's Remo and I'm ready to murder for you."

"Remo, it's me."

"Mark, I know."

"Is Chiun awake, too?"

"Wait a second." Remo thrust the phone in the direction of the snoring for a few seconds. "Even you had to be able to hear that."

"Wake him, please. We have a situation."

"Situation. Check." Remo hung up and said gently, "Little Father?"

Chiun stepped from his room, fully clothed, sandals on, just as fresh as if he had been up for an hour. "You could have at least asked him what kind of a situation requires our immediate attention." The small, old Korean man lifted the newspaper clipping with both hands before heading for the door.

DATA WAS POURING IN from Woods Cross Falls, Utah.
There were digitized voice recordings of the many people who had phoned 9-1-1 to report the attacks by a
pack of dogs on the retirement home, and there were
briefs entered by emergency response operators as they
received the calls. There were the initial police reports,
which were useless. There were on-the-scene media
briefs, which were speculative and sensational and
worse than useless. The only good information so far
came from the security firm that monitored Woods
Cross Hermitage. They had called in a detailed description of the attack as it progressed, watching it all re-
motely on their satellite video feeds.

"Any progress, Mark?" Smith asked.

"I'm getting the feeds now," Mark Howard said.
"Give me a minute to stage them to play simultaneously."

The door of the office opened and Smith adjusted his
foot. His screen went dark. At this time of night, it
couldn't be Mrs. Mikulka, or anyone else for that matter, except for the enforcement arm of CURE. Still,
until he was sure, Smith darkened his screen.

It was his enforcement arm. The two Masters of Sinanju slipped in from the dark outer office. Their feet
made no sound on the old linoleum and the door closed
behind them without an audible click.

The ancient, small Korean man stood before the
desk and bowed. "Good evening, Exalted Emperor."

"Master Chiun," Smith said with a nod. Long ago he

had given up trying to convince Chiun to not call him Emperor. He realized that it would be foolish to force the issue. A Master of Sinanju worked only for true leaders. They had contracted out to kings and princes, tsars, caesars and warlords. Elected presidents and prime ministers were now acceptable. Simple federal bureaucrats were not acceptable. The only way in which Chiun could justify serving Smith was by giving him a royal title.

The title was inaccurate, but Smith's authority was almost on par with an emperor's. He was, quite possibly, the most powerful individual in the United States government.

"Prince Howard." Master of Sinanju Emeritus Chiun bowed to Smith's assistant, then sat rigidly in one of the office guest chairs.

"Hey, Smitty," said the much less traditional Reigning Master of Sinanju, Remo Williams. "Hey, Mark."

Harold Smith announced, "We're monitoring another dog attack. This one in Utah. It may be the deadliest so far. Reports are just coming in."

Remo Williams became interested and seemed to forget about sitting down. "Pictures? Video? Reliable eyewitnesses?"

"We're just getting video from the off-site security company," Mark Howard said, and he found that Remo Williams was already standing at his shoulder. Chiun came behind Smith's desk to watch.

A nine-window video grid appeared on the displays,

dark and muddy except for a time marker in the lower right corner. Adjusting for the time-zone difference, the video was less than an hour old.

There were dimly lit halls, a well-lit, lobby-looking room with a young man at the information desk and a view of the outside front entrance. Nothing was happening anywhere.

"Hold on," Mark said.

Remo said, "Ah."

Mark scanned the nine screens. "You see something."

"Top right," Remo said.

Mark hunched over the top right grid window. It was a hallway that was pockmarked with night-lights and vanished into blackness.

"What?" Mark asked.

"Below it, as well," Chiun announced.

"Yeah," Remo agreed. "What do they look like to you?"

"I would see them more clearly," Chiun replied.

"Here?" Mark asked, tapping the middle right screen. "There's nothing there."

"Dogs," Remo said. "Maybe dogs. Canines, anyway."

"Where."

"They're in the middle, too. Bottom middle. They're sticking to the shadows. I can't see them very well."

Mark was frowning and moving his face low in front of the windows until he got in Remo's way and Remo moved him back.

Mark said, "Well, I don't see a thing. Dr. Smith?"

"No."

"They're there. What are they doing?"

"What? What are they doing?" Mark asked, fiddling with the video quality in an attempt to bring up the visibility. He saw only dark halls.

"They're coming out of that door to the stairs."

"How do you know it's marked 'stairs'?"

"I read it before they opened it."

Mark felt a little frantic. "I can't even see it!"

"They're coming out and just sort of gathering together."

"Staging for an attack," Chiun suggested.

Smith looked at the old Master, then back at the screen. "Where are they staging?"

"In the darkness, Emperor." Chiun tapped all the five windows showing dark, motionless hallways.

"We cannot see this," Smith said. "Mark, can you bring up the detail?"

"I'm trying. If it's there, I can bring it out," Mark promised, and began fiddling with the controls. One of the windows washed out with white.

"Put it back," Remo said tersely.

"We can't see it," Mark protested.

"Now nobody can see it. You can play around with it next time. Besides, they're getting ready to move out."

Mark Howard tried to pierce the vivid blackness of the hallway windows. All he saw were the red sparks of eyestrain.

"What's happening?" he demanded.

"They're waiting. They're pairing up," Remo explained.

"They are forming ranks," Chiun added.

"Why can't I see any of this?" Mark Howard demanded.

Then there was visible movement on the screen showing the information desk. The young man bolted to his feet, dropping a cartoon-colored novel on the desktop, and he cried out with a tinny sound.

Mark saw the dogs for the first time. They came for the desk clerk from either side. Two from the left, two from the right, nosing out through swinging doors and leaping onto the helpless clerk. The clerk disappeared behind the desk.

A dog rolled out, sprang to its feet and leaped behind the desk again. The young man sprang to his feet with the dogs clinging to him. One of them had its jaws clamped on his throat. When the young man crashed onto the desktop, the dog released its hold and the neck spouted blood. The young man reached for an electronic telephone with a lot of buttons. He was going for a red square on the lower front of the phone. He got the little plastic cover lifted from the red square before a set of jaws clamped down on his hand and crushed his bones. The young man raised his face and made a horrific noise from deep in his belly, and it came across the security video as a toad croak. One of the dogs landed on the desktop and shut the clerk up by clamping its jaws on the young man's face and tearing off his lower jaw.

The dogs sprang away in two directions.

"Did you see that?" Remo asked, tapping the image of the still twitching clerk. Mark Howard glared at him.

Now the other windows showed moving dogs that Mark Howard could see. They approached the doors and stopped. Sometimes they moved to other doors. Sometimes they let themselves in to the private rooms of the Hermitage residents, only to emerge seconds later with blood-soaked muzzles.

"Chiun? What do you think?" Remo asked.

"They are not wolves."

"Yeah. That's a relief."

"A relief?" Mark Howard asked. "This makes you feel relieved?"

"It could be worse," Remo said. "They could be wolves. Special wolves. Ugly, mutant wolves. But they're just dogs with remote controls."

Harold Smith said, "Once again, you feared Judith White had come back."

"Easiest explanation," Remo said. "But they aren't her wolves. They're dogs. All of them the same breed, in fact."

"What breed?"

"You got me," Remo said. "But they're all the same. They look the same. They move the same."

The murder continued inexorably. The dogs stopped at a door, then moved in or moved on. When they moved in, they often emerged with blood dripping from their muzzles.

"What makes you think they're being remote controlled?" Smith pressed.

"See the little boxes on their collars?"

"No."

"Wait." Mark Howard rewound the video in the reception area. The very dead clerk sucked in his lifeblood and came back to life, stood, fell down, stood again with dogs flying backward off of him. Then he sat back down and grabbed his book for a little light reading.

Mark paused the tape and moved ahead slowly until the dogs came into the picture. He paused when one dog was thrown out from behind the desk and picked it up. Mark froze on the beast, then zoomed in on the head and neck. The collar was wide and heavy, and small irregular components studded it.

"Could be anything," Mark said.

"Could be a little speaker. In fact, it is a speaker. Somebody is controlling those dogs from a distance by just telling them what to do."

"There's no evidence of that," Harold W. Smith said.

"Save for the voice that issues from the collars and in fact directs the activities of the brutes," Chiun said. "Fiddle with your knobs further and you shall hear the small voice that speaks."

"See that?" Remo tapped a window that was still running in real time. "See the pair of mutts go up to the door and sit there." A pair of bloodied dogs came close to the camera, rested on their haunches and allowed their gore-dripping tongues to loll out. "Now they'll get a command from their collars. It's either 'wrong' or 'strike.'"

"I'm getting nothing," Mark pulled on a pair of headphones and adjusted his volume. "No."

"Wait for it."

No one spoke until Remo said, "It's a 'wrong.' They'll skip that room."

"I didn't hear it," Mark said, frustrated.

"It's kind of quiet," Remo said. "They must have a heck of a security system to pick up the sound."

"Maybe you're hearing it incorrectly."

"Yeah, right." Remo rolled his eyes. Chiun looked pained.

The pair on the screen moved across the hall to another door, a little closer to the security camera. They sat and looked around, like any other bored dog waiting for its master's command. There were screams coming from other rooms now, but no sign of human life.

"It's a 'strike,'" Remo declared suddenly. "Whoever is in that room is dead."

"I didn't hear it!" Mark said.

"Nevertheless, the command was given," Chiun said.

The dogs were already dragging on the door handle, and when they opened it, the occupant began shouting at once. It was an old woman pleading for her life. The dogs, by the sounds of things, weren't in a listening mood. The woman croaked, and there was a thump. Mark Howard *did* hear the thump.

The dogs came into the hall again, but they didn't find any more doors to try. They sat on their haunches and waited until another command brought them to their feet.

"'Extract,'" Remo said. "The command is to extract."

The dogs loped into the blackness at the end of the hall. Remo Williams reported that the pack was stealing into the stairs again. Then the emergency lighting system at the hermitage came on, just in time for Mark Howard and Harold Smith to see the last of the dogs vanish into the distant stair doors.

The halls were empty again, except for one small, old man who stepped out and crossed the hall to another room, and emerged sobbing. He fell against the wall and allowed it to hold him up as he stumbled back and forth, unhinged by grief.

Mark Howard pressed his headphones tight to his chest and replayed the last few minutes of the dogs in the hall, then replayed it again and again. Each time he adjusted the sound in his headphones until it was so loud that it irritated Remo's ears just listening from a distance. Finally, with the volume cranked to an eardrum-shattering volume, Mark Howard's grim face pulled up into a triumphant grin.

"Aha!" he shouted. He whipped off the headphones. "I heard it!"

"Shh," Remo said.

"There are voice commands coming from the speakers on the collars," Mark hollered. With his ears ringing, he couldn't hear himself.

"Good, Mark," Smith said, "but you're talking too—"

"That's how they're controlled! It's as simple as a walkie-talkie!"

"Junior!" Remo snapped, making his own voice loud and piercing.

"What?" thundered Mark.

"You're shouting."

"I am not shout—" Mark's lips were pinched shut. He rolled his eyes wildly and tried to push back, but the Sinanju fingers were immovable.

Remo used his other hand to put a finger to his own lips. Mark nodded. Remo released him, but stood close to Mark's desk.

"It is a simple enough method," Harold Smith suggested. "The radio gives a spoken command to the dogs, and the dogs follow the command. They must be highly trained animals, of course."

Mark Howard was squinting at Smith, but he shrugged.

"In *The Doberman Gang* they used high-pitched whistles," Remo said.

"I believe that was a movie," Smith said. "Not reality. Which means it is not relevant to this situation."

"I guess walkie-talkie technology has advanced

since then," Remo pointed out. "Also, these dogs were meaner than the Dobermans. These dogs don't need machine guns strapped on their backs."

"Yes," Smith said. "And, in addition, the scenario you speak of comes from a *movie*. So it's not meaningful now."

"Did you see the Doberman movie with Fred Astaire and Barbara Eden and the midget?"

"Remo," Chiun said. "You are distracted."

"Just thinking out loud. The Doberman gang members were trained to do certain things and they didn't need to be guided too much while they did it. But the Utah dogs were being told what to do while they were doing it."

"They were still extremely well trained, obviously," Smith said. "But yes, there was someone monitoring their activity and making real-time decisions affecting the dogs' attacks."

"Dog snacks?" Mark Howard asked loudly. Remo raised his fingers threateningly to the assistant director's mouth and Mark clamped his mouth shut.

"But how did the controller know what to tell them to do?" Remo asked.

"Perhaps there were small video cameras mounted on their collars," Smith suggested.

Mark, still sucking his lips in like a toothless old man, snatched a piece of scrap paper from his desk and wrote a message rapidly, then displayed it.

"Six pee eight?" Remo read.

"GPS," Smith said. "Of course. A video feed from a dog's collar would be too erratic to stabilize, but a global positioning transmitter on the collar could feed back to the controller, who would track the dogs on a digitized map of the facility. He would know where each dog was at any given moment, so he could make the judgment as to whether their door was that of an intended victim. 'Strike' they go in, 'Wrong' they move on to another door."

"Neat." Remo didn't sound as if he thought it was neat. "So what makes one old folk in a nursing home a target for mutt murder and another not? In fact, what makes any of them targets?"

"We're still working on that," Smith said.

"And who's behind it? Still working on that, too?"

"Yes. Maybe we can find out by intercepting a controller."

"A controller? As in a dog trainer?"

"Yes. There have now been two major attacks in the area of Woods Cross. You will go to Utah."

"What of the killings at the golf stadium?" Chiun asked.

"Connecticut," Mark whispered harshly, but at least he didn't shout.

"That is nearer than Utah."

"Yes, there have been several attacks across the United States," Smith said. "Not enough to form a pattern."

Chiun nodded. Mark Howard seemed as if he wanted to say something, but thought better of it.

"Where in Utah?" Remo asked.

Mark Howard snapped out some commands on his computer, then gestured Remo behind the desk to see the names and addresses of facilities on his screen. Remo looked them over and his Sinanju-sharpened brain memorized the names, street addresses and telephone numbers. "Got it."

He forgot most of it by the time he walked out from behind the desk.

"Wise Emperor, have you considered that this place is itself a prime target for the brute packs?"

"I have," Mark announced.

Smith raised his eyebrows. "Unlikely."

"Perhaps you wish us to stay to guard your beloved inmates?"

Smith winced. "They're patients, Master Chiun. We do not call them inmates. The danger in the Eastern states is marginal. Folcroft is safe for the time being."

Mark Howard opened his mouth and closed it again. When it became clear the assistant director wasn't going to say anything, Chiun nodded.

Remo wasn't sure what sort of a vibe he was getting from Chiun or Smith or Mark. "Utah it is, then."

9

The city sidewalk evaluation was one of the Foreman's favorite tricks. He had instructed Maureen McIntyre to arrive at Times Square at noon and start walking.

You couldn't miss her, a freckled, pale woman with striking white eyelashes and eyebrows and hair a bleached-looking rust color. She was going incognito in sweatpants and a floppy sweatshirt, but still managed to attract leers from the suits eating hot dogs from the street carts.

The Foreman felt no twinge of danger as he fell in step behind her.

"Ma'am."

"Be off."

"I b'lieve yer the one I'm to be meetin' here, ma'am."

She looked sharply at him. His disguise was effective. Beard growth, a deep fake tan, well-worn cowboy hat, dingy jeans and stained, worn denim shirt. His sunglasses were almost black.

"You are him?"

"The Foreman, ma'am."

"You don't look like I pictured you."

"Glad tah hear it."

She slowed. "I don't believe it's you."

"Keep on walkin'. What's to believe? I'll go away if you want me to. No harm done."

She reached into her belt pack.

The Foreman didn't flinch.

She pulled out a mobile phone.

He had know that, whatever was in the pack, it wasn't dangerous to him.

She jabbed a few buttons. The phone in the Foreman's pocket vibrated.

"Excuse me while I take this call," he drawled. When he snapped the phone open, his voice changed dramatically. "Foreman."

She stared at him with the phone to her ear, and he guided her around a police car parked on the walkway. She put the phone away.

The Foreman tried not to be obvious when he checked her out through his dark shades. Maureen McIntyre had an exotic, Irish beauty that he had a hard time ignoring.

"Dang crank calls," he said, putting his phone back in his pants. "You want to explain what you have in mind, ma'am."

Maureen spoke in a low voice, afraid that some passerby might overhear the plot. She stiffened when he put his arm around her, but it was the embrace of a used-car salesman trying to unload an old Neon on a sucker. The Foreman bent low to catch every word.

Then he let go. "You want me to do in your own blood relation?"

"We're second cousins," she said. "Besides, Jack's never treated me like family."

The Foreman nodded. "He made you his number two in the Jackie Macks."

"You don't want tah know what I did to get tah where I'm at, Mr. Foreman."

"I see." The Foreman did want to know, but didn't ask.

"So? What do you want for the job?" She flicked a look his way.

"Nine hundred thousand, plus expenses. That's a twenty percent savin's on the second job, see?"

"I see."

"Too rich for yer tastes?"

"No. I'll pay it. But…"

"But what?"

"Maybe we could barter for a bigger quantity discount."

"Barter what?"

"I think you know." She reached over her shoulder, took his hand and moved it down. The Foreman found himself feeling the warm heft of her breast, and now his face was inches from hers.

"Ah see. Well, problem is, I never barter."

"Even when the goods to be exchanged are this valuable?"

He found himself exploring her breast through her

shirt, oblivious to the people around them. "It is quite nice."

"You must have an interest, Cowboy. Otherwise, why'd you meet me in person?"

"Ah do that, sometimes."

"Almost never, from what I've heard. I think maybe you had a crush on this pretty little Irish lass from the time you heard my voice."

"Well, Li'l Poke, I have tah admit you're easy on a man's eyes. And I like your ballsy style, trading favors for removal of your own cousin."

"Second cousin."

"Whatever."

"But I got standards that I adhere to."

"Don't say no. Not yet. Not until you've sampled the goods."

"I think that would be ill-advised."

"Do you *really* feel that way?" She moved his hand, so that he could feel something he'd like.

The Foreman's mind was in a state of flux. Why had he come down to meet the lovely Maureen McIntyre in person? Had he really needed to size her up—or was he just intrigued by the opportunity to meet the legendarily attractive organized-crime princess?

The truth was, the Foreman lived a solitary life, and he was lonely. And why not spend some quality time with an eager young lady? It wasn't as if she was a risk.

The Foreman knew when a lady was dangerous, just like he knew when *any* kind of danger threatened his person. He wasn't getting bad vibes from Maureen. Only very pleasant vibes.

"Got a place in mind?" he asked.

She smiled and directed their footsteps to the nearest Hilton Hotel.

10

Jackie Mack had the feeling he was being followed. It pestered him all afternoon, from the moment he left the restaurant where he had lunch and began the rounds of his places of business.

He even called ahead to have the places watched by independent observers—but nobody ever saw a sign of a tail on Jackie's car.

He switched to another car, and then another. There was still no sign of anybody tracking him, and nobody could have kept up with all his car switches and evasive maneuvers.

He felt better when business was finished. It was time for a little unwinding at Carlotta's place.

THE FOREMAN wasn't frustrated by a few hours spent wandering around Jackie Mack's Brooklyn territory. He might tail a man for a week before catching him at an unprotected moment, but the moment would always come.

There had been a moment early in the day when it looked as if he had an opening. Jackie Mack was entering the jewelry shop under a set of upscale row houses. The shop was on Maureen's list of Jackie's business operations. The Foreman made his typical approach—he walked right up to the place.

He didn't try to conceal himself or to watch for surveillance. He didn't need to. It was either safe or it wasn't, and for the moment, it felt perfectly safe. He tried the door. Locked, but it hadn't closed all the way. He went inside the jewelry store and made his way to the stairs and started up them.

Then he felt the danger, distant but coming closer. The Foreman turned around and left the way he had come.

Sure enough, a bunch of Jackie's men arrived a minute later and marched inside.

It was like that sometimes. Jackie was upstairs, above the jewelry store, alone, and he had posed no danger to the Foreman. Maybe he was on the john or had his back to the door. Only the arrival of Jackie's armed friends created the danger.

If they'd been a few minutes later, the Jackie Mack job would have been a done deal.

No big deal. There would be plenty of opportunities later. There was nobody on the planet who was safe from the Foreman one hundred percent of the time. No matter what kind of security they had in place, there was always a minute here or there when the safeguards were missing and the subject was unprotected.

The Foreman had never met a man he couldn't kill, sooner or later. The only sense of urgency came from his wish to please his Maureen. He'd known her for just a few hours and he was smitten.

After their initial romp in their hotel room, the Foreman had asked Maureen McIntyre to tell him everything about Jackie's movements on a typical day, and that's when she'd told him about Carlotta's apartment.

Jackie spent time at Carlotta's apartment every afternoon, no matter what, and the Foreman knew that offered him the best opportunity to make the hit.

Sure enough, the place was danger free—at least, free of danger to the Foreman. Old bullet holes in the first-floor apartment manager's office showed that it had seen its share of mayhem.

The Foreman climbed to the fourth floor and found Room 436. No danger here. Carlotta was unguarded. Why guard a tramp like Carlotta Dell?

He tried the door. Locked. He knocked. No answer. No twinge of peril. He picked the lock on the rattling old knob and stepped inside. The place was empty. He made himself at home.

His phone vibrated and he pulled it out.

"Hi, Cowboy," Maureen purred. "Where are you?"

"Hangin' out in Ms. Carlotta's shower."

"Really? How exciting. Is it a nice place?"

"Nah. To be honest, it's sort of disgustin' and filthy."

"Do you think you can handle a little more filthiness."

"I can handle it, whatever it is, Li'l Poke."

"See, Cowboy, I figured out how to get my little

camera phone to stand up just right on the dresser. You hang up now and I'll show you."

The pictures started coming. Of Maureen. She had the thing shooting out pictures every half a minute. It took her just five pictures to have all her clothes off and then she started going into poses.

They sure as shootin' were what you'd call filthy.

She was at home, in the apartment she shared with Jackie McIntyre, on Jackie Mack's bed, doing those things for the Foreman while he lay in wait to take Jackie Mack's life away. That sort of made it even more perverse.

The Foreman was intrigued by this woman. Why, she was enjoying herself. She seemed to really like him, or at least, she liked the odd relationship they had made.

Wouldn't last, surely. Just as long as their business arrangement. Still, Maureen already seemed inclined to do more than satisfy her part of the bargain. Hell, sending him dirty pictures wasn't a part of the deal at all. She was doing it because she wanted to.

Could he, the Foreman, the man without an identity, the man no danger could touch, and her, the strangely alluring and kinky Celtic crime queen, somehow make something together?

He never would have thought so, but then, he had never been with a woman before who was interesting and strong—and nonperilous.

He heard the key in the lock. No danger. It must be

Carlotta herself. The Foreman reluctantly snapped the phone shut on a particularly lurid, shell-pink image of the young Maureen. He put the phone away and replaced it in his hand with a stiletto.

Carlotta entered the bathroom, used the facilities, and departed without ever noticing the dark shape behind her shower curtain.

Soon the Foreman felt the prick of danger. It was small, just what would be expected with the arrival of a known killer like Jackie Mack.

Jackie Mack entered the apartment with his own key. He didn't need to use the facilities before he and Carlotta got down to the task at hand.

Carlotta was a giggler, but it was all forced and fake giggles like a porn star pretending to enjoy herself in an X-rated movie. Jackie Mack must have been able to tell Carlotta was pretending.

How different it was from being with Maureen. Say what you want about their odd coming together, Maureen genuinely enjoyed their sexcapades.

What would make a man want to leave a ball of fire like Maureen at home for a skanky crack addict like Carlotta?

Well, there was no figuring some people, the Foreman thought as he crossed to the bedside in two long strides and punctured Jackie Mack's middle with the stiletto.

Jackie Mack looked over his shoulder. He saw only a stranger, then his eyes rolled up into his head.

The Foreman drove the blade deep so it pierced the crack addict, too. She'd stopped giggling and then stopped breathing. The Foreman left them entwined.

The hint of danger that Jackie Mack had broadcast when he arrived was now gone. It was perfectly safe for the Foreman to walk out of the place.

As he strolled down the street, he opened his phone again, and there were lots more pictures.

11

There had sometimes been unusual visitors to Folcroft Sanitarium. For years, there had been the old and diminutive Asian man who came and went with his young companion. They spurred tremendous gossip among the ranks of permanent residents of Folcroft, which only intensified during their protracted absences.

Sarah Slate was a different kind of visitor. She appeared out of nowhere and at once began making her presence felt among the patients. At first she was simply seen on the grounds in the company of the hospital assistant director. She always spoke kindly to others, and began chatting with residents in the halls and public rooms. She charmed them all. She even managed to stay friendly as she rebuffed the amorous invitations of Larry "the Lecher" Leebok, a decorated World War II veteran with debilitating emphysema and an infamous libido.

Sarah Slate cemented her reputation with the residents with a dramatic act of heroism. It happened soon after her arrival, when the grounds of Folcroft were haunted by a malevolent presence.

Some said it was a raven. Some said a spirit in the shape of a bird. Whatever the creature was, it was winged and big and dangerous—and it spoke. It attacked the residents, it lurked outside their windows and it chanted strange, ominous words that terrified all who heard it. Sarah Slate had marched into the wooded areas on the grounds of Folcroft, a young woman, unarmed and alone, until she tracked down the creature in its lair. Then she had called for a security guard with a shotgun. The creature, whatever it was, was real enough that it could be killed—and one blast from a twelve-gauge did the job nicely. Sarah brought the remains out of the trees in a sack, and the haunting ceased.

To this day, the residents could not agree on the creature—what it was or why it came to Folcroft.

"It was just a bird," said old Mrs. Benali.

"That was no ordinary bird," trilled the elderly Mrs. Thorn-Mullet, of the Long Island Thorn-Mullets. "Ordinary birds don't speak."

"I never heard it speak." Mrs. Benali sniffed.

Gordon Hemmingsville tapped his cane on the tiled floor of the sunroom. "I did!" He tried to make his voice thunder. At one time he could really resonate. Not anymore. His voice was pinched and flat. "It threatened me. Wanted to chew my brains out. It told me so."

"All right, Gordon, keep your diaper on," Mrs. Benali said.

"I won't sit here and be called a liar!" Gordon Hemmingsville looked around with his wrinkled lips pursed. "Where's the damn nurse?"

"But it could have been a talking bird," Mrs. Benali said, trying to sound reasonable. "We had big violet birds in the aviary at home that look like our bird, and they're just parrots."

Mr. Hemmingsville looked angry. "You're blind as a bat. The bird wasn't any colors. It was black as coal. It was a raven, as evil as anything out of Edgar Allan Poe."

"You saw it?" Mrs. Thorn-Mullet gasped.

"I did," the man replied.

"And it was truly black all over?"

"Black as night. With beady little eyes. And I'll tell you one thing—there's no such thing as a black parrot."

Mrs. Benali smiled. "A mynah bird, that's what it could have been. They're black. They talk better than any parrot."

"I don't have to sit here listening to this." Hemmingsville announced. "Nurse!"

The problem with Mrs. Benali was, she was so damn practical. Everything had to get boiled down to the most reasonable explanation. Nobody could ruin a pleasant afternoon of gossip and speculation better than Mrs. Lucinda Benali.

"Why not ask Sarah about it?" Mrs. Benali suggested. "She saw it better than anybody else, in the light of day. She must have sat and watched it for minutes until the security man came to shoot it."

"She has been asked," Mrs. Thorn-Mullet said. "She doesn't like to talk about it."

"It must have been awful for her," piped up Tom Offenbach, who had been one of the infamous Offenbach playboys of Manhattan in his day. His party days ended in the hippie era, and after a few drunken decades the Offenbachs installed cousin Thomas in Folcroft for thirty years of medical observation.

"Why awful?" Mrs. Thorn-Mullet demanded.

"She picked up the pieces with her own hands," Offenbach pointed out. "There was blood on her hands when she carried the bag out of the trees. Did you all see the blood on her hands? Think of it, the sweet young girl gathering the remnants of that bloody carcass," Offenbach said with a shudder.

"Pshaw," Mrs. Thorn-Mullet said. "You misjudge our Ms. Slate. You don't know her."

The sunroom grew quieter and many wrinkled old eyebrows rose high on their foreheads at the insinuation.

"Why, Ellen, what do you know that the rest of us don't?" Mrs. Benali asked.

"I know Sarah Slate may be a very sweet girl, but she has a backbone that is iron," Mrs. Thorn-Mullet said. She tapped the top of the wood table next to her sofa seat. "*Iron.*"

Mrs. Benali shifted forward in her wheelchair. "Whatever are you saying, Ellen?"

Mrs. Thorn-Mullet looked pleased and secretive.

"Let me tell you," she said, but then her face fell and she looked over their heads.

"Hi, Mrs. T-M. Time to flex those muscles."

The big, butch physical therapist swooped Mrs. Thorn-Mullet off the couch like a gorilla and carried her off to the water therapy suite.

"Damn!" Offenbach snapped. "She did it again! The old bitch is always dropping a bomb right before they come to take her to therapy. I don't know how she does it."

"She watches the clock, Tom," Lecher Leebok said.

"What clock?" Offenbach demanded.

Leebok pointed at a spot on the wall. Offenbach squinted at it and made out the oval of an oversize clock, but the hands were too blurry to read. "Damn superior bitch. You know what will happen next time we try to bring it up, don't you?"

"What?" asked Mrs. Benali who was a rookie to the Folcroft's long-term residents.

"Alzheimer's. She gets it maybe once a month."

INDEED, the next morning after breakfast, when the small knot of long-term resident gathered in the sunroom, Mrs. Benali brought up the subject of Sarah Slate.

"Yes?" Mrs. Thorn-Mullet said.

"You were going to tell us about her."

"She's a sweet thing," Mrs. Thorn-Mullet said.

"About her family," Mrs. Benali said. "You had something to say about them."

Mrs. Thorn-Mullet had a blank look on her face. "I'm sorry, dear. I don't know what you mean. I'm afraid I might be getting the Alzheimer's."

Mrs. Benali reminded Mrs. Thorn-Mullet of the entire conversation, but the old woman played dumb.

"Cut it out," Offenbach whispered to Mrs. Benali. "The more you pester her, the longer it will take for her memory to come back, quote-unquote."

So the subject was dropped for days, until Mrs. Thorn-Mullet suddenly regained a scrap of her fragile memory. Sarah Slate herself had just come through the sunroom. She greeted them all by name and left the room sunnier than it had been.

"Such a sweet girl, and not at all like the rest of her family," Mrs. Thorn-Mullet mentioned.

Mrs. Benali nodded politely and continued her crossword puzzle.

"Did you know the Slates of Providence?"

Mrs. Benali looked up. "Oh, why, yes, I do recall meeting a Mr. Leonard Slate of the Providence Slates. That was a long time back. I didn't realize Sarah was from that family."

"Sarah *is* that family now," Mrs. Thorn-Mullet said. "The rest of them are gone. Killed off."

Offenbach was trying to conceal his interest. "Military men?"

"For starters. The Slates were involved in every kind of fool adventure you can imagine. They have been forever. I believe there were four households of Slates in Providence when I was a little girl. But they risked themselves in foolish stunts—it was like a disease in the family. I think half their number died on mountain climbs over the years. And on African expeditions and in the North Pole and the South Pole. A whole branch of the family tree vanished in South America about the time I came of age. I remember my mother giving me advice about the Slate boys."

"What kind of advice?" Mrs. Benali asked, entranced.

"She said they were very charming boys, and very wealthy, and that if I married a Slate I should count on being a widow sooner rather than later. But she said even the Slate women were expected to be careless thrill seekers."

"Sounds like the ideal husband." Mrs. Benali sniffed. "Dashing and wealthy and dead before the luster fades."

"But none of the Slate boys wanted a girl like me," Mrs. Thorn-Mullet said with a dismissive wave. "I was too domestic. You would never find me mushing dogs in the South Pole."

"Sarah doesn't seem like that," Mrs. Benali said. "And why is she working at Folcroft if she has all that money?"

"Why?" Mrs. Thorn-Mullet asked. "Mark Howard, that's why! I certainly hope she marries him, too. He's a very stable, likable young man. He's not a risk-taker. He is just what our Sarah needs."

"So why aren't they planning a wedding?" Lecher Leebok asked. "What's holding him up? A girl like that, he better make up his mind and give her a commitment. She's too pretty to leave hanging."

"Oh, yes," Mrs. Benali said.

"We ought to give the boy a nudge, know what I mean?"

"Mr. Leebok, are you suggesting we interfere in the love lives of those young people?"

"Damn straight," Lecher said.

Mrs. Thorn-Mullet pursed her old lips approvingly.

"Mr. Leebok, that is one of the most romantic things I've ever heard, and even more surprising that you are the one to say it."

Leebok looked at the floor. "Well," he said, "sometimes people need reminding to take a look at what is right in front of their face. I kind of wish somebody had taken the time to do that for me once or twice. I might not be a bachelor at seventy-eight."

Mrs. Thorn-Mullet smiled broadly, and Mr. Offenbach couldn't help noticing that she had her own teeth. "Larry, I think you've finally outgrown your playboy lifestyle and are ready to settle down."

"Ellen, you're right as rain, honey."

THE DIRECTORIAL OFFICES of Folcroft Sanitarium were silent for almost an hour. Mark Howard monitored the embarkation of Chiun and Remo at the airport, and the on-time takeoff of their flight to Salt Lake City. Only then did he announce, "I've used a security obfuscation on you, Dr. Smith."

"I assumed you did, which may have ruined its efficacy," Harold Smith said. "What's your rationale?"

"The pattern of East-states attacks is not as I reported to you earlier. The final two attacks were in New York State, both within fifty miles of Folcroft."

"Yes."

"The pattern shows that further attacks could also be in New York State."

"There are many facilities in New York that fit the target profile."

"I know. Chances are Folcroft will not be targeted."

"If Folcroft were to be attacked, Remo and Chiun must be elsewhere," Smith said, although he knew he was stating the obvious.

"I understand," Mark Howard said.

"If we're targeted, but escape tragedy because Remo and Chiun interfered, it would be disastrous."

"I know, sir," Mark said just a little too loudly. "It would attract attention."

"Exactly."

"CURE would be compromised. At the very least, we would be forced to abandon Folcroft immediately. At worst, we would need to silence any surviving Folcroft patients who were exposed to Remo and Chiun, then shut down CURE entirely."

"Exactly. You did the right thing hiding the knowledge of the attack pattern from me, Mark," Smith said, his voice sour and somber. "However, I suspected that you did it. Master Chiun may have sensed some dissembling."

Mark nodded somberly. "Well, they're en route to the other end of the country now. We'll just need to keep them from coming home until it's safe again."

Mark understood the reasoning, but he found it hard to accept the sacrifice of human lives at Folcroft. If the dogs came, the death toll would be high without the Masters of Sinanju on the premises. What were a bunch of dogs to the Masters, no matter how well-trained?

Without the Masters, Folcroft would be as vulnerable as Woods Cross Hermitage, where the body count was at forty-three confirmed.

"Mark, keep in mind that Folcroft is statistically unlikely to be one of the targets."

Smith's sour pronouncement didn't make Mark feel any better.

REMO WATCHED as the newspaper clipping rolled into a tight tube, which vanished in the sleeve of Chiun's kimono.

"I guess it wasn't a good time to show that to Smitty?" Remo asked.

"No," Chiun agreed, "but there shall be a good time." The old Master turned his gaze out the window of the aircraft.

Remo tried to look anywhere except at the little screen mounted inches from his face on the seat-back of the next row.

"Oh, miss?"

Three flight attendants arrived in a jiffy, including one from the next cabin.

"Yes sir," purred the trim, peach-painted older woman.

"This is my row," announced a well-proportioned younger attendant.

"I'm shift leader."

"So what? It's my row."

"What can I do for you?" asked a young woman with green cat eyes and skin as rich and dark as burnished teak.

"Uh," Remo said, "hi."

"Hi."

The other two interrupted their argument and formed an instant, unspoken alliance against the dark-skinned beauty.

"Hey, you butt out."

"It's her row, too," Remo said. "*You* butt out."

"But I have seniority," the younger woman pleaded.

"I'm shift leader," said the older one with the mask of makeup.

The dark-skinned woman had an unaffected smile and a nametag that said her name was Mala. "What can I do for you, Mr.…?"

Remo found himself smiling back. He couldn't help it. "Schatzie. Remo Schatzie. I was just wandering where my legroom went."

"Pardon me?"

"Last time I flew on this airlines there was more legroom. You had commercials, remember? Now, with more legroom?"

"Yes, of course. But it was a limited-time offer."

Remo sharpened his gaze. "If I didn't know better, I'd say you were telling a big fat fib."

"Honest injun," Mala said.

"You're Indian? Or an Indian?"

"Both."

"Interesting," Remo said, and ignored the petulant, extended sigh of annoyance from the seat next to him. "I'm part Native American myself."

"Really? I'm sorry about the legroom, Remo. They readjusted the seating last week. I think they hoped nobody would notice."

"It's okay," Remo said. "I'll fix it. What about the TV? How's it turn off?"

"It doesn't."

"But I don't want to watch it, Mala."

"But the airline wants you to watch it, Remo. It's got lots of commercials."

"But I don't have the headphones on to listen to the commercials."

"These commercials are designed to impact the viewer even without sound. After all, you can't help but look at them."

"That's kind of sleazy," Remo said.

"Yeah."

"Speaking of sleazy." The other two attendants had slipped away and were now busily working their way down the aisle with a noisy beverage cart. Remo couldn't help noticing they were barely addressing the other passengers. He also couldn't help noticing they had removed their undergarments and undone more uniform buttons. The movement of the cart turned into a fast walk. The bottles rattled menacingly.

Remo gently and swiftly lifted Mala off her feet and held her above his head. The other attendants were too startled to respond, and they kept right on going. He put Mala down when the coast was clear.

"You're a strong one," Mala said, never losing the polish in her green cat eyes. "Can I get you anything else?"

"No, thanks."

She left without a backward glance.

"Quite a display," Chiun said.

"How would you know? You were looking out the window the whole time."

"You were practically drooling."

"Just being friendly." Remo got to work on arranging his accommodations. One thing he knew about electronics was how to turn them off. With a quick tap, the screen became covered with fine cracks and went dark.

"I thought you were tired of stewardesses."

"Most of them, yeah." Remo got to his feet and leaned over the seat in front of him, holding on to the seat backs and exerting a measured amount of force. Then he jiggled the seats, very slightly, very rapidly, until the brackets holding them into the floor tracks loosened. He nudged the seats forward a full foot, then pressed them down to jam the brackets immovably in place.

There had been a woman in those seats, but she was on a trip to the washroom. When she returned she couldn't get into her row again.

"What happened?" she demanded to anybody who would listen.

Remo glanced up.

"Did you see what happened?"

Remo shrugged stupidly and went back to his in-flight magazine as the younger, braless flight attendant hurried back to address the crisis.

The harried passenger showed her how her seat row had been moved forward until it wedged into the next row.

"It must not have been secured properly," the attendant said, flustered. "You may sit in this aisle. She indicated the empty seat beside Remo.

"Lot of legroom, now," he said in a friendly way, showing her how far he could stretch out.

The woman sneered at him. She had dyed black hair and lips the color of eggplant. She took the seat beside him and jumped onto her feet again.

"The video's busted!"

An empty seat was found for her elsewhere.

"The cross-breed Indian woman is not for you," Chiun announced.

"I didn't say she was. I was just being friendly."

"And she was responding to the invisible vitality of a Master of Sinanju who has no self-control."

"Hey, I try," Remo said defensively. "I can do it when I think about it, and then I'm good for a few weeks. Then I stop thinking about it all the time and it comes back."

It was a strange thing, this hidden vitality that radiated from a Master of Sinanju like super female-attractants. This was not as wonderful a thing as it sounded. Remo was constantly harassed by women. Flight attendants had always been the most troublesome. Remo assumed it was the close confines and limited air circulation that increased the phenomenon.

Chiun didn't have this problem. Years ago, he had learned to turn off the attractant. He was dismayed when Remo failed to learn this skill, even after years of training.

"Who'd have thought this would be the one Sinanju lesson I could not learn to do with my eyes closed?" Remo said.

"There are other lessons you have not yet learned," Chiun said, his eyes on the aircraft wing. Chiun didn't trust aircraft wings in general. They wobbled uncertainly in their flimsy metallic sockets.

"What I mean is, this is the one thing I haven't learned to do without thinking."

"I see why that would be an inconvenience. Your nature, of course, does not put much priority on thinking."

"Come on, Chiun."

"And yet, I understand your meaning. You have not yet incorporated this skill into your subconscious."

"Yes. That's it. Everything else is in my subconscious."

"No thinking required."

"Exactly," Remo said. "What other lessons did I not learn, by the way? Didn't I take all the required classes?"

Chiun turned to his protégé. "Sinanju is not an academic degree, nor a military rank."

"I know that."

"It is a destiny. It is an art, honed by a thousand Masters who came before you. Consider the vastness of the wisdom they accumulated."

"I'm considering it."

"Why do you think that you shall ever absorb all their accumulated wisdom in a single lifetime?"

"I guess I won't. I can't. No one could."

"It takes wisdom to understand one can never be perfectly wise."

"So why keep trying?" Remo concluded.

"Only a fool abandons his pursuit of wisdom."

Remo leaned over and examined the sleeves of Chiun's Korean robe, which hid his hands. "You hiding fortune cookies in there? Sound like you're reading fortune cookies."

"Insult me if you wish," Chiun said. "But regard my words, Remo, for this is one aspect of Sinanju in which you do not excel. You do not seek out new learning."

"Compared to you?" Remo said.

"Naturally, compared to me. Whom else would you compare yourself to? What other peer do you have?"

Remo thought about it. "So I have to strive to be as good as you?"

"What greater aspiration is there?"

"So what are *you* striving for?"

"We speak of you."

"You speak of me. I speak of you."

"I wish to speak of you, for your future concerns me."

Remo sighed. "I thought we were talking about the flight attendant."

"We never were," Chiun said somberly.

Remo glowered at the broken video screen while Chiun monitored the wing over most of Ohio.

"Are you still learning new Sinanju teachings, Little Father?" Remo asked.

Chiun turned to Remo again.

"I know you'll say yes," Remo said. "So explain to me how you do it. How do you keep learning?"

"There is no how."

"I'll need to know this, Chiun. Someday you'll retire. How will I keep learning if I don't have you? How do you keep learning now, without another Master guiding you?"

Chiun's expression was strangely bright, but he said nothing.

"What?" Remo asked.

"I am pleased."

"By what?"

"You, my son. You asked a most erudite question."

Remo tugged the sleeve of the Indian attendant as she strolled by with hot coffee. "What's 'erudite' mean?" he asked her under his breath.

"Incisive." He didn't let go and she added, "Learned. Well-informed."

"It's a smart question, you mean?" Remo said to Chiun.

"Yes," Chiun sighed. "And I shall not provide you with the answer."

"Because why?"

"I will not say why."

"Well, thanks for clearing it up."

ONE DAY, Remo would need to know how to teach those lessons to his own student. More importantly, he'd have to teach himself those lessons. Chiun would have to retire, eventually. And Chiun wasn't exactly young. Even by Sinanju standards, Chiun was quite old.

Remo didn't want to think about that.

So how did Chiun go about teaching himself new Sinanju lessons?

By studying the scrolls? Remo studied the scrolls himself. Not as often as he should, and not as often as Chiun, but often enough.

Through meditation? Remo meditated almost as much as Chiun. Was Chiun getting something out of it that Remo wasn't?

Why wouldn't Chiun even tell him the reason he wouldn't tell him how he taught himself the Sinanju lessons?

There were two possible reasons anytime Chiun was being closemouthed about something. One, he wanted Remo to figure it out, and learn something in the process. Two, he didn't know the answer himself. Three, he was just plain ticked off at Remo. Okay, three reasons.

Right now, Chiun didn't seem specifically ticked off, so it wasn't number three. It wasn't number two, Remo thought. Chiun just wasn't acting the way he acted when he didn't know the answer himself. Which meant it was one.

So, figuring out how Chiun taught himself the lessons of Sinanju would itself be a lesson taught to Remo by Chiun.

This was getting complicated. All he wanted was a simple answer. Complicated things didn't work well inside his head, and he had to talk it through to figure it out—and Chiun wasn't talking.

"Maybe I should get a parrot," he announced.

"We had one and you detested it," Chiun replied as if they had been talking about parrots for hours.

"A purple, foul-mouthed vulture isn't what I have in mind. Maybe a little green thing. Just something I can talk to."

"Even a lesser parrot will learn to outwit you in conversation, my son. Perhaps a stupider animal."

"What do you suggest?"

"A decorative carp?" Chiun raised one eyebrow.

"I can't talk to a goldfish."

"A housecat?"

"Too stuck up. Besides, you'd never be okay about living with a litter box."

Chiun nodded seriously. "Regardless of the beast you chose, it shall not dwell within my home."

"What's the point, then?" Remo asked.

"Get a dog. Perhaps one of the killing dogs. They are valuable, purebred animals, and they share your vocation. They are even skilled at the task, considering they are but trained brutes. You may keep him in a pen near to our home, so long as you clean up after it, feed it, walk it and teach it to remain absolutely silent at all hours of the night and day."

"Gee, that'd be swell, pops."

12

Maureen got the ball rolling by calling Jackie's men. She and Jackie Mack were supposed to meet over dinner, she explained. "It was an important meeting. He wouldn't have missed it."

The men respected Maureen and they observed her authority, but they knew that she was a distant second in command. The idea of the important meeting that none of them knew about, was her way of setting the stage for an elevation of her own importance.

"We got no idea where he is," said Robbie Rollins. He'd been the last one to see Jackie at his final stop on his daily rounds. Rollins had natural leadership skills— more of a natural leader than Maureen, in the eyes of the Jackie Mack gang.

"You don't have any idea where he was going after he saw you?"

"He didn't tell me nothin'," Rollins insisted. He was covering up—Rollins knew where Jackie went every afternoon. Everybody except Maureen knew, as far as Rollins knew.

Maureen called the other Jackie Macks. She used the important meeting explanation again.

"Rollins was the last one to see Jackie, but he says he doesn't have any idea where Jackie went next."

All of them tried to come up with their own explanation. They couldn't tell her he was out boffing another woman.

"Something's wrong," she added. "Robbie is acting really strange-like."

None of the others would try to defend Robbie's strange behavior.

"Ever since Jackie and Robbie had that big fight, I been worried there might be violence between them," Maureen added.

None of the men would admit that they had not been privy to news of a major argument between the top man and his number three man.

"Let me know what you hear."

There was worry in the ranks, and they were thinking about how Jackie Mack had thought somebody was tailing him in the afternoon. Somebody went to check on Jackie at Carlotta's, where they found Jackie and Carlotta just as the Foreman left them.

Before they could decide what to do about the whole mess, the cops arrived, and the Jackie Macks let them have it to themselves while they figured out what to do next.

MAUREEN WAS WITH the homicide detectives for hours. She'd appeared in public several times during the afternoon—during breaks in her solo photo sessions—so she wouldn't be a suspect. She still had some hints to drop the cops.

When she finally returned to the apartment she had shared with the late Jackie McIntyre, the Foreman was waiting for her.

"I've got a surprise for you, Li'l Poke."

"Show me, Cowboy." Her clover-green eyes danced.

He displayed his mobile camera phone with great drama.

"You made pictures for me?"

He nodded. "Pictures that I couldn't send over the phone lines. Look."

The first shot was of the deathbed. The next picture was a close-up of the gray mattress. It was a word scrawled in blood.

"I used his hand to do it when he was dead. See what it says?"

"Rollins," she breathed. "Rollins! You framed Robbie!"

"A known association of Mr. McIntyre. They'll search Rollins's place, I promise you that."

She put her hand to her mouth, knowing the good news hadn't stopped coming. "What'll they find at Robbie's house?"

"Well, Li'l Poke, I may have jes broke into Robbie's apartment and dropped my pants in his laundry basket. We're about the same size. And I couldn't wear them anymore because I got two little drops of blood on the cuff. One from each victim."

"Perfect! Oh, God, are you the best Foreman an Irish girl ever had or what?"

She showed him her appreciation.

He didn't have much time. It would be a busy night for the Foreman. He had a dog show to stage. First, he went about performing the task that Jackie Mack and Maureen had argued about hiring him for.

TOMMY JOHANSSON ran the adjoining quadrangle of Brooklyn blocks. The Tommy Johns and the Jackie Macks were not friendly, and Jackie McIntyre had coveted the Tommy Johns territory.

Tommy Johns died at home with piano wire embedded in his throat.

Robbie Rollins was arrested at about the same hour, and when they showed him the bloodstained slacks in his laundry hamper he claimed they weren't his. He didn't know how they got there. The arresting detectives got a laugh out of that.

Robbie Rollins was finished in this town, even if the law eventually acquitted him. He'd still be a suspect to the Jackie Macks. He'd never gain their trust enough to return to the fold.

Maureen had a good night's sleep. Tomorrow would be a big day.

THE FOREMAN had his little movie player propped on the dashboard, showing one of his favorite old Cary Grant movies.

He glanced over at the display on the backpack in the passenger seat. It showed a white grid over a topographical map of the area, and it showed a number of tiny dots converging on an icon of truck. The truck was the Foreman.

The Foreman didn't need to count the dots. The system counted them for him. All the dots were present and accounted for. All were still moving at a normal pace.

They had finished their strike and were on their way back, none of them missing, none of them injured enough to slow them down. There was no hint of danger to the Foreman himself.

Sometimes, this job was almost too easy.

ANY OTHER SENSIBLE criminal would have said the foreman was nuts for doing what he was doing. What he was doing was waiting in the parking lot of the Knowlton Public Library in Knowlton, New Jersey. It was midmorning on a weekday, with all kinds of people coming and going. Nobody could possibly miss the big white panel truck that was pulled in with the engine running across four parking spaces.

Common sense said that news of mass murder at the Knowlton Historic Rail Museum would spread through the town fast, the police would be alerted without delay and it wasn't smart for the murders to make themselves known. Common sense didn't sway the Foreman when he knew, without doubt, that he was perfectly safe where he was.

Always knowing when he was safe was the thing that made the Foreman better than anybody else in his line of work.

He had decided to personally handle the strike on the Annual Knowlton Railfan Meeting because, on paper, it looked like one of the riskiest excursions. It was a high-profile target, in a well-heeled community. Lots of upper-middle-class, middle-aged Knowlton retirees were Railfans. The local police force was known to be effective and well-equipped.

But the Foreman found the town was danger-free. He could park where it was convenient. He chose the library for its easy access to the public grounds that bordered the old railroad station that was now the Knowlton Historic Rail Museum.

Maybe a lot of police were out sick today. The Foreman didn't really care about the why. He was watching his movie.

IT WAS A CURIOUS ability. In his youth, back when he still had a name, he had investigated the nature of the talent. It was too perfect to be a natural instinct, he decided from his reading on animal senses. It was too reliable to qualify as precognition—ESP couldn't even be scientifically verified but it was so inconsistent.

Seeing into the future was something the Foreman could do, in his own way. He didn't know what the future held, only when the future might be dangerous. And he could always change what his sense foresaw.

He was a teenager, driving his first car, the first time it really struck him how powerful the sense was. He loved that car. He was cruising through town with some buddies, out late on a Friday night. He felt the sensation of danger, the sensation he had experienced off and on most of his life. He pulled the car to the side of the road, taking shit from his friends because he couldn't explain what the hell he was doing.

A white Chevy had been driving alongside them until he pulled over, and they all witnessed the white Chevy get broadsided by a speeding tanker truck that ran a red light.

That truck crushed the white Chevy, then tumbled onto the car and burst into flame.

The boys in the car knew they had cheated death. If they hadn't pulled over, they would have been alongside the white Chevy. They would have been smashed and they would have burned, just like the doomed couple in the white Chevy.

It was clear to the other boys that their friend had somehow foreseen the crash and had saved their lives. They wanted an explanation that he couldn't give them.

"Did *you* see it coming or did you just *know* it was coming?" one of the boys kept asking him.

"Nothing like that. I just knew all of a sudden that I should pull the car over."

What he didn't tell them was that he had felt the danger in his body. It was a shrill sensation, but not quite like sound. It was as if he were feeling the beep of an alarm clock. It was the same thing he had always known, in much smaller ways.

When he was a kid, he knew when to throw spitballs in class without getting caught. He knew when not to throw spitballs because the teacher was about to turn around to catch him in the act. He knew when the cops were watching him and he knew when it was safe to speed.

He had always gotten away with stealing candy bars from the convenience store. After the accident, he began to seriously test himself for the first time, and began stealing more-expensive goods from local department stores. There were times when his instinct told him to take nothing, and there were times he could pick up a television and walk right out the front doors of the store.

He *never* got caught.

He began having fun with his skills. He stole ridiculous items. He took stacks of clothing from the most expensive men's store in town. He took refrigerators, a trampoline, entire cash registers and paper lunch sacks filled with jewelry.

His favorite feat was when he brought a big gas can into a local hardware store, filled the tank on a two-thousand-dollar lawn tractor and started her up.

Later, he read the police report in the paper and found out why it was safe to do something so bold that particular morning. The manager had run to the bank to get change, and the only employee in the store at that moment was a young checkout clerk. She was so intimidated by what was happening that she was helpless to react.

He drove the rumbling lawn tractor down the aisle and laughed when the twin front doors open to let him out as terrified customers fled in all directions.

No one in the store was able to ID him. The police had no clues. The investigation went nowhere.

The Foreman could steal virtually anything, he grew bored with theft. He turned to bigger crimes. He found murder to be easier than stealing, and more lucrative. He became a hit man.

His reputation spread. His name was known throughout his state. He became one of the most wanted men in the country. Although he was never in danger of being apprehended, being a wanted man hurt business. Half the people who hired him were dangerous in and of themselves, since they were tempted to turn him in for the reward. He walked away from more and more jobs.

He relocated. He dropped his name. He forgot his past, which was easy and painless. There were no friends or family that he really wanted to keep in his life. He took new names and new identities, and never kept them long.

As he specialized in putting together teams of experts to achieve impossible missions, he gained a new reputation. Now he was the Foreman.

For a price, he could steal any object, break into any building, kill any person, and do it without leaving a trail. His network of experts stretched across the country and around the world.

Even his most trusted people didn't know who he was. He was just the Foreman. The man who spoke in different voices, who had a different face, each time you met his—if you ever actually met him.

He paid his people well, which made his people willing to put up with his strange behavior. Sometimes he would put months into a certain plan only to pull out of it as it was getting under way, then starting with a new plan.

The money helped his people overlook his strangeness.

He was known to have masterminded some of the biggest cons on the planet. It was rumored that the Foreman had been behind the massive fraud perpetrated by a sports television network. The rigged events had killed many contestants—and earned millions for the network.

And yet, the network had been exposed. The Foreman, for the first time, had failed his objective.

Maybe so, but it didn't mean the Foreman had trouble finding more work. Just now, he had a high-paying temp job as a dog trainer.

The Foreman had personally helped to choose the targets. There were more than a thousand possible targets for his five nationwide dog teams. The Foreman's expert handlers knew how to assess a target—and they knew when a target was a risk. They could pull out of a strike at their own discretion.

Some of them would get caught, of course, because none of them could avoid risk with the perfection of the Foreman. He, the Foreman, personally tended to the riskiest targets.

One such target was the Railfan convention. There happened to be many Railfans gathered with the same sort of health insurance. The Foreman's sponsor insisted that the Railfans had to be targeted. The Foreman didn't argue. Just took the job personally.

It should have been exciting, but it wasn't. He was glad he had his movie player.

He paused it. Cary Grant froze midsmirk. The Foreman stretched as he strolled to the back of the truck and raised the door. The dog pack emerged from the trees and leaped gracefully into the rear of the truck.

A woman in a matronly dress was walking to the library, but she stopped to watch the progression of animals, which seemed to float off the ground when they jumped.

She looked like a librarian. Probably was a librarian. The Foreman gave her a nod and dragged the door down, then stepped into the cab and drove away.

The town was coming alive with the wail of sirens. Police cars, ambulances and fire trucks hurried down the crowded streets of town to the scene of the murders.

The Foreman paid them no attention, and the cops never noticed him.

He got a twinge of danger when he turned onto a county road, so he turned back, made for the expressway. No danger. He headed home, arrived at his rented country house without further delay and off-loaded the dog pack.

They trotted into their fenced kennels and settled in for bowls of chow.

13

"Lou MacMayor here."

"It's me. The Railfans are history."

Lou MacMayor was president of the Institute of Nationalized Humane Health Care, and he was watching the news in his office. "Channel 4 says there's thirty-six dead. They are really making a big stink about this."

"What did you expect? So many dog attacks in so little time makes people excited. It doesn't matter."

"It does if any of it gets traced to you or to me," MacMayor said, nervously tapping his fingers.

"They will not to trace it back to me," the Foreman said. "I've left it up to you to choose targets that will confuse the investigators."

"I know," MacMayor said. "Just getting a little nervous. What next?"

"We are on schedule," the Foreman said. "We have five teams operational now. More dogs arrived yesterday and we'll have them in the field within twenty-four hours."

"How many more teams? How many more dogs?"

"Ninety animals came in last night—enough for two

teams. We're staging one in California. The other one will go to the Florida Gulf Coast."

"Florida's good. Lots of retirees," MacMayor said. He hated retirees. Retirees were red ink waiting to happen. "Give me some numbers. Where are we at? What are you forecasting?"

The Foreman didn't like to give MacMayor hard numbers, but MacMayor needed them. Numbers were what he lived for.

"We're culling an average of one hundred subjects daily at our current rate," the Foreman said. " That rate will increase to approximately 170 per day with the addition of the new teams."

"Wait," MacMayor said. He opened a desk door and raised a self-leveling shelf holding MacMayor's old-fashioned adding machine. It was his pride and joy. It had been with him throughout his career, like a close friend.

"One hundred per day, plus 316 subjects removed prior to today. Sustain that two more days, then up to 170 per day. Sustain that rate for five days. We are up to approximately thirteen hundred subjects. If fifty percent of the subject are INHHC enrollees, that's seven hundred. Estimate a lifetime claim payout for each of about three quarters of a million dollars. Nice. We've saved the company a half-billion dollars already, friend."

"Wrong," the Foreman said. "You base that on unreliable forecasts. I've told you many times that our progress should be sporadic."

"How high could the daily cull-rate reach?" Mac-Mayor snapped, his hands sweaty with glee.

"With our larger teams, hitting larger targets, we can expect the cull rate to rise to 225 per day. Or they could drop to less than fifty."

"Depending on what?" MacMayor asked.

"Depending on the response. There will be a nation-wide reaction to the attacks. Security will be increased at the kinds of facilities we're hitting. We'll need to slow down."

"We can't slow down," MacMayor said. "We have financial goals to meet, my friend. Every day we cull a solid 125 sickies from the rolls is a day we save a hundred million dollars for the company. Understand?"

"You saw yourself." The Foreman said. "People are screaming about our activities so far. They'll put armed guards on every nursing home and hospital in the nation."

"Ha! They can't. Too many of them, not enough security."

"Of course," the Foreman said. "They won't stop us. But they *will* slow us down and, no, I cannot forecast how much."

"I thought you knew what you were doing out there," MacMayor growled.

"Better than anybody. Even I haven't done this kind of thing, MacMayor, as you well know. Are you not satisfied that I'm delivering what I promised?"

"Yeah, yeah, you're doing great. Call me tomorrow," Lou MacMayor said.

MacMayor hung up and looked for answers in the dull paint of the adding machine. Then he began punching the keys again. He made a couple of forecasts. The first was conservative, based on the number of INHHC enrollees removed from the ranks. Most of the enrollees were sickies-in-waiting. They had some sort of a life-threatening disease already inside them. That was what that dogs were able to sense: cancer; infections; tumors. The dogs could sniff out that sort of sickness even when it was dormant, even when it was years away from showing itself to the conventional tests of modern medicine.

Based upon the kinds of diseases the dogs could identify, MacMayor could estimate the average dollar amount that each enrollee would suck from the company while they died. He came up with an estimate of three quarters of a million dollars each.

That amount covered the full course of treatment for their disease, from the testing used to diagnose the illness, through the pointless years of treatment, until the illness finally killed the enrollee.

Nobody sucked up more insurance dollars per day than a dying cancer patient.

MacMayor was an insurance-industry lifer, and for years he worried about the problem of the sickies. They cost the company a fortune, and they always died anyway, no matter how much money you gave them.

He toyed with the idea of funding the development of a special test for all INHHC enrollees. ID the sickies that way, and drop them. He decided this might be construed as inhumane. It might even cause a backlash. Perfectly healthy, premium-paying enrollees would end up leaving INHHC.

Besides, no single blood test could find so many diseases. It would take extensive testing of each and every enrollee, and that would be so expensive it would negate the potential profits.

The answer came to him from a TV program about alternative medicines. He hated alternative medicines, but you always had to know what the nutcases were into. The show was an enlightenment to MacMayor. It featured a Swede named Peter Ohly, and his amazing, cancer-sniffing elkhound. The dogs found disease in patients, sometimes years before medical testing could find it.

And the dogs were trained to hunt and disable Swedish caribou.

What a combination of talents! The answer Mac-Mayor was looking for.

By the time the program ended, MacMayor knew his plan. Buy those dogs. Buy lots of them. Train them to find disease. Train them to kill the diseased. Every time a sickie was removed from INHHC ranks, and removed before the disease had cost the company one dime in claims, the company's bottom line was lifted up. When you started adding the savings for hundreds and thousands of enrollees, the savings added up.

It added up to billions of dollars in recovered losses. Now *that*, MacMayor thought, was a fiscally responsible health-care program.

Rollins was in jail, and Maureen McIntyre had assumed control of the Jackie Mack organization. Before anyone had time to express doubts about her leadership abilities, Maureen announced that she would continue with the plan Jack McIntyre had formulated to take control over the Tommy Johns territory.

"We had all kinds of plans for it. It's what Jackie and I were supposed to meet about on the night he was killed," she explained before the gathered heads of the Jackie Macks. "He was ready to bring all you boys in on it. Jackie even wanted Robbie to lead the whole takeover. He never suspected a thing."

She looked contemplative. The men, her men, gave her a moment to compose herself.

"I know Jackie's not even cold in the ground," she said loudly, "but we never dreamed Tommy Johns himself would be taken out of the picture so soon. We can't let this chance slip away without making a grab for it. We need to make our move now, while the Tommy Johns are trying to get themselves reorganized."

"But how do we do that?" asked one of the Jackie Macks boys—one who might have trouble taking orders from a freckle-faced, big-boobed babe with a brogue.

"Easy, lad. We get with them and convince them it's in their best interests. I've already arranged a meetin'."

THERE WAS NOT TIME for the Jackie Macks to think it over. Maureen was working fast. They rendezvoused with the Tommy Johns at the Border Restaurant. A late lunch was served in the private room in the back.

The meeting went down as badly as could be expected. The leadership of the Tommy Johns showed no signs of internal conflict, even with the famous Tommy Johansson dead. The new leader, Tommy's brother, was firmly ensconced and his men were showing him all due respect.

"You're not seriously asking us to put ourselves under your authority?" Gary Johansson asked.

"An orderly transition will keep the Tommy Johns area from turning into a battleground," Maureen McIntyre explained.

"Who's gonna be battling?" Gary Johansson asked with an incredulous cheek tick.

"You all will."

There were chuckles.

"Honey," Gary said, "I think you need to see the light. We're solid. We're fine. You Irish, maybe you ought to be looking at your own situation in terms of leadership and all."

Maureen nodded seriously. She didn't see her own

men fidgeting nervously behind her, but she knew they were thinking she had made a major error in judgment.

"I ask just one thing," Maureen announced. "I ask that you not give me an answer, one way or the other, until this time tomorrow."

Gary Johansson thought about it. "Fair enough. Out of respect for my old friend Jackie, I'm gonna do as you ask. I—we—all the Tommy Johns—we'll wait until tomorrow to give you an answer. We'll all meet here again for a nice breakfast. Maybe things will have changed by then. Maybe you, the Jackie Macks—will have a new outlook on things, too. You know?"

Maureen didn't need to turn around to know that, indeed, the Jackie Macks were already reconsidering a lot of their options.

"Until tomorrow, then," she said, beaming.

MAUREEN WAS BUSY making funeral arrangements for her cousin as the rest of the Jackie Macks got together for dinner at a little Irish place. They met without Maureen McIntyre, their erstwhile commander, but she was the name on every man's lips.

"We give her the boot. We do it nice. No hard feelings."

"But she was Jackie's number two. He thought she had what it takes."

"You saw her today. Made us look like morons. She doesn't have a clue."

"You don't know that. Maybe we'll be surprised when we meet them Tommy Johns tomorrow."

Laughter.

"We give her the boot."

"Yeah. But we do it nice. No hard feelings."

"Yeah."

"But we'll have to off her."

"Oh sure, she knows everything about our business."

"But quick, you know, nice."

"Yeah. No hard feelings."

15

Eileen Mikulka brought tea and a prune yogurt on a flimsy plastic tray. She had a sandwich, too. Tuna-fish salad. The cafeteria did an acceptable tuna-fish salad if you got it on the first day.

The office was silent, the two men poring over copies of profit-and-loss estimates for the fiscal year.

Oh, dear. Mrs. Mikulka hoped there wasn't some sort of irregularity.

The director of the Folcroft Sanitarium, Harold W. Smith, tolerated simple financial losses with cool practicality, but he was most disturbed by accounting irregularities. What with all the problems among other companies, with missing millions of dollars frittered away by bad accounting and fraudulent management, Mrs. Mikulka sometimes worried about similar problems popping up at Folcroft.

It was highly unlikely that Smith would have allowed irregularities on his watch.

But something seemed to be engrossing Smith and his assistant director, Mark Howard. Mark was such a nice young man. Mark got the tuna-fish sandwich and a green salad. Smith got the prune yogurt.

"Thanks, Mrs. M.," Mark said.

She put the tray on Dr. Smith's glass-topped desk.

"Mrs. Mikulka?"

"Is something wrong?" She could tell there was. He was staring at the prune yogurt.

"Why the change in the yogurt?"

Mrs. Mikulka examined it. Had she brought the wrong flavor? Impossible. She had delivered prune yogurt to this office for literally decades.

"It's differently sized. Smaller."

"Oh, dear. I hadn't noticed. I'll get another one."

"No. Thank you. I probably won't eat the whole thing anyway."

"Dr. Smith, if I may say so, it's no wonder you're not feeling well. You haven't taken your constitutional in days."

"I've been quite busy."

"This is no excuse for a man of your age."

Smith appeared uncomfortable and tried to avoid looking at her, or at Mark Howard.

"Neither of us are spring chickens," Mrs. Mikulka added cheerfully.

Indeed, Mrs. Mikulka was showing her age. The woman had been Smith's secretary for many years and she was well past the age of retirement. She had been cutting back her hours, no longer coming in at the wee hours of the morning as she used to.

Way back when, Mrs. Mikulka and Dr. Smith always arrived at Folcroft when the halls were still silent, and well before the rest of the day crew came in.

When Mrs. Mikulka arrived each morning, it had been her habit to bring Dr. Smith his breakfast of prune yogurt. How many thousand times had she brought Dr. Smith his prune yogurt?

Now, she came in too late to bring Smith his prune yogurt for breakfast. He only asked for it when his stomach was upset.

There were some elderly people who took care of themselves and there were some who didn't. Mrs. Mikulka knew she was one of the former and she knew Dr. Smith was one of the latter. The man dedicated all his time and energies to the job of running Folcroft Sanitarium.

The truth was, Mrs. Mikulka cared about the old sourpuss, and she was too old to care about keeping her thoughts to herself.

"How about one o'clock, Dr. Smith?"

"One o'clock?"

"For your afternoon constitutional."

"One o'clock. Yes. I'll make a point of it. Thank you, Mrs. Mikulka."

MRS. MIKULKA closed the door behind her, the office went through a metamorphosis. Dr. Smith pushed his paperwork aside and touched a tiny control under the lip of the desk to illuminate the large flat panel displays mounted under the glass desktop. It came to life with windows of various kinds of data—everything from standard web browsers to specialty data feeds.

Mark Howard was behind the second desk in the crowded little office. The top of his desk swung open to his own set of displays. Until recently they had been bulky old cathode-ray tube screens, which weighed so much they kept wearing out the hinges and hydraulic springs, making them squeak when the screens were opened and closed. No more. He had finally fit the desk with new flat-panel displays, making them more lightweight and quicker to hide away—not to mention easier on the eyes.

Mark Howard and Harold W. Smith were looking at many of the same data feeds from the vast data-crunching mainframes buried deep in the basement of Folcroft Sanitarium. The mainframes, called the Folcroft Four, were magnificent intelligence-gathering systems. They ought to be—they used the best parts scavenged from the latest state-of-the-art supercomputer systems.

Right now, the Folcroft Four were probing the semi-secure case files of the Federal Bureau of Investigations and various local law-enforcement agencies.

The photos on Mark Howard's screens would have been most disturbing to Mrs. Mikulka had she seen them. It was a messy pile of dogs, all of them shot to death, some with shotguns, which made for messy wounds.

"We've got mostly mixed breeds in the Utah stray kill. Only one of the dogs had a collar, but with no identifying markings. Several had open sores scars that indicated wounds that had healed without veterinary treatment. Two had advanced heartworm infestation. All had burrs and parasite infestation. Everything is consistent with a pack that's been in the wild for some time."

"What about the bloodwork?" Smith asked.

"Nothing out of the ordinary. No rabies, lots of standard infection and unhealthy concentrations of various pollutants. There's nothing here that's notable. I don't think these were the dogs that hit the plant."

"Why?"

"There are no dogs here that fit the physical profile of the eyewitness accounts from the factory. We have thirty witnesses who saw compact, brown and white and black dogs, with collars. They all agree that the dogs were of the same breed. Nobody said anything about seeing a Rottweiler or a boxer. The pack of strays had a poodle in it, of all things. There are a couple of mixed-breed animals that might have fit the description of the dogs that made the attack, but only a couple."

Harold Smith nodded thoughtfully. "What do the locals think?"

"They're being cautious and politically correct. They're lauding the deputies that wiped out the pack, but they're making it clear that there could be more killer dogs on the loose."

"I agree. These aren't the dogs that attacked the plant. Any ideas, Mark?"

Mark Howard shook his head. "I've got nothing so far, Dr. Smith."

"Any inclinations?"

Marl made a wry face. "Sorry, nothing there, either."

Smith nodded. He had come to accept Mark Howard's capabilities. The young man had premonitions sometimes. They came and went. While Smith, and Howard, were loath to place a label on these occurrences, they might have been called clairvoyance, extrasensory perception or psychic ability. As a man of science, a man who had been clinically diagnosed as having almost no human imagination, Harold W. Smith was not interested in using words that carried so much weight in supermarket tabloids. Mark had something better than that—something real.

"Who's this?" asked the man who answered the phone.

"Remo. Schatzie. Who's this?"

"Hafner. Call me Jim. Tell me about yourself. Where were you born?"

"Hi, Jim Hafner, I want to talk to Smitty."

"Remo Schatzie wanted Smitty. The reasons were a mystery, but soon the entire world would know why— the sordid tale of these two men and the secret that binds them together."

It was just the CURE computer talking, pretending to be a real person. The idea was to intercept wrong numbers without making the caller suspicious. Therefore, the computer would simulate a deli, or a pet store, or a law office or a convent.

"I don't know what the hell you are supposed to be," Remo commented.

"Biography writer. Big market. Everybody wants a biography for their blog site so they can show the world what an interesting life they've had."

"Not me, James. It's been dull as dry toast from day one. Now, where's Smitty?"

"Listen, I can make anybody's life sound interesting. Guaranteed."

"Hello?" Remo demanded. "Is there a human being listening in on this conversation?"

"What's the problem, Remo?" asked Harold Smith.

"Your phone system is the problem. It tries to annoy me."

"I think not."

"It does too much of the talking. It's supposed to let me do the talking, so it can match my voice print, right?"

"Its first priority is to misguide accidental callers."

"Whatever. We're in Utah. Where's the mutts?"

"We're expecting an attack in Bountiful. There are three prominent and well-funded retirement homes there."

"That works out, since there's three of us."

"There is?"

"Yeah. I finally have a protégé. Little Korean kid that Chiun imported for me. He's sharp as a tack and mean as a snake."

"You didn't."

"This kid's a killer. Really a killer. Which explains why he's an orphan. Anyway, he's got what it takes to be Sinanju, so I started giving him the back story on the plane trip."

Smith was silent.

"Hello?"

"Remo, I think you're joking."

"You think I'd joke about sending a homicidal kid into a nursing home?"

"I think you would, yes."

"You're right. I would. It's a joke. It's my way of getting you back for making me talk to the computer every time I call. Okay, give me the names of the nursing homes."

Smith automatically gave Remo the information for finding the three nursing homes in Bountiful Utah, that had come up on the list of probable targets.

"Remo," Smith asked, "what is the likelihood of you actually adopting a protégé in the near future?"

"That's my business."

"Do you have a candidate?"

"Butt out, Smitty."

"Remo, this is very much my concern. CURE will be affected."

"CURE will have to deal with it."

"If I recall," Smith said with great sourness, "you intend to take a Korean child as your trainee."

Remo shrugged. "Except for one time, Sinanju Masters always started out as little Sinanju kids. I'd say it's a good bet I'll stick with that tradition. My life would be hell if I didn't."

"I see," Smith said. Mark, listening in, happened to see Smith's lips go pale.

"Or maybe a Sun On Jo kid," Remo suggested.

Smith's head snapped up.

"They're Sinanju, too."

"But a child?"

"Sure. Sinanju can't be learned by adults. We've always done it that way. Except for once."

"I would have thought that Winston would make an ideal trainee," Smith suggested carefully.

"Winston's all growed up. And he's a jerk. I don't think he'd have the patience to learn Sinanju and I don't think I'd have the patience to teach him. Plus, he hates your stinking guts. You wouldn't want him around."

Smith nodded. "I see. And Freya?"

Remo Williams didn't know where this was going, but he saw no harm in playing it through and figuring out what was on Harold W. Smith's mind. "Freya just might be trainable," Remo admitted.

"Yes?"

"She's fast as lightning, quiet as a cloud. She's got guts. She's fearless."

"Sounds ideal."

"Not ideal. First of all, she's an adult. Second, she's a she. No Mistresses of Sinanju are allowed by ancient tradition."

"A tradition you would be in a position to alter," Smith pointed out.

"Third—and here's the clincher, Smitty—no killer instinct. She has the skills, but she doesn't have in her heart what it takes to be an assassin. It'll never happen."

Smith considered this and half turned in his chair, looking out at the surf of Long Island Sound.

"Can I go now?" Remo asked.

"Does she have children?" Smith said.

"Hey, this really isn't any of your business," Remo snapped. "No, she doesn't have children. She's not even involved with anyone."

"Winston?"

"Have kids? No."

"But those children would be ideal candidates? I'm merely trying to plan for the future."

"Why? What difference will it make?"

"Much difference," Smith said. "It would change your employment with CURE. I would have great difficulty sending you into the field with a child at your side."

Remo laughed harshly. "You, Smitty. You're the most heartless, emotionless bureaucrat on the planet. You could send a kid on an assassination as easily as you could shoot some poor, innocent computer repair guy who learns your business."

"It is different with minors," Smith stated simply.

"Minors? You mean kids? Well, you can fire me when it happens, okay? I'll get work somewhere, even with a protégé."

Smith knew it was perfectly true.

"That wouldn't be necessary. I would specify which missions the trainee could accompany you on."

"Don't make me laugh. You can't do that. No emperor, no matter how much gold he ponies for Sinanju services, gets to interfere with internal Sinanju affairs. Sinanju training is about the fieldwork."

"You can't take a child in the field," Smith snapped sourly. "It's irresponsibly dangerous."

"It's the only way to mold a Master."

"I think not. I think it is simply the tradition, Remo. You should get an adult protégé."

"I get it," Remo said. "It would be inconvenient for CURE to have a kid on board."

"It would, but that's not why I suggest it."

"I've had enough of this conversation. Forever. No more talking about protégés with me, got it, Smitty? I'll pick who I want, when I want, and *then* I'll tell you about it. You'll either deal with it, or we'll get a job somewhere else."

"Remo, answer me this," Smith said. "Would *you* have what it takes to put a young boy in that kind of danger? Will you have what it takes to risk the life of a child, not once but repeatedly? Because it will take years for a boy to learn the skills he needs to handle himself in the field."

"It's the way it is, Smitty. Sinanju Masters have been trained like this since the beginning of recorded history. Hundreds of them."

"With one exception," Smith reminded him. "You were not trained that way. You haven't experienced it. How will you make yourself do it?"

"I just will," Remo said out loud. "It is the Sinanju way, and it is that way for a reason. It must be done and it will be done."

When the call was finished, Smith withdrew several antacids from his desk drawer and chewed on them. His stomach felt like it was full of churning acid, but the conversation had actually gone better than he had planned.

16

Jack Cartfeld parked his van at the far end of the grounds of the Nineveh Retirement City. He turned the engine off and waited for minutes with the windows open. There was no sound out of place in the deep night of northern Utah.

Cartfeld crawled into the rear of the truck through the felt-covered dividing wall. When he closed the flap, he was in an enclosed room without windows. He turned on the overhead lights and began unlatching crates. Each of the dogs emerged and presented itself for his inspection.

Cartfeld wasn't inspecting the dogs, but the dog collars. He flipped on the power, checked the tiny diagnostic lights that told him that the charge was full and all the components were operational.

Each dog left the van through the rear, where an open hatchway was covered with curtains of black strips to block the light. They moved into the shadows of nearby tall grasses and waited for the entire pack to be ready.

Cartfeld returned to the cabin and flipped on the pack of electronics on the passenger seat. All the signals were reaching the unit. Everything was ready to go.

Then Cartfeld noticed the flickering of his police radio lights. The sound was down all the way, but there was a lot of traffic out there tonight in Nineveh. He spun the volume.

"—Retirement City," somebody said.

What was that all about?

"Is this another booze bash, Randi? Over."

"Looks like it, Sheriff," the dispatcher said. "Over."

"Heck," radioed the sheriff. "Fine. I'll check it out."

Cartfeld jumped out of the truck and jogged to the rear. "Inside," he ordered. "Inside."

The dogs left the stillness of the weeds and leaped back into the truck.

Cartfeld snapped the hard door in place and took off in a hurry.

THE NINEVEH RETIREMENT City was taking no chances. It had hired extra mobile flatbed trucks with generators and mounted lights to flood the outlying grounds. Extra hired security teams strolled the inner grounds, where no extra lights were added as a courtesy to the sleeping residents.

"Real good thinking," Remo observed. "They light up the far-out areas, where there's not enough people watching, then they put lots of extra eyes in the dark areas where somebody could slip through in the shadows. Like us, for instance."

Remo and Chiun had been delayed mere seconds at the periphery of the overlit outer grounds, until they found a place where no electronic surveillance was at work and the strolling patrol was in absence. They simply walked across it, in all the pale, garish light, and were unseen by man or machine. Then it was a simple task to stay in the shadows as they glided among the crowd of alert guards near the building.

"Although, maybe not everybody could get through the way we did," Remo admitted.

"A pack of stealthy brutes could come here, just as we did. But we have wasted our time," Chiun commented. "There are no dogs here."

"Not yet. It's early. Let's wait."

Chiun stopped in a grassy area where the trees made deep shadows, and he descended into a cross-legged position, tucking his hands in his sleeves and closing his eyes. Remo lowered himself just as gracefully to sit across from the Master Emeritus. He reached out with his hearing and his sense of touch, letting the environment flow into him.

He heard it all. The hush of the breeze on a thousand leaves. The quiet conversation of the guards a few feet away. The hum of the ventilation inside the retirement home.

He felt it all, too. The breeze was a speckle of signals against his skin. The sway of the trees created soothing pressure waves that no human being, save himself and Chiun, was trained to feel. Gravity itself was a constant companion, always there to orient Remo Williams, whether he was sitting still in meditation or airborne in the midst of an attack, and it was one of the most useful tools to a Master of Sinanju. It gave him a constant reference point—and yet gravity itself was an entity that changed in ways so subtle that even Remo could scarcely sense it.

This sensory input—sound, feel, all of it—was with Remo Williams at all times. The same pressure waves that told him about a swaying tree could also tell him about a bullet rushing at him at supersonic speed.

In the stillness of this night, his hearing reached even farther than usual.

He heard a large engine approach, come to a halt, then turn off. It was a van or a pickup truck, maybe three miles out. He and Chiun had hiked through that area some time ago, and it didn't seem like the place anybody should be at this hour. Unless it was a security patrol. But it didn't act like a security patrol. But if it were someone intent on offloading a pack of killer dogs, it would be a good place for it.

There was a kind of movement in the vicinity that Remo couldn't really hear.

Then the truck started up again and pulled away.

Why'd he do that?

"Scared off by all the lights?" he asked out loud.

"It is most likely a pair of young people filled with alcohol and lust and looking for a private place to exchange their diseases," Chiun said, speaking in a whisper too soft for the nearby patrols to overhear. "It is they who were scared off by the extra meaningless lights."

"I suppose so," Remo said.

They listened as the vehicle drove away. Drove fast. It stopped hard and the tires scraped on gravel.

And there was another sound.

"What was that, Little Father?"

Chiun said nothing as the barely heard vehicle finally faded away.

"Chiun, I heard something just then. Did you?"

"Perhaps."

"Was it a dog?"

Chiun was silent.

"I thought I heard a dog," Remo said. "If there was a bunch of dogs in a van and that guy slammed on the brakes and they went flying, and one of them yipped. That's exactly what I thought I heard."

Chiun nodded at last. "Then we should waste no more time here."

GET FREE BOOKS and a FREE GIFT WHEN YOU PLAY THE...

Lucky 7

SLOT MACHINE GAME!

Just scratch off the silver box with a coin. Then check below to see the gifts you get!

YES! I have scratched off the silver box. Please send me the 2 free Silhouette Bombshell™ books and gift for which I qualify. This female action-adventure series features strong, sexy and savvy women caught in high-stakes situations! I understand I am under no obligation to purchase any books, as explained on the back of this card.

300 SDL EE24   **200 SDL EE2S**

FIRST NAME   LAST NAME

ADDRESS

APT.#   CITY

STATE/PROV.   ZIP/POSTAL CODE

7	7	7	Worth **TWO FREE BOOKS** plus a BONUS **Mystery Gift!**
🍒	🍒	🍒	Worth **TWO FREE BOOKS!**
♣	♣	♣	Worth **ONE FREE BOOK!**
🔔	🔔	🍒	**TRY AGAIN!**

Order online at www.eHarlequin.com

(BOM-L7-06)

DETACH AND MAIL CARD TODAY!

The Silhouette Reader Service™ — Here's how it works:

Accepting your 2 free books and mystery gift places you under no obligation to buy anything. You may keep the books and gift and return the shipping statement marked "cancel." If you do not cancel, about a month later we'll send you 4 additional books and bill you just $3.99 each in the U.S., or $4.47 each in Canada, plus 25¢ shipping & handling per book and applicable taxes if any.* That's the complete price and — compared to cover prices of $4.99 each in the U.S. and $5.99 each in Canada — it's quite a bargain! You may cancel at any time, but if you choose to continue, every month we'll send you 4 more books, which you may either purchase at the discount price or return to us and cancel your subscription.

*Terms and prices subject to change without notice. Sales tax applicable in N.Y. Canadian residents will be charged applicable provincial taxes and GST. Credit or debit balances in a customer's account(s) may be offset by any other outstanding balance owed by or to the customer.

If offer card is missing write to: Silhouette Reader Service, 3010 Walden Ave., P.O. Box 1867, Buffalo NY 14240-1867

BUSINESS REPLY MAIL

FIRST-CLASS MAIL   PERMIT NO. 717-003   BUFFALO, NY

POSTAGE WILL BE PAID BY ADDRESSEE

SILHOUETTE READER SERVICE
3010 WALDEN AVE
PO BOX 1867
BUFFALO NY 14240-9952

NO POSTAGE
NECESSARY
IF MAILED
IN THE
UNITED STATES

17

"It was lucky we heard him at all," Remo explained. "And we may be wrong."

Smith sounded less than assured. "Master Chiun heard this, too?"

"Not that's he's admitting. Look, the truck had to get on County Road HH North. Just tell me what's the next good target in that direction."

Smith was searching. At the next desk Mark Howard was doing his own rapid-fire data crunching as he listened in to the conversation.

"Tufted Convalescence is nearest."

"Government supported," Mark responded.

"So what?" Remo asked. On the phone he could hear Mark's comment as well as he could hear a dog yip at three miles.

"Not worth investigating," Smith explained.

"Not worth saving them because they're a charity case?"

"Not worth assassinating if you're working for the

insurance industry," Smith replied, obviously finding the topic a waste of his time.

"I see," Remo said, although he didn't.

"You're not on a rescue mission, Remo."

"Wouldn't dream of it."

"Villanueva Retirement Facility," Smith said.

"Or McCullan Oaks Center," Mark added.

"Both possible targets," Smith agreed, then looked across the desks to his assistant and said, "Mark?"

It was a test of the both of them. Harold Smith had already decided, in what little time he had, on which of the two targets was the most likely to be hit. He wanted to know Mark Howard's assessment—and why. It would test the decision-making of both men.

Harold Smith would analyze this crisis after the fact, critically and without emotion, to determine how well both of them had performed.

Mark Howard had an admirable success rate when it came to crisis decisions, but not as good as Smith's.

"Villanueva."

"Why?" Smith asked.

"Larger population of terminal patients, result of a wing closure and shifting of healthy patients to a sister facility in the next county."

"Agreed. Remo?"

"What? I was supposed to make sense of all that?"

"Villanueva."

"Congratulations. I'll buy you a housewarming present. Does Mrs. Smitty like vanilla candles?"

"I'm not buying a new house. I'm talking about the Villanueva Retirement Facility, the next most likely target. Here are the directions."

Remo listened, then announced, "That's a long way for a close target. Is there a shortcut?"

Smith explained that there was not a shortcut, and hung up. He plotted the route, searched the police bands in the vicinity and kept himself busy. There was only so much that could be done for the time being.

"Uh-oh," Mark Howard said.

"Yes?" Smith asked.

"Hold on a second." Mark snatched up the phone and dialed a local number.

"Mark?" Smith asked.

"Have to call home."

"Home?"

"It's me," Mark said. "Hi. Listen, would you do me a favor and look in the liquor cabinet?"

Smith was staring at him. Mark Howard tapped a button that put the conversation on the speaker. "What's in there?"

"Not much," said the voice of Sarah Slate. "That coconut rum stuff. The champagne. One wine bottle opener."

"Booze. I mean, any more booze?"

"Uh, no, sweetie."

"Oh. I thought I bought something today. I mean, I didn't mean to buy it. But I think I bought it. And I didn't even remember buying it until just now. But maybe I didn't."

"Oh," Sarah said. "The Scotch?"

"I bought Scotch?"

"It's not in the cabinet. You left it out. I'm having some. It's not a bad single malt."

"What's the name, Sarah?"

"The name of the Scotch? McCullan."

Smith sat up straighter.

"Read me the label," Mark said.

"McCullan Single Malt Fine Oak Highland Scotch Whiskey. Was it a gift, Mark? Is it okay if I have some?"

"Fine. I'll call you later." Mark Howard cut the line. "Dr. Smith?"

"You bought it today?"

"Yes. I went out for a few groceries, and came back with a bottle of McCullan Fine Oak Single Malt. Eight hours later, we're given a choice of McCullan Oaks Center or Villanueva."

"And we chose Villanueva," Smith finished slowly.

"Sorry," Mark said sharply, angry with himself. "It just popped back into my head."

"Yes," Smith said.

"You agree it's not a coincidence?" Mark asked. "I don't drink Scotch. I didn't even know Sarah did. Stuff wasn't cheap, either."

"No coincidence, Mark, not at all."

Mark Howard had to get over being mad at himself before it occurred to him that Smith was taking it all pretty well.

"If one of them would just carry a phone we could

call them up and get them on the right track," Mark pointed out.

"True," Smith said. "But they don't."

Mark watched the data coming out of Utah. All was quiet. Nothing on the police bands except for some drunk and disorderly—coincidentally, it was at the Nineveh Retirement City.

No alerts came from the minimal security systems at McCullan Oaks Center, or Villanueva, for that matter. The night stretched on interminably.

"Hey, Smitty, we're sitting here with our thumbs up our butts," Remo said in a quiet tone when he phoned in finally.

"Be assured that *I* am not doing this hideous thing, Emperor," Chiun hissed close to the phone.

"Figure of speech," Remo said. "Nothing is happening." The phone system told Smith and Mark Howard that he was calling from the courtesy phone in the front lobby of Villanueva.

"We were mistaken," Mark announced. "The target is not Villanueva. It's McCullan Oaks Center."

"Ah, crap," Remo said. "What happened?"

"Nothing yet," Harold Smith said.

"It's been hours," Remo said. "Maybe there's no attack coming."

"It is McCullan, and Mark plotted an overland course for you. You'll need to cover 403 miles over mostly scrubby terrain."

"No problem. But what makes you think it'll happen at all?"

"Please make haste for McCullan Oaks, Remo," Smith said.

"Fine. We're off."

Remo hung up.

"You sound more sure of this than I am," Mark commented.

"What you did was meaningful."

"I just bought a bottle of overpriced liquor."

"It was entirely out of character for you. The fact that you forgot about doing so makes it more significant."

"It makes it a useless gesture." Mark sulked.

"I think not."

"What if there's no attack on McCullan Oaks or anywhere?" Mark complained.

"Then I will assume that the attack was going to happen, but was averted," Smith said matter-of-factly.

"Even I don't trust my psychic powers that much, Dr. Smith," Mark said.

Smith looked at him. "Perhaps you should."

DR. HAROLD W. SMITH didn't believe in psychics—at least, not the kind of charlatans who advertised on television. Nor the kind who put neon signs in their windows. But he did believe in Mark Howard. The man had some true mental ability that affected him in curious ways. It allowed him brief insight. It sent him messages that he couldn't always understand.

Smith didn't know how Mark's ability worked, but he had a feeling that his messages came from his subconscious. The young man, Smith believed, was receiving knowledge from his abilities, but his abilities couldn't feed this knowledge into his mind in direct ways. For whatever reason, it disguised the knowledge in clues that Mark's subconscious directed him to provide for himself.

Mark Howard had been reluctant to admit to Dr. Smith that he even had this ability, and since it came to light, Mark was often frustrated that he couldn't get better control over it, to make it truly useful to the work of CURE.

But sometimes Smith wondered if Mark's subconscious wasn't providing him exactly the right kind of information in the right way to do, in fact, the most good.

Smith pulled up the entire McCullan Oaks online security system to his under-glass display. It consisted of several basic window and door alarms and a couple of Web-based security cameras that covered perhaps maybe a quarter of the square footage. A tank could sneak into McCullan Oaks without being seen on video.

But it was all Smith had to work with.

CHIUN AND REMO slipped across a few miles of scrubby terrain before the scent of dogs was carried to them on the wind.

"Dogs," Chiun said. "Haste is called for."

Remo skimmed overland as fast as his feet would carry him, and that was very fast. He caught up to Chiun as they reached the ten-foot chain-link fence that marked the boundaries of the center. The fence was hidden in the scrub, and it didn't slow them for a second. They stepped up and over it, and continued racing like shadows.

They followed the scent of many, many dogs.

JACK CARTFELD didn't want to pull out of a second job in one night, but he would. The guy who hired him, the guy called the Foreman, appreciated caution above all else.

First sign of trouble, Cartfeld would call for an evacuation.

He was listening to the police bands and keeping a hard eye on the position display. On the screen, McCullan Oaks was reduced to a bunch of schematic lines on a grid, and the hounds were dots on the grid. The dogs were deploying in the hallways, taking their positions in readiness to commence their attacks.

The last of the little dots stopped in their staged positions. They were still.

Cartfeld evaluated their staging. His display was programmed with the room numbers of viable targets. They displayed as green on his screen. Unworthy targets were in red.

Hounds Five and Six were at a red room number. His radio base station had a send button for each dedicated pair of dogs. He pressed the Five-Six-Send button and said, "Wrong. Wrong."

He pressed the Eleven-Twelve-Send and ordered, "Strike. Strike."

There were more commands. The dog-dots began moving as they carried out their orders.

And then the dog-dots began to behave most strangely.

CHIUN SEPARATED from his protégé, leaving Remo to move to the adjoining wing.

It was necessary, and an inconvenience, that they must concentrate on preventing the killing of the residents of the asylum.

Emperor Smith had curious motivations, which extended beyond the annihilation of his enemies. Chiun knew that the victims of the killer mongrels must be saved to appease Harold the Mad King. To allow the dogs to spill the blood of these innocent people would have riled him. In fact, Smith would have seen it as negligence on Chiun's part.

Chiun knew that Remo shared these sentiments. If Chiun did only what he was supposed to, by all standards of Sinanju duty, it would mean only that he would seek out the enemy and smite him. That was the role of the assassin.

In fact, it would have been best to allow the creatures to perform their deed first. Without being alarmed by the Masters' presence, the animals would behave normally and lead the hidden Masters to their handler.

But such could not be the case. There must instead be confusion and diversion. Save the inmates, which meant revealing their presence to the dogs, and thus losing all hope of easily finding the handler.

There was a certain kind of foolishness in such an enterprise—and once upon a time Chiun would have been sure to point out just how foolish.

He no longer bothered wasting his breath. He wasn't the kind of man to belabor a point, even when he was correct.

Chiun found a side door with only two narrow windows. The security glass was reinforced with embedded steel webbing. When Chiun cut into it with his impossibly tough and sharp fingernails, the glass was like stretched paper cut by a straight razor—it melted away, and Chiun caught the perfect square pane, leaning it against the wall. Then he slipped inside.

Even Chiun didn't look small enough to slip through the slot where the window had been, but through it he went, without so much as snagging the embroidery threads on his fine Korean robe. The break-in was accomplished in seconds, then Chiun slipped along the darkened corridor, following the smell of dogs.

They were clean dogs, recently bathed in chemical soaps, but they still smelled like dogs. Chiun tracked them easily, then veered off the trail to find an entrance corridor. A single dog held the door open. A wise move, to keep the escape route open. Another creature was breathing noisily outside, near the door but out of sight.

Chiun appeared to the door-dog not like a person, but like a curtain floating in the wind.

"Ur?" the dog said.

By then, the human being that floated like a fluttering curtain had reached it, and touched its ridged canine skull with one finger. The dog didn't know anything else, and it didn't make a sound when it collapsed on the floor. Chiun stepped outside long enough to dispatch the second animal.

The four-year-old brute was one of the best-trained canine hunters in the country, and it never even knew it was in danger. Its alertness simply transformed to blackness.

CARTFELD DIDN'T understand the alert. He had seen it during training. A little blinking X had come up where Hound Eighteen had been. Now, what did the blinking X mean again?

He glanced at the tiny laminated card taped to the control panel. It was his cheat sheet, and he found X near the bottom: "X equals Dead Dog."

Oh shit. Oh yeah, oh shit! Dead dog. There were motion detectors on the animals, sensitive enough to determine within a few seconds if an animal had ceased to breathe or move.

Then Hound Nineteen became a blinking X too.

How did that happen? Were they shot? They must have been shot. But the other dogs weren't reacting and they should have been reacting to the sound of gunshots. They were trained to react to gunfire.

Whatever it was, it was trouble. Time to call home the hounds.

CHIUN RETREATED down the hall to the mass of dogs, which suddenly became a rumble of activity. It wasn't Remo who had bumbled into Chiun's wing and sent the canines into a mindless stampede. It was the orders coming from their radio collars.

"Extract," Chiun heard. "Extract, come on!"

The dogs trotted together in Chiun's direction—a fast but orderly retreat, not a mad dash. Chiun stepped behind a door and allowed them to pass.

After all, there was no need to alarm them further. Tonight's massacre was clearly postponed.

THERE WAS NO HESITATION when they reached the dead animals at the door. A pair of brutes wedged themselves into the opening above the carcass and pushed it open. More dogs grabbed the carcasses in their teeth and they all hurried away from the building.

Chiun followed with interest. Would they lead him so easily to their handler?

This was the only pack that had appeared in the night thus far. What of the numerous beasts in the next wing, which Remo had gone in search of? Why were they not being extracted, as well?

Doubtless, Remo had complicated everything to the point of chaos. At any moment, Chiun expected to hear the savage snarls of a dog pack gone mad. He pictured Remo rushing from room to room, snatching would-be victims from snapping fangs. The pack would then emerge in a state of confusion and mayhem, and the panic might affect Chiun's well-ordered pack, too.

Remo Williams's bleeding heart could be such an inconvenience.

"EXTRACT, dammit."

The muffled commands were coming from twenty-two collars. Twenty-two dogs were not obeying the command. Four pairs of the beasts were staying put in front of the apartment doors, baring their teeth.

"Extract."

One of the rebellious dogs snarled viciously at the air. His partner snarled, too, and snapped. The other dogs were waiting for the rebels, looking about uncertainly. They didn't know how to handle it.

"Extract! Extract!"

The biggest pair barked and snarled as if they were about to tear the walls out of the place. Clearly, they didn't want to extract. Their blood was up.

The big pair turned on each other, snarling and biting, then went for the door. The female clamped down on the handle and dragged it down with its body weight, then the male shoved through the door—and stopped cold.

The male was withdrawn from the door like a tick being pulled out of somebody's forearm. The creature was too stunned to resist. It found itself levitated in the air, hanging by the scruff of the neck in front of a human being.

The human being tapped it on the snout with his forefinger.

"Bad dog!"

The brute transformed into a snarling, biting, writhing spider of a creature—then Remo gave it a quick shake. Bones popped and the brute went limp.

Its mate overcame its surprise and lunged for Remo's ankle—but the ankle vanished at the last possible instant. The female's teeth slammed shut on empty air, then Remo's leather shoe squished its head like a bug.

The other rebel dogs had a target for their blood mania—and their better-behaved pack members joined in. The pack closed in for the kill. The compact, muscular bodies flew into Remo Williams and tried to latch on to his arms and legs, clothing, neck, anything they could get their fangs into.

"Sit," Remo said, flinging a big beast to the carpet with such momentum the creature's ribs shattered and pierced its fur.

Remo swatted another animal against the wall.

"Stay."

The dog corpse embedded in the wallboard and, in fact, it did stay. Remo stepped aside from a flying pair of animals and gave them a little nudge, which sent them cannon-balling into a bunch of attackers from the other direction.

The force of the collision was tremendous. Bones snapped and dogs dropped. Remo poked at a pair of furry bodies that sailed between his legs, and they became bloody, spinning bone bags.

"Roll over. Good dog."

He caught one by the neck and used it as a snarling battering ram.

"I kind of like dogs, actually," Remo told the beast. It tried to get its teeth into Remo's thick wrists. "I thought I'd have qualms about killing a bunch of dogs. After all, you're just trained to be bad, right? But I have to say, you're making it easy."

The dog twisted so violently it dislocated bones in its shoulder, but it got what it wanted—it could strike. It closed its teeth on Remo's forearm with strength that had been known to break the legs of adult caribou.

"Bad." Remo twisted the creature like a strand of taffy, and before it made good on its chomp, the bones that still fit together inside the dog came apart.

"Extract!" the voice repeated from the collars.

The sound was low, and seemed to come from the neck of the brutes and from their very bones, too. Ah, the little devices directed their electronic sounds into the dog's neck, making the sound reverberate subtly through their bodies.

The survivors backed away from Remo.

"It's time to ask yourself one simple question. Am I a good puppy? Or a bad puppy?"

The dogs held their ground, snarling. One of them tugged on the ear of a dead dog and let go again.

Remo came at them.

"It's neutering time."

The survivors turned tail, leaving Remo Williams alone with eighteen bloodied, broken dog carcasses scattered around him.

A door opened and a wide-eyed woman in an oxygen mask stammered, "Are you the dogcatcher?"

"Catcher? Catching them is too good for these filthy mutts. Have a good evening, miss."

Remo left as the other doors were slowly, tentatively starting to creak open.

THE FOUR BEASTS flew to the door, where they joined up with a pair of anxious-looking door-dogs, then the group raced over the ground without seeming to even touch it. Remo kept a few paces behind them, keeping his footfalls quiet enough to be unheard even by dog ears. He wanted them to get wherever they wanted to go. After all, he didn't really have a grudge against these dogs.

He wanted the people who made them into what they were.

18

The dogs flattened to the ground to slither under a small cutout in the fence. Chiun went to the ground and spider-walked through the same opening, then was on his feet close behind the pack.

The pack, however, seemed not to know where it was to go. It turned gradually away from the fence.

Ah. Clever. The pack was describing a large circle, and no matter what direction the wind blew, the pack would catch the scent of any pursuit. Chiun stopped to see what would happen next.

His scent he couldn't erase. So the dogs would sense him. There was no point in attempting to hide from them. He would simply wait them out.

The dogs caught the scent of the Master of Sinanju from a hundred yards, and they whimpered in concern, coming to a bedraggled halt at the top of a slight hill. Several of the pack turned to face him.

Chiun stood silently, awaiting their interest to fade. He wouldn't quarrel with these beasts. He only wanted to accompany them to their handler.

But the beasts didn't continue on. Several of the brutes circled excitedly and came back down the shallow hill, raising their snouts into the air.

There were yips and snuffles. More of the dogs came trotting hesitantly down the hill. The little radio commands had fallen silent. Maybe the creatures were lost without their human leader directing their movements.

But that wasn't it. They were attracted to Chiun's scent. The old Master felt vaguely disgusted.

"You invade my privacy. Slink home to your keeper."

Their excitement was growing. They came down the hill together, the entire pack, their attention fixed on Chiun.

Master Chiun glowered at them.

"What do you want of me?"

For answer, several of them raised their grotesque snouts, drew in snuffles of air and yipped with agitation.

AND THEN CHIUN UNDERSTOOD. The old Master of Sinanju was filled with a riot of thoughts. He was disgusted and violated by the filthy brutes. He was filled with wonder and fear at the dogs' message to him—and he knew the message could not be true.

They closed in on him, as if he were just another of their victims. He was more than a subject to be diagnosed and annihilated if found to be tainted.

"Foul, unclean creatures, "he said miserably. "Filthy, foul creatures."

The pack encircled him. They all had his scent now,

and it aroused the bloodlust in them. It had not been so reprehensible a few minutes ago. Now, Chiun knew it was an abomination.

The animals were confused by their quick retreat, but they couldn't escape the passion raised by the smell of the old man's blood. They were trained to know this scent and to kill when they found it. The scent and the need to kill were one and the same. The need was over-powering. They could not disobey it. They snorted and snuffled and converged on the old man.

Chiun stared over them, to the place where his pro-tégé appeared from the trees. Only a few dogs were left from Remo's wing, but those animals romped up to pack about Chiun and drank greedily of the smell. The effect it had on them was obvious—they became ex-cited, slavering beasts, craving for the kill.

Chiun's ancient hands flashed about at the creatures, and his saber-like fingernails, the Knives of Eternity, laid waste to their flesh. So many of them collapsed during the instantaneous onslaught that they seemed to simply fall over in waves at his feet. As fast and as ferocious as they were they could not understand the speed of the attack.

Chiun suffered none of the offenders to live. He reached out for the beasts that bolted away, snatched them up and flung them down so that they shattered when they hit. He used the bodies of some to batter the animals that held their ground, until not a one of them remained alive.

19

"Who's in charge this time?" Maureen asked the knot of drawn-looking men across the table at the Border Town Irish Italian Restaurant, which did indeed sit on the border of the two territories. They were in the same private dining room, but the Tommy Johns' side of the table was only half as full as it had been the night before. Gary Johansson's chair in the middle was left unoccupied.

"No one is in charge," said one of the Tommy Johns.

"He's right. Nobody."

"I wouldn't even know who's next in line."

"Me, either."

There was an uncomfortable silence.

"Sorry to hear about Gary," Maureen offered.

"Yes."

"Thank you."

"Tragic."

The Tommy Johns sat in silence, but the Jackie Macks were just as stunned. The news had started pouring in from their neighborhood next door and it just kept on coming.

Gary Johansson was dead. Stabbed through the heart

with his own fireplace poker. Two related Johansson's men in the Tommy Johns organization were found dead within hours.

The Tommy Johns met in an emergency meeting at two in the morning, and at 2:06 a.m. the storefront pawnshop burst apart. Broken gas main, apparently.

There weren't many top-level Tommy Johns left after that.

"Somebody's in line for the top spot," Maureen insisted. "Who is it?"

The Tommy Johns tried to not answer. They mumbled and stuttered.

Maureen slapped her hand flat on the tabletop with a crack. The place settings jumped. The Tommy Johns' attention riveted on her. The Jackie Macks watched her, too, astounded by her commanding presence.

It was amazing how differently you looked at a person after they commissioned mass murder.

"Who do I have to shoot to get an answer out of you people?" Maureen was clearly out of patience. "If you don't have a leader, can you at least agree on one man to speak for the others?"

"Well."

"Yes."

"I guess we could."

"You." Maureen pointed to the man closest to the vacant middle seat. "You're the spokesman. The Tommy Johns promised me an answer today and I want the answer. Are you in with the Jackie Macks, or are you *out*?"

When she said "out," she pulled her finger across her throat.

"You have two minutes. Why don't you discuss it among yourselves."

The surviving Tommy Johns got into a quick huddle.

Maureen got to her feet and stretched, then turned away from the Tommy Johns and leaned her bottom against the table and smiled to her men. "Guys, I'm sorry I couldn't let you in on the whole plan. Jackie thought it was better for you guys if you kept your hands clean."

The Jackie Macks nodded slowly. "We appreciate that," said Alvin Dean.

"Yeah, sure and we do."

"Thoughtful of you."

"Don't thank me," Maureen said. "This is all Jackie's doing." She said it in such a way as to convince her men that the doing was one hundred percent hers.

"Jackie was a saint."

"Sure and we're gonna miss ' im."

"Thank heavens we got you to carry on, Maur."

"Yeah."

"Yeah!"

"To Maur!"

They grabbed their breakfast beers and toasted her.

She smiled humbly, then took her seat again, facing the Tommy Johns.

"Well?"

"We're in."

CASHWORD

$2

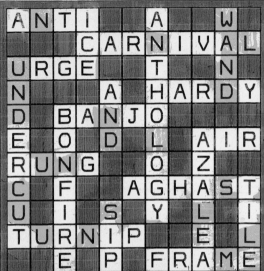

A	N	T	I			A			W
		C	A	R	N	I	V	A	L
U	R	G	E			T			N
U	N		A		H	A	R	D	Y
D		B	A	N	J	O			
E		O		D		L		A	I	R
R	U	N	G			O		Z	
C		F		A	G	H	A	S	T
U		I		S		Y		L		I
T	U	R	N	I	P			E		L
		E		P		F	R	A	M	E

LETTERS

O X J B T I Y V Z
W E H C F R A P G

WIN UP

PRIZE LEGEND

FIND	WIN	FIND	WIN
3 WORDS	$2	7 WORDS	$50
4 WORDS	$5	8 WORDS	$100
5 WORDS	$10	9 WORDS	$1,000
6 WORDS	$25	10 WORDS	$35,000

HOW TO PLAY CASHWORD

1. Scratch the CALL LETTERS to reveal 18 letters.
2. Match the corresponding letters on the Crossword Puzzle by removing the scratch-off material covering the matching letter.
3. Scratch three or more complete words in the CROSSWORD puzzle, win corresponding prize in Prize Legend. The entire word must be uncovered to win corresponding prize. In the CROSSWORD puzzle, every lettered square within an unbroken horizontal or vertical sequence must be matched with a CALL LETTER to be considered a complete "word". Words within words are not eligible for a prize.

PRIZES MUST BE CLAIMED BY NOVEMBER 19, 2007.

Instant prizes of $2, $5, $10, $25, $50 and $100 may be paid by any Lottery retailer.

Prizes of $1,000 and $35,000 will be paid at any Lottery Office or licensed Claim Center, or may be claimed with a Ticket Receipt Form from any Lottery retailer.

Approximate overall odds are 1 in 4.82.

All tickets, transactions and winners are subject to Lottery rules, directives and state law and any prospective and uniform changes thereof. Liability for void ticket is limited to replacement of ticket or refund of retail sales price. This ticket is a bearer instrument.

Odds of winning a prize and the number of winning tickets produced are established before ticket sales begin, and will change as prizes are won. Tickets may continue to be sold after all top prizes have been claimed. Visit our website for remaining top prizes. Printed in Michigan.

If you bet more than you can afford to lose, you've got a problem. Call 1-800-270-7117 for confidential help.

Join PLAYER CITY™, the Michigan Lottery's VIP Club at **www.playercity.net.** Membership is FREE!

_____

WINNER'S SIGNATURE

_____

NAME (PRINT LEGIBLY)

**MICHIGAN LOTTERY REVENUE
SUPPORTS EDUCATION.**
www.michigan.gov/lottery

**GAME NO. 866
CASHWORD**

0-866-063732-035

"All of you?"

"All of us," the spokesman said.

The others agreed eagerly.

"If I may?" said the spokesman. "To Maur!"

"To Maur!"

The Tommy Johns upper ranks—what was left of them—were ushered around the table, where they merged with the Jackie Macks.

HOURS LATER, the Foreman cursed himself for the fool he had been.

What had he been thinking?

He had been wearing rose-colored glasses for days. His whole relationship with Maur had taken on the aspect of a fairy tale in his imagination—Christ, he even thought of himself as the mysterious knight who had stolen into the life of a dysfunctional kingdom and smitten the exotic Celtic princess.

They would throw their little kingdom into turmoil, then set it right again. Their extreme natures were the very things that made them capable of manipulating the kingdom, as well as the very thing that attracted him to her, and her to him.

The truth was all too clear, but only after the whole wonderful fairy tale came crashing down around him. She was not a princess, just another street thug who happened to be spectacular naked. He was no knight— just a freak with good self-preservation instincts.

It was his instincts that revealed the truth to him

even as he was feeling more content than he had felt in years. They were in the afterglow of a rambunctious session that left Maureen panting in his arms.

"You okay there, Li'l Poke?"

"This lassie couldn't be better, Cowboy." She sat up and looked at him.

"What's the matter?"

She swung her leg over him and sat on his pelvic bone. "Hey, Cowboy, let's keep doing this. Let's be together forever."

"Aw, Poke."

"Listen, I'm not asking you to marry me. You don't have to live here. You don't have to tell me your name. You can just be Cowboy forever. I don't care. I just want you with me."

The Foreman was stunned.

"Just do what you do. You do the behind-the-scenes work. I'll run the scene in the front. It'll all work out just like it did today. And every time it works out we'll celebrate like this."

He just stared at her.

"We'll keep it a business arrangement if you want, Cowboy. We'll have a standing contract or something. I don't care just so long as we keep doing it just like this. You and me. Please, Cowboy."

"You had me at 'Hey, Cowboy,'" he said.

She grew a broad, happy smile, and in the glow of streetlights coming into Jackie Mack's apartment, she was as pale as a corpse and as lovely as a bride on a magazine cover. She rocked on top of him, he responded, and they consummated their new life together.

The Foreman didn't know if he had ever been happier.

She collapsed into an afternoon siesta. The Foreman nodded off, contented, then his eyes sprang back open.

He felt the warning instinct. Danger. It was a whisper, but it came from *her*.

Oh, God, it had been there, in the back of his brain, itching him, and he had ignored it. It had come into being when she'd asked him to be her partner—and he had agreed. He had avoiding recognizing it. He had tried to not feel it, but it was growing and it couldn't be ignored any longer.

She was the danger. Their commitment to form a bizarre sort of marriage was enough to make her a danger.

The alarm grew like rising voltage. His flesh was crawling where her skin touched his. He hurried out of her bed.

She was a ghostly vision of loveliness, so entrancing that, for just a moment, the whistling danger warning was muted.

Then it was there again, amplifying. The Foreman hurried into the bathroom and stared into the mirror. He was naked and exposed and utterly at risk.

But why? he demanded silently. Maureen wasn't trying to trap him or defeat him. She wanted him to keep doing what he did, come and go as he pleased. She wasn't even asking for his real name. What better arrangement could a freak like him ever ask for?

But she was a danger.

"What kind of danger?" he demanded of his own reflection.

The mirror didn't answer.

"But how did this happen," he mouthed. "She wasn't a danger before. Why didn't I sense it before?"

His reflection seemed to give him a look that said, "You idiot. Think about it."

He thought about it. He didn't sense danger in her before that moment, because Maureen had not been a danger to him until that moment. The commitment made her dangerous, because the commitment obliged him to her.

So that's it? I can't ever have a girlfriend, because the very fact that she's my girlfriend makes her dangerous.

But he had had girlfriends. It was just that they had all been milquetoast. Submissive, or at least docile. Never before had he been with a woman who was in any way willful.

"Fine, then," he announced in his mind. "No commitment. I'll keep my distance. I'll stay away. I'll come to Maureen on no terms but my own."

It didn't matter. The commitment was not promises, only an emotional tie. The rising siren of alarm told him that his promises changed nothing.

She was lost to him. He understood it at last. He

could no more stay, with the alarm constantly screaming in his mind, than could a goldfish swim in a piranha tank, no matter how affectionate he felt to the
piranha. One day or another, the piranha would get
hungry enough, and that would be that.

"I'll leave," he announced. "I'll never see her again.
All my girlfriends from now on will be docile little
cows. No more strong women."

"Who you talking to, Cowboy?"

The door creaked open. Maureen was standing there,
but it was an entirely different creature from the Maureen he knew and, yes, loved. He gulped. He loved
Maureen, and Maureen was dead to him now. The thing
in the bathroom door was a furnace of danger, so hot it
burned him even from here.

"Cowboy? Something the matter?"

He made a choking sound, then barreled into her
and past her, into the room. The screaming danger
almost sent him into a panic. He stumbled and fell on
the bed. He tried telling himself that it was not
Maureen that had become a shrieking demon, it was
how he saw her now.

It didn't work. Whatever it was once, it was a shrieking demon now. Every moment he spent near it was a
moment of danger.

He stumbled out of the apartment. She called his
name and it was like a fire-heated nail penetrating his
brain. He fell into the elevator and descended.

Somehow he'd had the common sense to take his

pants with his wallet in the pocket. He put them on and hurried into the sunlit street, falling into a cab.

He was on the far side of town when he realized the sense of danger had fallen low—but hadn't vanished. He bought a T-shirt and flip-flops at a convenience store, then headed for the airport. He was on the next plane to Boston.

Something was horribly wrong. He got halfway across the Logan terminal before he truly believed that the sense of danger was still there.

And he knew why. Because *she* was still there— back in Brooklyn, waiting for him.

He didn't want to think what that meant.

The Foreman got on the first nonstop to Dallas/Fort Worth. He sat in a waiting room at Dallas/Fort Worth Airport, unable to believe that he could still feel the warning.

For the first time, the danger wasn't localized. It wasn't a danger he could run away from, because Maureen's very existence was a danger to him. As long as she was, he would want her, and as long as he wanted her she was perilous to him.

Even now, he longed to go to her and hold her.

The warning blasted like an air horn and he grabbed his head. Then the Foreman headed to the ticket counter. He got on the same plane, heading back to New York City.

He found her. He told her how much he cared for her as he gripped her neck and forced his thumbs into her throat. She looked so confused, so betrayed, and more than anything he wanted to explain this all to her—but there wasn't time. He couldn't live with the shrieking danger for another instant. He had to end it now.

The instant she was dead, the warning went from unbearably strident to absolutely nothing. He was safe from her at last.

Well, he tried to tell himself, it had been good while it lasted.

A temporary descent into idiocy.

A few laughs, a few bedroom thrills, but now it was time to move on. It was time to bury himself in his work.

After all, he had a kennel full of dogs in Upstate New York just waiting for another hunting trip.

20

"Christ, Chiun, talk to me, would you?"

They were on the flight from Salt Lake City back to New York. Chiun turned to him. "What would you have me say?"

"Just talk to me about this! What does it mean?"

"It means nothing."

"It means something."

There was a cough from the next row and Chiun turned his head away, leaving Remo feeling very alone. His mind was working on everything he had seen, desperately looking for an explanation that meant something different from what he thought it meant.

But he had seen the dogs react to Chiun. They were trained to smell disease in human beings and they had reacted to Chiun as if he were fresh, raw meat.

Chiun saw it, too. He had obliterated the dogs out of embarrassment more than anything else.

Remo weighed the problem in his head, unable to get through the mess it all made up there. He was reliving the incident with the dogs and he was considering what

Chiun had said about lessons learned. How did a Master of Sinanju keep on learning his lessons even when he no longer had a Master? How did he keep learning when he was the Master and he had his own student, who was depending on him for wisdom?

Remo felt a twinge of despair. How could he ever be responsible for imparting wisdom to a Sinanju Master-in-training? He didn't have wisdom. He didn't even have common sense.

And now Chiun was sick? Chiun was dying? How could that be? Chiun couldn't die. He was Little Father, Remo's Little Father. Chiun was *the* Master of Sinanju. He couldn't die.

Remo wanted to spin the old man around in his seat and say, "Look, you screwed up! I don't have what it takes. I'm too dense to be somebody's teacher. I don't even think I would be a good assassin without you around."

How selfish would that be? How selfish was this whole train of thought—it was all about how horrible it would be for him if Chiun wasn't with him anymore.

He folded his arms and slumped in the seat and stared at the little reading light in the ceiling.

When he closed his eyes, he had a dream-memory. Nothing fantastic—just a word-for-word replay of something that had actually happened some time ago.

REMO FOUND Sarah Slate packing her suitcase in the rooms where she had been living with Mark Howard in the private wing of Folcroft Sanitarium. It was just across the hall from the rooms Chiun and Remo shared.

"What's going on?" Remo was alarmed. "What happened?"

"Nothing happened," Sarah said. "Just packing up."

"You're going home?"

"Home to Rye. Mark's apartment."

"Oh. Okay, then."

She seemed amused. "You thought I was moving back to Providence?"

"Yeah."

"That would distress you?"

"Kind of."

"Really?"

"I'd probably be asked to off you."

"Oh." Her amusement died on her lips and she continued stuffing folded clothes into the suitcase. "What's up, Remo?"

"Nothing."

"Why are you here?"

"Just visiting."

"Are you going to miss having us here?"

"Sure. Why not."

She opened a hospital chest of drawers and extracted more clothing.

"Can I ask your opinion about something? In secret?"

She turned and leaned her butt against the drawers. "Okay."

"You won't tell Junior?"

"Not if you ask me not to."

"Okay. What do you know about IQ tests?"

"Not much."

"There was a book that came out about IQ tests and how some races of people seemed to do better than other races did."

Sarah Slate shook her head slightly, as if she was trying to clear her confusion. "This isn't what I thought you wanted to talk about."

"Now, there's something wrong with it. Something I'm not getting. What's wrong with it?"

"Wrong with what? You've lost me, Remo."

"The whole idea is wrong somehow. Not wrong because it is all about race, but wrong because it just doesn't make sense. But why doesn't it make sense?"

Sarah Slate still wasn't up to speed, but she put her hands behind her head and stretched back, considering the problem. Remo couldn't help noticing her belly button peek out from under her blouse.

"What kind of intelligence are they talking about?" Sarah asked.

"Just IQ. What else is there?"

"There's a lot more. There are different kinds of intelligence."

"What?"

"They teach it in Psychology 101. There's spatial reasoning and logic and geometric. These are all kinds of intelligence. But just think about it and you'll know that there has to be lots of different kinds of intelligence. There are people who can design computers but they can't identify an obvious literary symbol in a simple verse. I could give you a hundred examples like that. So, what is IQ anyway? It's something somebody made up. It's just a number. You can't score a person's capabilities like a basketball game."

"I think I get it," Remo said.

"Maybe you can measure a person's skill at long division. But some people can perform long division on paper and some need an abacus. Which one's smarter? And that's just talking about long division. Think about all the different skills that you could point to to say somebody is smart. Nobody's smart enough to figure out how to measure all the things that makes someone else smart."

Remo snapped his fingers. "I get it. You can't measure it. You can't say somebody is stupid because nobody can ever know all the ways there are to not be stupid."

"What's this about, Remo?" Sarah seemed to have run out of patience.

He understood a little bit better about himself. He wasn't stupid. Okay, maybe he was stupid in some ways. But in a lot of ways at least he had some kind of aptitude. He had aptitude to learn Sinanju, both the physical skills and the mental skills.

Chiun knew he had aptitude, too. No matter how poor he thought Remo's intelligence was, Chiun must believe Remo had aptitude.

Remo was walking, talking proof of it. Because Chiun, the wise old Master of Sinanju that he was, would never, ever have trained Remo if he thought Remo didn't have aptitude.

He was awake again, wondering why he'd had that mundane little dream. Did it tell him something? Was the dream reminding him that he knew he wasn't stupid?

Okay, so he wasn't stupid, but he wasn't wise, either, and that's what he was worried about.

Or was it? Why was he worried about being wise all of a sudden?

Was there something else he should be getting from the dream memory? Was his memory flawed, or was Sarah Slate getting goo-goo with him that day? Christ, he hoped not.

Didn't he hope not?

He didn't want Sarah Slate to be goo-goo about him. Even if he did, he still didn't, because Sarah was supposed to be goo-goo about Mark Howard. Hell, how had he got on this line of thought? This is not what he was supposed to be thinking about.

He sat forward, frustrated beyond belief. What the hell was he supposed to be thinking about? He wasn't sure anymore.

He really *was* stupid.

21

The black waters of the Bykal Alean were frigid, even this time of year. Rjuven Ystadwas terrified of the ocean, and to him the ink-black waters were like the putrid petroleum sludge of Satan himself.

He put his paddle in wrong and a few icy droplets splashed onto the bare skin of his face. He made a quick little sound and wiped it off fast, as if it were acid that could burn him.

"Get a grip, Rjuv." Herschel was in the second kayak, not far off, although he could have pulled a hundred yards in the lead if he had chosen to.

"Sorry."

"I honestly don't know if you should be out here on the open water."

"I have to be," Rjuven said. "It's the only way for the truth to be revealed."

"Yes, but it's also a good way for you to get yourself killed, and then you won't be revealing nothing to nobody."

"That's why I have you with me, Hersch."

"Against my better judgment." Herschel paddled easily, his paddle dipping so gracefully into the ocean waters that it was a like a spoon stirring a rich, thick syrup. How'd he get so good at this? They had both taken the same kayaking course last summer. How come Herschel was so good at it and Rjuven wasn't?

Because Herschel was good at everything and Rjuven was good at nothing.

"You're wasting energy," Herschel said. "Put the paddle in the water at the least amount of an angle. See?"

"Yes. I took the same lessons you did."

"I'm trying to help you, Rjuv. We've got a long voyage ahead of us and I don't want you killing yourself or me. Now, reach higher before you put the paddle in the water, and bring it down more directly. Reach. Sharp like a knife. Good."

"I got it. Now leave me alone."

"Okay. I sure hope you know what we got ahead of us, Rjuv. It's a big ocean out there."

The suffocating walls that towered on either side of the Bykal Alean finally ended and opened into the vista of the black, heaving ocean.

The Gulf of Bothnia was angry with the world for what it was doing to her. If mankind wasn't excreting its industrial wastes directly into her waters, then it was poisoning the land and the streams that seeped into the fjords and eventually leached into the sea. Not a hundred miles north of where they were at this very minute were toxic lead mines. Just another hundred miles south were filthy zinc-mining operations and iron-ore excavations.

Sweden didn't have much in the way of manufacturing. The land was spared that evil—at least when compared to nearby nations. Only the winds that swept the Baltic Sea kept Germany's pollution from choking off all life in Scandinavia.

Scandinavia was on the verge of industrialized suicide—and this in one of the environmentally cleanest parts of the Western world. The land was positively pristine compared to the grimy conditions in Germany and the sulfuric slop that coated the British Isles from one end to the next. Italy's air was full of the fumes of incinerating plastics. In France, the air on the streets was a cloud of carbon monoxide and carcinogens—not to mention the dangerously high levels of radioactivity from their nuclear power plants. There was a reason Paris was called the City of Lights, and it had nothing to do with strands of holiday bulbs draped on the Eiffel Tower—it was because the very walls and soil and streets of the city practically glowed in the darkness. That's just how radioactive the place was.

Rjuv had taken the Tour of a Self-Destructing Europe soon after he joined the Greener Sweden Activities Organization. Any doubts he could possibly entertain about his environmental philosophies—and he didn't have any—were erased on his three-day, nine-nation bus trip on the European Continent. There was no time for seeing historical sights. No opportunity for dining in fine restaurants.

"Listen, friends," said Guirdag, "Lingering anywhere in Europe is the last thing you want to do. For every hour you spend here, your life will be two hours shorter. That's been proved by scientists at the Greener Sweden Activities Organization Laboratories in Trundheim."

The famous labs. A lot of explosive research results came out of the Trundheim facility. Not a month went by that the crack staff of environmental researchers didn't publish some new revelation about the dire state of the planet's ecology. Rjuv had never been to the facility—he lived in Trundheim, but could never seem to find the place. Later he was told the location was kept a secret.

"If the governments of the United States found out where our think tank was situated, they would come in and sabotage us, no doubt," Guirdag explained. "Or the British secret service or even the United Nations. We give one of them a bad black eye each time we make a discovery. We expose the lies in their environmental policies. We make a mockery of them. How long do you think we would last if they were able to locate our laboratory and research school?"

Confidentially she informed Rjuv that, in fact, the facility might not be in Trundheim at all.

"I think it is really up north, in Troms, maybe. Safe from foreign eyes."

Guirdag was a wise, well-informed hunk of a woman. Rjuv hung on her every word. When she insisted he book passage on the Tour of a Self-Destructing Europe, he complied, even if it meant maxing out three credit cards. The cost was high, and the amenities were few and far between.

"Remember, this is not a trip for pleasure," Guirdag said. She organized the tour, including the booking of the charter bus. "Think of this as your college education, preparing you for your career as professional environmental protectors. We go so that you can see and smell and taste the poison that drags Europe into the grave day by day. We go to help you see the wisdom of your decision to dedicate yourselves to lifelong activism. And you *have* made this decision! Yes?"

It was at the orientation meeting of the Buskerund Regional Branch of the Greener Sweden Activities Organization, that Rjuv heard about the Europe tour for the first time. Clearly, all of those who truly wished to dedicate themselves to the cause were expected to go on the tour—otherwise, how would they know the scope of the problem?

Rjuv had not, in fact, decided that this should be what he dedicated his life to. In fact, until today he had not thought about dedicating his life to any one thing. But that was before he met Guirdag. That was before she revealed to him the true scope of Earth's ecological affliction. Her exhortations transformed him from environmental hobbyist to fervent activist.

So when she pointed a finger at him and demanded to know if he was dedicated, he answered, "Yes!"

She gave him a stern smile that said, "You have shown you are a worthy man."

Reward enough. Then she moved on to the frail woman in the next seat, with her limp hair, gnawed fingernails and visibly chapped lips. "And you! Are you dedicated?"

She practically curled up in her seat. She had no choice, really. "Yes," she peeped.

Guirdag gave her a smile, too, but it was not the same smile. It said, "You are spared—for now."

After that, the rest of the new recruits followed the crowd. Nobody wanted to defy Guirdag.

Part and parcel with their commitment to the cause was their commitment to take the European bus tour. "Sign up now. You will find the money later. This I know. Determined activists find a way."

There were those who hesitated visibly about signing the tour agreement. Guirdag said nothing, but walked away from them and came to Rjuv. He was eager to put his signature on the bottom of the contract.

"You are a rich college boy?" she asked loudly.

"No."

"You have much money in your bank account?"

"No." He wasn't sure where this was going, but it was for the benefit of the others. That signified that Rjuv was being made an example of. A good example. He was Guirdag's pet, and that made him feel extraordinarily happy.

"Where will you get the money for this trip, then?" she asked in the voice of an actor trying to reach the farthest row in the upper balcony.

"I do not know. But I will get it. I do what I have to do. This is too important to miss."

He had a feeling it was exactly the right thing to say. The look on Guirdag's face told him he was right. Her eyes radiated satisfaction, then she turned on the others. "One man made his pledge and one man stands by what he said! Are there others who will keep their promises?"

Another signed up. And another. Every time one of them signed up, it became harder for the next one in line to back out. Guirdag had to skip over a couple of them as they continued to hesitate, but she came back to them, time and again, until they had all signed on the dotted line.

"How can somebody go to join a protest movement and end up buying a time-share package?" Herschel asked.

"It's not a time share," Rjuv insisted. "It's an important facet of my education. If I'm going to dedicate myself to the cause of saving this planet, I need to know the scope of the true problem."

"Wait a second," Herschel said. "Since when are you dedicating yourself to saving the planet?"

"Since today. I guess I forgot to mention that part of it."

"I guess so."

"I've always been into environmental stuff, right?"

Herschel shrugged. That was true. Rjuv had been running the school's Campaign to clean up Kongberg when they met at the age of twelve. They had been friends ever since, although never really best friends. Still, they were both accepted to university in Trundheim and it was natural to share costs on road trips and a student flat.

"This is really going to interfere with your studies," Herschel pointed out.

"I can do both. This is too important to not involve myself in."

"Whatever," Herschel said. "But I still don't get the whole bus-tour thing. You've been to Paris and Rome and we were in Germany for two weeks last year."

"But I was there to enjoy myself. This time I'm going to educate myself. Besides, we're going to other countries, as well. Eastern European countries. That's where the real problems are brewing."

If Herschel had been Rjuv's best friend, he would have belabored the point. Tactfully, he shrugged off his roommate's idiosyncrasies and went on with his own life. He drove Rjuv to the terminal where the bus tour commenced. It was an early May morning, the air snapping with cold, but neither the chill nor the dilapidated condition of their transport could dampen the enthusiasm of the new junior environmental activists of Sweden.

"See you Monday," Rjuv said excitedly as he opened the door, before the car had even come to a complete stop.

"Have a blast," Herschel said uncertainly when Rjuv was pulling his knapsack out of the car.

On Monday, Rjuv's phone call rolled Herschel out of bed an hour after he crawled into it.

"What's happened?" Herschel was alarmed.

"Nothing happened except you didn't pick me up at the terminal."

Herschel took a moment to collect his thoughts. "You're back already? In Trundheim?"

"Yeah. I told you eleven-thirty on Monday night, remember?"

Herschel said, "You mean the trip is *supposed* to be over already? It wasn't shortened for some emergency?"

"Of course not."

Herschel drove to the terminal. Rjuv's face was long and limp like an old dishrag.

"I'm still trying to understand this, Rjuv," was the first thing Herschel said. "You knew all along that this trip was going to be nine European countries—plus a ferry ride to and from Sweden—and that it was going to be just three days long?"

"More than three days. More like eighty-eight hours."

"But you must have been driving constantly."

"We hardly ever stopped," Rjuv agreed. "Except for some security checkpoints in Czechoslovakia and Romania."

"But where's the fun in that?" Herschel said.

"It wasn't supposed to be fun. Our goal was to get in, expose ourselves to the poisons for educational purposes and get out as quickly as we could."

"What could you possibly learn from it?"

"I didn't expect you to understand."

"Well I hope you didn't pay a lot for that little adventure," Herschel said.

"It was worth every penny."

"Did you at least get decent meals?"

"They were just fine." Rjuv never told Herschel that all members of the tour had packed along their own rations.

"You look like hell, Rjuv."

"I'm fine, but you know how vacations are. I'm more tired than when I left." He forced a laugh.

The truth was, the grinding of the bus's antiquated gearbox had made sleeping almost impossible. Everyone had slumped over unconscious during the precious quiet hours on the ferry from Denmark.

Rjuv had to admit, though, the trip had been rushed and not as enlightening as he would have liked it to be. Although Guirdag exhorted her enlistees to breathe and taste and see the airborne poisons as they crossed each new border, Rjuv had been able to taste and smell only the diesel fumes of their own sputtering bus.

But Guirdag kept his spirits high, and when she left him standing at the bus station, the last to catch his ride home, she had rewarded him with a few words of personal encouragement.

They had a dinner date for the next weekend.

That was a year ago. Rjuv had slowly disengaged himself from his studies. He and Herschel had signed up to learn sea kayaking as a way to impress girls, but Rjuv only went to two of the three classes. Herschel was surprised when Rjuv brought up the idea of a camping and kayaking trip at the inlet near Trom. It turned out there was Greener Sweden Activities Organization business to be taken care of in the vicinity, but Herschel went along.

The problem was that Rjuv had become a zealot. He was hyper-focused on environmental causes.

"For God's sake, Rjuv, talk about something else."

"Like what?"

"School. Football. A joke you heard at the pub. Girls with big tits. Anything."

Rjuv tried to think. He couldn't think of anything.

"You, my friend, are brainwashed," Herschel said.

"I am not."

"There's nothing left in your life anymore except the organization. You stopped going to all your classes. You don't go to the pub anymore. You don't tell jokes. You don't go on dates. What do you have going on in your life besides the clean-up cult?"

"Don't call it a cult."

"Answer the question."

Rjuv said, "I'm going to bed. You should get some rest, too. We're off in a few hours."

Hershel should have let the idiot go off on his own, but he had a sinking feeling Rjuv would never make it back alive. Rjuv wasted his energy and wore out fast. It had always been this way when they played sports in school, and it would be that way on the swells of the gulf.

All to save a bunch of ugly little grouse. Scandina-

vian Speckled Mud-Loving Grouse, Rjuv called them.
Nearly extinct. Just a few pockets of them survived on
the isolated islands off the coast of Sweden. The biggest known population was on the island called Stord,
privately controlled by one of the most respected and
connected men in Sweden. Peter Ohly was a Stockholm
aristocrat, with old money and a distinguished pedigree.
Nobody seemed to believe he was a very bad man.

"We've been trying to nail that bastard for years,"
Guirdag had snarled one evening at the activists center.
"He's wiped out the grouse there, he and his dogs. He
keeps a pen of them on the grounds and lets them loose
when anybody comes nosing around. He's even got the
POWs convinced that he still has a thriving population."

Protect Our Wildlife was a group in Oslo. They were
negotiators—Guirdag called them *inactivists*. Their
ideals were good, but the Greener Sweden Activities
Organization didn't trust them and neither did Guirdag.

"They're a little too cozy with the Riksdag and the
ombudsmen, if you ask me. Always talking about working together with elected officials and advancing our
goals within the framework of the law. There's no time
for that kind of mincing about when whole species are
being exterminated."

Rjuv understood better when he watched an Oslo
Channel 1 documentary that included an interview with
the infamous and duplicitous Peter Ohly. Guirdag
showed the video and hit the pause button as Mr. Ohly
was giving the film crew a tour of his dog runs.

"He must have a hundred dogs in there."

Guirdag made a raspberry sound. "A hundred. He's the world's biggest breeder of Swedish elkhounds. He publicly acknowledges producing twenty litters a year. But the numbers don't add up. Look at those pens. Almost every one of those pens has a breeding pair."

Rjuv tried counting them as the video resumed. "Fifty breeding pair."

"Seventy. Now look at the space he's got penned in. Look in the background. This film crew was never allowed onto the far side of the island, but look at this." She produced a grainy digital photo of a rugged island coastline. A small herd of elk, maybe twenty animals, was surrounded by ten times as many stubby animals. At first he thought they were sheep.

"Dogs!" He had never seen so many dogs in one place before. Hundreds of them—and as he looked closely, he could see that they were tearing the elk to pieces.

"That's right. Swedish elkhounds, every one of them. We think he gives them the occasional elk herd just for sport."

"What's he doing with all of them?" Rjuv asked. "They're not puppies. He can't sell them. Why so many?"

"Who knows?" Guirdag said. "He's a madman. What I do know is that the grouse population doesn't stand a chance with all them mutts having free run of the place. We could have Mr. High and Mighty Peter Ohly arrested, if we could only get proof."

The quality of their one elk photo was too poor, she said. Boat patrols had yielded nothing and had been chased off by Ohly's private security.

"You need someone to sneak onto the island," Rjuv pointed out. "Get good shots of all the dogs running free."

"Yes. That would do it. You volunteering?"

"Maybe I am," Rjuv said.

HE TOLD HER his plan, and something strange happened to the fair and strong Guirdag. Her face, always so stiff with determination, relaxed. Her eyes, always steely, brightened and grew positively girlish.

She showed her appreciation of the idea. Rjuv was almost always trying to get her to show her appreciation, and she relented to his desires on perhaps a monthly basis. No more than that.

This was an unexpected treat. She had shown her appreciation just two weeks ago. Rjuv remembered it had come during a commercial break during the evening newscast from Vasterbotten.

"You would be so big in my eyes if you did that thing," she told him afterward. "*So* big."

HERSCHEL STAYED CLOSE as they left the imposing walls of the bay behind them.

Rjuv began to paddle frantically as his kayak was lifted up, up, up, then descended sharply. He was going down!

"Relax, Rjuv," Herschel said. "Just some swells."

Rjuv reached the bottom of the trough and found

himself on the rise again. He willed himself to paddle slowly, keeping a regular rhythm.

"Sorry. My first time on the ocean."

"I thought you went out with your brother when you went home last year."

"Oh. Yeah."

"You told me you did."

Rjuv had forgotten the lie. The reality was, he had gone home to ask for money. His parents had given him holy hell for "squandering money he didn't have" on a "fool mission." He tried to defend himself, but they wouldn't listen. They claimed to be environmentally aware, and they voted the Green Party ticket and everything, but they were hypocrites in the end if they couldn't see how much Rjuv needed to do what he had done.

"Two thousand euro for a holiday in Italy and Romania?" his father exclaimed. "Somebody made a hefty bundle of cash off you, my boy."

In the end, they agreed to make his minimum credit card payments and keep paying for his share of the apartment, so long as he stayed in school and kept his grades up.

If he hadn't needed cash so badly he would have told them to go to hell. But he did need cash. He needed a way to support himself—for the time being. Something would come up.

He couldn't come back and tell that sob story of a cuckolded son to Herschel. Herschel always seemed to have his act together. Herschel never had to ask his family for financial support. Hershel never needed to follow some stinking cause. So he told Herschel about an idyllic family visit, with quality time with Mom and Dad and some kayaking with his kid brother in Kongberg.

"Well, the truth is, we stayed in the strait all day," he admitted to Herschel. "It was really calm. Not like this. This is like a hurricane."

"It's a real maelstrom, all right, " Herschel said, and rolled his eyes in the dark. "Actually, this is protected water, Rjuv. Nothing like the North Sea."

"Fine. Whatever." Rjuv's nerves were frayed already. His paddle always seemed to hit the water just a little off center. Herschel stayed close behind to keep an eye on his roommate.

The island of Stord loomed ahead of them. With steady progress, they would be on the shore by moonrise.

22

But the moon rose and kept rising for a long while before Rjuv managed to paddle himself onto the shores of the little rocky island in the Gulf of Bothnia. He flipped out of the kayak when he was scraping rocks under the plastic hull, then staggered onto the gravel beach and fell on his back, breathing hard.

Herschel grabbed Rjuv's kayak before it went back out to sea, then dragged both boats high onto the shore. He sat on a rock and drank a bottle of water. Rjuv was still huffing and puffing. He ate a power bar and a salami sandwich. Rjuv finally started to catch his breath.

The guy just didn't know how to work smart, Herschel decided. He wasn't much fitter than Rjuven, but he had only been invigorated by the crossing, not physically wiped out. How the hell would Rjuven have the strength to get himself back to the mainland shore?

The answer? He couldn't. Which meant Herschel would have to tow him in.

"Come on," Herschel said. "Let's get this over with."

Rjuv didn't answer. He was fast asleep.

PETER OHLY HEARD a curious commotion. It was the disturbance of many unsettled dogs.

There was no barking. The packs were trained well enough to keep their yaps shut unless there was a real reason to sound off. But something was bothering them. They were restless in their kennels, murmuring, growling, pacing. One hundred powerful, highly sensitive animals could make a hell of a lot of rustling around.

He swung his feet out of his Gøün bed carelessly and the bed swayed. The bed was a streamlined impressionist reinterpretation of the Stockholm ultra modernists industrial design movement, executed in pewter, hand-plated with bronze. The bed riveted the eye but had barely enough mechanical integrity to hold itself together if Ohly did anything as drastic as getting into it or out of it. The one time he actually tried to get a partner into the thing it collapsed when the activities were just getting started. The young lady lost the mood and, worse, the bed required expensive repairs by the original artist to get it back into original condition.

Ohly placed his feet flat on the floor to steady the swaying of the Gøün bed. He flipped on the light outside his private bedroom. The lamps flooded the kennels. A hundred pairs of eyes turned in his direction and became demonic red.

Several were trotting the length of their runs. Others

were pawing at the chain link. Not one of the animals was asleep.

He grabbed the phone and dialed his man on the dock. He had no idea there was a disturbance.

"The system's all green lights."

"Get in the water. Something is going on."

"Yes."

He hung up and looked out the window again. The more agitated dogs were calmer now.

Nothing to worry about, right? He wasn't doing anything illegal. Right? He was just raising dogs.

What was the worst that could happen? Some sort of a raid by the police? Why would they? And if they did, they would find nothing. Peter Ohly was innocent of wrongdoing. Maybe not once, but now he was, and he would make sure he stayed that way.

Oh, wait. The cave. The police would probably find the cave, and that would get Ohly in a lot of trouble.

He needed to get the cave cleaned out.

BORAS LUND sweet-talked *Bergsa* as he stroked her little rump. She responded eagerly. She was a good girl, his *Bergsa*. He treated her with love and tenderness, and she was always ready for him whenever he needed her.

She purred for him. The secret was in the lubrication, he liked to tell the guys at the pub at Sunsvall on his days off. Keep her rear parts lubricated with good, natural oils and she'll always come through for you. None of those synthetic lubes for Boras and his pretty little *Bergsa*.

He steered her away from the dock and kept *Bergsa* in the middle of the pass, far away from the reflectors nailed to the rock on either side. Those rocks would love to sink their teeth into *Bergsa's* firm white flesh. Pull open her heaving fiberglass bosom. Her clean, well-oiled innards would slide out and scatter in the rocks.

He'd never let that happen to her. He used special care not to turn too soon as he emerged from the pass. There was a rocky outcrop that lurked just below the waves, hoping for a taste of sweet fiberglass meat. Boras wouldn't give the evil rock the satisfaction.

Boras was a believer in old ideas. A Christian he was, like all good men these days, but the stories that were a part of his family for generations were too resilient to be easily dismissed. There was something to them, the tales of the people of the rocks and the sea. His grandma, when he went to sea, would tell him to watch for the *sjöjungfru* in the rocks. He believed in *sjöjungfru*, just as he believed in the trolls on land, and knew what *sjöjungfru* was capable of. But he would never let the nasty sea ladies take his sweet *Bergsa*.

He swept the shore of the island with his spotlight, looking for intruders.

RJUV SAT UP with a gasp.

"It's a patrol boat."

"Patrol boat? As in coast guard?" Herschel asked.

"Private security."

"You didn't say anything about security."

"We have to hide the kayaks."

Herschel knew now was not the time to argue. He hoisted his kayak overhead and trotted it into the bigger rocks at the top of the shoreline, tucking it out of sight. Rjuv didn't have the energy left in him to get his own kayak overhead, so he was trying to drag it. The noise of the rocks seemed amplified. Herschel lifted the other end and they put it away behind the boulders, then flopped on the gravel alongside them.

The little boat was already swinging into view, stabbing at the shore with a white-hot spotlight. The craft hummed like a purring housecat, while the spot sizzled at one spot on the shore, then gyrated crazily to another spot, then to another.

"It's not just a nightly patrol, Rjuv," Herschel hissed. "They know we're here."

"They couldn't know. We came in silent and dark."

"They could have infrared motion detectors or something. Whatever, they know and they've got a boat looking for us. I never would have come if I knew it was gonna be dangerous."

"Quiet."

"Now you're going to start being cautious."

But Herschel shut up. The spotlight flashed across the shore and stopped nearby. It lingered for five seconds, eight seconds, then seared down the beach, penetrating the gaps in the rocks like laser beams and blinding them temporarily.

Then they were in darkness again and the purring of

the boat diminished like a contented cat slowly drifting to sleep.

"We're fine," Rjuv said. "He missed us."

"I SPOTTED 'EM," Boras radioed. "Rocks all wet from the tide edge into the rocks where they walked. Bet they have some little boat hid up there."

Peter Ohly swore. "How many?"

"Who can say? I saw one trail of water, but it could have been made by one or twenty."

"Christ! Call the others."

"I called them already."

"Move in and check them out," Ohly snapped. "We have to know what we're dealing with."

"That'd be the death of this pretty boat of yours, Mr. Ohly. Vicious rocks lurk along the shore. They hunger for her sweet flesh."

"All right," Ohly said. "Keep circling. Watch for any other sign of them."

"This little girl is strong, but too comely for her own good. The rocks have the passion to tear into her."

Ohly snapped off the phone.

THEY CAME OUT of the dormitory stretching and yawning.

The barrel-chested Welshman with the old-fashioned bushy mustache led the way to the Second Kennels, which were in the soft-rock depressions that turned the island into a two-mile-wide soup bowl. As recently as a few hundred years ago the bowl was filled with rainwater—a rare freshwater island lake. Then a fissure opened in the rock and the water drained out.

Now the Second Kennels were at the bottom of the bowl, where they could not be seen from the water or even from the living areas of the island. Only an aircraft would have spotted the kennels—but only if it was looking for something unusual. The kennels were camouflaged above and on the sides.

The dogs in the Main Kennels were restless. Mr. Ohly was walking the floors, too. They could see the light on in the bedrooms on the top floor of the steel-and-glass nightmare he called a home.

The dogs in the Second Kennels were as alert, but outwardly they appeared more calm than their parents—and they were all offspring of the breeding pairs in the Main Kennels. These were the result of the hidden litters. For every litter that was registered with the strict Swedish kennel club, three litters were never revealed. These animals had bloodlines just as pure as their official siblings, and their skills and training were far superior in some interesting ways.

The Welshman with the handlebar mustache pulled out a ring of oversize keys and unlocked the front run in the hidden kennels.

Two sleek animals, an all-white female and a patch-work male, waited for his instructions.

"Liv. Död. Come with me."

The dogs named Life and Death marched out of the enclosure. From other chain-link dens, more dog pairs emerged and followed the corridor that took them by the den of the lead pair and outside.

Liv and Död sat at the Welshman's heels. Their pack formed ranks behind them.

The other men and women hurried to unlock all the gates. The pack assembled outside the enclosures, sitting quietly. It had taken less than a minute to form ranks.

Then the Welshman said, "Come."

The dogs, and the other trainers, obeyed.

"I'M LEAVING," Herschel said.

"I'm staying. I have to get proof of what's going on here. We're talking about the annihilation of a species."

"Not a species. One flock of a species. Not even nice birds. You're gonna risk getting shot over a couple hundred feathered rats. I have news for you—they're wringing the necks of that many birds every day in Stockholm for Grouse under Glass at the nice restaurants."

"We'll discuss it later. I'm gonna get some pictures." He flipped on his camera.

"Of what? You expecting to find a pile of rotting grouse?"

"I expected to find an overpopulation of elkhounds. Hundreds of them. Trained killers."

WHO'S THE FOOL? I'm the fool, Herschel thought. I should be heading for the shore, grabbing my kayak, putting it in the water. I should be getting the hell out of here.

But leaving Rjuv behind could very well be a death sentence. His roommate would never have the endurance to paddle all the way back to the mainland.

"If I tricked you into coming back to the boats with me, then I could knock you on the head with a rock, put you in your kayak and tow you back to the mainland. But you'd probably fall out and drown."

"I'll go with you willingly after I have taken pictures of the dogs."

"Hundreds of dogs," Herschel added. "Hundreds of trained killer dogs. You're going to take some flash photos of them, then leave."

"They'll be in kennels, or pens," Rjuv said.

"You hope."

They were ascending the rocky hillside that rose from the shoreline, and they came to the top, catching their breath. Herschel stopped breathing and hissed at Rjuv.

"I guess you were wrong about the kennels."

"Yes."

On the windswept, treeless island, they could see the mass of animals streaming across the land, their coats glistening in the moonlight. The animals were split into packs. Each pack was led by two dogs, with a human being flanking the leaders.

One pack circled the island clockwise while the others circled counterclockwise. Another pack came up the middle. All of them converged on the place where Hershel and Rjuv were catching their breath.

"I was right about there being a lot of them, though."
Rjuv raised the camera.

Hershel snatched it away. "Are you freaking insane?" he whispered. "Come on."

He started back down the steep, rocky hillside. It wasn't quite steep enough to be called a cliff. The descent was much faster than the climb up had been, since they gave no heed to the minor scrapes and bruises that came from sliding down the irregular rock face as fast as they could go. Herschel felt a sharp, stony edge slice his leg through his water-resistant thermal suit and into his skin. He ignored it, like all the other little pains he collected on the way down. But when he collapsed on the gravel, he found it hard to get to his feet. His leg was stiffening.

He forced through the pain and limped at top speed to the place where the kayaks were hidden.

Then the dogs came—another pack, circling the island at shore level. They noiselessly leaped around the boulders and the kayaks, and the pack came to a halt facing Hershel and Rjuv.

"What do you want?" Hershel shouted at the stern-faced woman who accompanied them. She was as lifeless and unresponsive as a butler at a formal dinner party. The two dogs at the head of the pack stayed on their feet and stared Hershel down.

Rjuv snatched the camera out of his chest pocket and snapped a picture. The flash transformed the brooding pack into stark, red-eyed demons for one heartbeat, then the darkness masked them again.

Hershel steeled himself for the rush, but the flash didn't send the dogs into a fury of violence.

Rjuv took a few more snapshots.

Hershel heard the sound of breathing behind him and turned. He made a startled sound when he found another pack within a few paces of them.

The man who flanked the pack leaders was something out of a comic strip from the 1940s. He was in fitted black trousers, highly polished hiking boots of mahogany leather and a turtleneck sweater that looked fine enough for a black-tie dinner party. His mustache was a huge, bristling affair.

Hershel couldn't help himself. The stress was too much and the man was just too comical. He laughed sharply.

The leaders of the pack shifted on their paws.

"What are you supposed to be?" Hershel asked.

The man said something in what might have been English. Hershel spoke pretty good English, but he didn't catch a word of it.

"Who are you people?" Rjuv demanded in English. "Are you all a part of the environmental holocaust being perpetrated here?"

The man with the bushy mustache chuckled. The dogs standing at his shins were not amused. They growled and stepped closer.

"Liv. Död. Stand down."

The dogs backed off.

Now it was Hershel's turn. He guffawed.

"Life and Death? I must be missing something. Where's 'life' come into the picture?"

"We will show you the life," she said with an American accent. It was the woman handler in the other pack. She was close to them now. Hershel realized their stalling had been for a purpose. The packs had spread out on the shore. There was now a ring of animals between Hershel and Rjuv and the frigid waters of the Gulf of Bothnia.

"Advance," the man with the mustache said.

The dogs crowded toward them. Hershel and Rjuv backed away.

"These animals were trained in two stages," the American woman explained. She sounded like a guide in a museum. "The Swedish elkhound has unequaled olfactory talents. It can smell the presence of disease in the human body. It can even be trained to smell out cancers and infection in the body at early stages, far too early for medical science to detect."

Hershel was trying to make sense of the lecture as he painfully limped away from the approaching line of attack dogs.

"The first stage of the training teaches the dogs to make such diagnoses," the woman continued.

"Admirable work," Hershel said. Maybe he could polite these people into sparing his life.

"We are the trainers in charge of the second phase of the dogs' education. We teach the dogs to work in organized units. They work in pairs and the pairs can be grouped in units comprised of two pairs, four pairs or as many as twenty pairs of animals. We take advantage of the natural hierarchy that develops among the animals."

"Yes?" Hershel said agreeably as he was backed against a rock and struggled around it. The dogs were now shoulder to shoulder.

"They learn that during group exercises and operations they must subvert their need to fight for position in the extended pack. A natural leader rises to the top."

"What kind of exercises?" Hershel asked. His leg was screaming. He was against the cliff. He looked up and saw the top of the cliff was packed with more dogs and their handlers. Hershel's idiot roommate Rjuv was tapping his camera, trying to get the flash to charge up.

The dogs kept coming. The man with the funny mustache gestured down the beach. The dogs were leaving an open walkway. The prisoners were supposed to go that way. Hershel staggered down the beach cooperatively, with his roommate tagging along.

"Exercises such as this," the woman explained. "But this is not typical. The exercises that the dogs are trained for are to cull disease carriers. They can follow their noses to the disease carriers and exterminate them."

"Disease-carrying elk?" Hershel said.

The woman smiled. "Who would possibly benefit from culling the elk herds?"

"You mean, people? You're going to kill people?"

"Oh God, oh God," Rjuv said suddenly. "Herschel, there were attacks in the United States. A bunch of people were slaughtered. Everybody said it was trained dogs that did it."

"They were going to die anyway," the woman said pleasantly. "These are the last packs to go out. We've been training the animals for more than four years. All the others are already in the United States. Hundreds of them."

"But why?"

"Because health-care costs are out of control," the woman said. "I know. I used to have HMO coverage. The premiums were ridiculous! Do you know how much it costs to keep alive a patient with lung cancer during the two years it takes for him to die? It can be as much as a million dollars. And the death is not pleasant. So truly we're bestowing a great mercy on someone by giving them a quick death, in contrast to the lingering agony of a life that is sustained artificially in a hospital."

"Why are you telling us this?" Rjuv demanded.

"To keep you distracted during the walk down the beach," the woman said, looking positively buoyant. "But now we're here."

She nodded.

Hershel and Rjuv turned around and found themselves at the mouth of a sea cave. The man with the big mustache said something—again, in English, but his speech was too tortured by his Welsh accent to be understood. He flipped on a battery lantern and set it on a nearby boulder.

It illuminated the inside of the shallow cave, which

was sealed off by a gridwork of iron bars hammered into the rocks and bolted together. The inside was no bigger than a shower stall, and it was filled with the jumbled bones of decaying human beings.

Hershel gagged and threw up his energy bar and salami sandwich. Rjuv hacked on an empty stomach.

A new voice explained, "They're the first set of trainers. They taught the dogs to sense the disease. They thought the animals were being trained in a great new experiment in proactive health care."

The man who spoke was standing above them on a narrow ledge above the cave. He was wearing silk pajama pants and a sturdy wool sweater.

"I'm Peter Ohly," he added, speaking Swedish. "Proactive health care is one of the stupidest ideas ever conjured up by capitalist societies. If you have some poor soul who's doomed to have his guts eaten out by cancer, why in the name of God would you give him life-sustaining treatment? All it does is extend his suffering. Right?"

"Right," Hershel said.

"I'm glad you agree. See, we were sure that the phase one dog trainers would resist the idea of merciful euthanasia. That's why they went in the cage." Ohly glanced significantly down over the cliff edge at his feet. "So I guess I want to ask you men, how do you feel? Do you think we're doing the right thing?"

Hershel didn't think they were doing the right thing,

but there was no point in being disagreeable at this moment.

"Oh yes, it's the right thing."

He elbowed Rjuv. Don't be an idiot, Rjuven, he thought, trying to force his thoughts telepathically into Rjuv's brain.

"Oh, yes, right, I agree one hundred percent."

Ohly smiled and clapped his hands. "Wonderful. Come on, you guys. Let's get you fixed up."

He waved them up the cliff. Hershel couldn't believe their luck had turned around one more time. They weren't going into the cage! He was so filled with relief that he was able to keep the pain at bay as he did the one-legged hop up the series of uneven steps carved in the rock.

Ohly came down a few steps and took his hand. "Nasty scrape. You're losing a lot of blood."

"Yes."

"The crabs will just *love* it," Ohly said.

"What?" Hershel said. Then Ohly maneuvered him a little to the left and gave him a quick shove. There was an opening in the rock at Ohly's feet. Oh. So this was how you got into the cage in the rock. Hershel bounced through the opening, then he fell until he landed on snapping bones. His skin was covered with the smeared, rotting flesh of many human beings.

He tried to scream, but just then his roommate landed on top of him, knocking the breath out of him. Rjuv did enough screaming for the both of them.

Ohly leaned over the opening. "Sorry. I'm sure you're nice people, but I just couldn't be sure that you were on the team. By the way, would you tell me why you're trespassing on my island in the first place?"

"To protect the Mud-Loving Grouse, you devil!" Rjuv shrieked.

Ohly chuckled. "Good God, man, the grouse know enough to stay away from the kennels. I have thousands of them. They've practically overrun the place. I went to great lengths to prove this—television interviews, aviary biologists roaming the whole island. Took a hell of lot of logistics to clear the pups out so it could happen. But I guess that wasn't good enough. Let me ask you this?" Ohly crouched, looking down into the hole. "What will it take to get through to you people?"

Hershel was in shock, so he didn't answer. Rjuv, who had just found his finger lodged in the gelatinous gunk filling the eyeball socket of a human skull, couldn't answer the question, either.

Ohly left. The tide came up. Rjuv tried climbing and jumping up, but it was hopelessly out of reach. The dogs on guard watched his acrobatics with little interest.

Despite his weakness, Hershel struggled to his feet when the water level rose. He'd die of hypothermia in no time if he stayed down there.

"When the water rises high enough, we'll climb right on out," Rjuv said.

"Won't get high enough," Hershel said, his teeth clattering together. "We'll freeze long before."

"We're not going to die," Rjuv insisted.

"We are going to die. Like Ohly says, why go through all the agony?" Hershel slithered down the bars, landing in the messy gazpacho of brine and chunks of softened human beings.

"Don't give up," Rjuv said.

"Can't stand up anymore anyway," Hershel said. "Can't feel the cold."

But, to his surprise, he could feel it when the crabs arrived.

They smelled fresh meat.

23

Guirdag looked at the images on the screen of her computer.

"They're beautiful. They're perfect. I'll send them to the BBC and the Americans and everywhere. Then the Swedish government will have to send out a rescue team."

"It will be too late, Guirdag. I'll be dead in a matter of minutes."

"Speak up. I can't hear what you're saying."

"I have to whisper. There are guards outside. I'm afraid they'll take away the phone."

"What? They take what?"

"The phone," Rjuv said a little louder. "I'm afraid they'll take it before I say what I have to say. Hershel's dead. He drowned ten minutes ago. He keeps bumping into me. There are pieces of dead people all over me. The water is so cold I'm already numb. I can't hold the phone out of the water much longer."

Indeed, it sounded like his jaw was frozen, giving him a drunken slur.

"Yes?"

"I love you, Guirdag. I love you with all my being. I couldn't leave this life without telling you that. And I want to ask you—is there any chance you feel the same for me?"

She was flipping through the images. Dogs and more dogs. "Are you sure you are dying?" she asked.

"Please, don't think of that now. There's no chance for me to escape. My time is almost up. I can't make my hand hold on to the phone. I'm only seconds away from drowning. Please, tell me."

"Yes, I love you, too, Rjuven. Very much."

"Thank God. I am so happy. I can die happy. Good-bye, my sweet, precious Guirdag."

"Yes, bye then."

"My love, goodbye my love. Goodbye."

"Yes, love you, too, good-bye."

There was a sob. It was a cry of pure happiness. And then the connection was lost.

Sheesh. He better be dead, because he'd be unbearably clingy and sappy to her if he made it through. Not to mention, she'd feel obliged to show her appreciation many, many times.

The pictures were really good. Dramatic, convincing, startling. And they were all hers.

She picked up the phone and dialed her contact at BBC News, Stockholm office—only to hang up again.

The pictures were hers. All hers. Rjuv had done an admirable job getting them and he'd died for the cause, but they were hers now. He was dead. Drowned. She checked her watch. Probably drowned by now, but for sure in another few minutes. The point was, he was beyond caring what she did with the pictures.

Maybe nobody had to know about Rjuv and his roommate right away. Maybe the cause would be served better if she played the game differently. By differently she meant *profitably*.

Guirdag began e-mailing thumbnails to all the media contacts in her address book. Subject: "Now accepting your bid."

SHE WAS TOO LATE to make the morning editions in London. A tabloid paper there would front-page it the next day if she gave them exclusivity.

She didn't respond to that. News, she knew, had a tendency to get old fast—even before it was printed. The editors would get over their enthusiasm for a particular story, especially if something even more sensational happened along.

It wasn't even midnight in America. Plenty of time to get into their morning papers. She began e-mailing newspapers with a one-hour bidding deadline. Somebody had to bite, right?

Somebody bit.

It was *Today in the U.S.A., The Nation's Newspaper*, and they were at once eager to get their hands on the pictures and reluctant to trust a source they had never heard of. They agreed to the price—but wouldn't transfer the cash to her bank account in Sweden until they examined the full-size digital images.

EDITOR OSCAR SHANNON stood over the shoulder of his acquisitions editor.

"If they're genuine, they're gold," Kelly Hark said.

"If they're genuine, we'll double our print run," Shannon groused. "But I'm not changing the front-page layout until I see them and until Charlie sees them."

Kelly transcribed the message to the contact in an e-mail and sent it. Her e-mail program bonged when another message arrived at the same time.

"Our office in Stockholm." Hark opened the message and read the contents. "They know who she is—the Swede with the pictures. Some sort of environmental activist."

"She told us that much," Shannon said impatiently. "Can we trust her?"

"Their file is skimpy on her. Says they're trying to track down the reporter covering the Swedish greenie movements. They think she knows the contact. Give them ten minutes."

"Ten minutes is a lifetime," Shannon huffed. "They must be Web-filers."

Web-filers was Shannon's nickname for the new breed of news reporters who typically filed their copy directly to electronic news journals and RSS feeds. They didn't think like newspaper people, who had production deadlines to meet on a daily basis. They didn't have print deadlines, so when it came to dealing with newspapers they thought they had all the time in the world.

There weren't many real newspaper men in the world, men like Oscar Shannon. He remembered a time when newspapers were the real thing. Back in his day, the idea of a nationwide newspaper was exciting and new. One nation, one newspaper—that was innovation. That was the way of the future. Everybody getting the same news at the same time. Nobody could spread the news across the country with the speed of *Today in the U.S.A.* The Internet? Hell, he loved the Internet. It let their reporters file copy instantly. No retyping of blurry faxes. It really streamlined their operations.

He remembered meeting the U.S. vice president who had invented the Internet and shaking his hand. "E-mail's the greatest tool a news publisher ever had."

"Now, you just wait and see," the vice president said in ponderous monotone. "I'm working on something new. I call it a Global Web of Text and Graphics. It will let you put pictures on the Information Superhighway along with words, and leave it somewhere for everyone to see it."

Shannon remembered holding up the reception line at the White House dinner party. "Now, why would I want to put a picture in an e-mail? And why would I want to let just anybody see my e-mail before they go in the paper?"

The vice president smiled. "But what if you could put your newspaper, pictures and all, right on the computer of anybody who wanted to see it?"

Shannon was appalled. "Why do that?"

The White House social coordinator stepped in to

move the reception line along and Shannon never got his answer. He worried over the idea at dinner, but it was a laughable notion, anyway. He sent the vice president a thank-you note. "Novel idea of yours, this worldwide Web of text and graphics," he scrawled on the card. "But don't quit your day job. Take care, Oscar."

He got a note back. "Thanks for the thanks. I like your name. Mind if I use it? Sincerely, Al."

Shannon wrote an even shorter note. "Knock yourself out. Oscar."

Imagine his chagrin when the nightmare materialized. A World-Wide Web. And there were newspapers putting their stuff on the World-Wide Web.

"Free news is a fucking Communist notion," he complained at the press club.

"Oscar," said his much younger managing editor, "you gotta catch up. It's 1994. Communism is yesterday's news and the World-Wide Web is tomorrow's."

"Yer nuts," Oscar growled. "Those papers that give their news away? Out of business. One year I give them. Mark my words—you'll never see *Today's U.S.A.* giving news away free."

By 1996 they were giving it away free. A decade later Shannon was still bitter about it. That son of a bitching vice president and his damn inventions. Now the same vice president was turning into a media mogul—running a cable company where people used the Internet to pick their own TV schedule. It started up about the same time that *TV Guide* stopped putting in TV listings. The world of media was going bonkers.

"Oscar!" his acquisitions editor snapped. "What do I do?"

Oscar snapped back to the present. Kelly had asked him a question about the Swedish character reference. Nothing had come in yet from the reporter who supposedly knew her and ten minutes had elapsed. Damn Web reporters.

"What's the production guys' take on the pictures?"

"They did a quick analysis. The graphics experts agree they're not digitally manipulated, but that doesn't mean the shots weren't staged."

"There's at least a hundred dogs in some of these shots. Wouldn't be easy to stage." Oscar said.

"She's asking fifty grand for full exclusive rights. That's a lot."

The money was the third worry from the top of the list. Number one was running them, then having them exposed as fraudulent. Number two was *not* running them and letting somebody else get all the benefit.

"Buy 'em. Put them on front page."

"Great!" Hark took care of things.

IT ALL FELL APART within hours. Kelly Hark got the bad news from Sweden. It was from the reporter who covered the Swedish greenies. She had finally been tracked down in Norbotten, which the Swedes claimed was a big city in their country.

The reporter's e-mail said, "The one with the pictures is a con artist. Don't give her a dime. Look what she tried to sell me a few months ago."

Attached was a photo of a hairy ape man trudging across a field of snow, dragging a gaggle of birds on leather lines. The caption was, "The Wildman of the Swedish Laplands is not a myth! Here's the proof that the *snowmannen* exists. He was photographed while tending his gaggle of pet Ground Dwelling Tundra Grouse, also highly threatened. The proposed expansion of the Hultfred zinc mines will wipe out both species! Bidding for exclusive rights to this photo start at one thousand kronor."

The *snowmannen* photo wasn't as good as the dog pictures, what with the visible zipper seam beneath the wild man's furry butt.

Kelly didn't want to be the one to tell Shannon. She didn't think she could stand one more of his rants, and this would be a doozy. Her only other option was to quit this very minute.

She thought it over, then sighed and went into his office.

"PULL THE FRONT page!" Shannon bellowed.

"Too late. You know that."

One problem with a national newspaper was that it was printed in a dozen different cities. Shannon was the manager of the nationwide operations, but he didn't have complete authority over the regional guys.

"It's a staged picture," he said.

"Doesn't matter," said the guy who ran the regional office in Washington, D.C. "Once the print run starts, the print run does not stop. That's policy."

Shannon kicked his desk. The steel warped. "Fuck policy. We will *not* put a paper on the streets with that front page. Understood?"

"You authorize the cost of reprinting the whole damn edition and I'll do it. Understood?"

Shannon called the budgeting and finance department.

"The expense will be huge," they said.

"We'll look like idiots if we put it on the streets."

"Did you use the standard disclaimers? These are *purportedly* the same dogs terrorizing the United States? The dogs are being trained in Sweden, then shipped to the U.S., *according to sources*?"

"Of course we did."

"No problem, then."

"Yes problem! I'm a journalist. I don't run a damn tabloid! We'll be held up to ridicule."

"No such thing as bad publicity."

In the end, the D.C. edition went on the streets with the pictures of the Swedish dogs blown up on page one. New York and Boston did, too. Detroit was late going to press, and they were able to pull the page in time. The other editions were an hour behind the East Coast and they were able to replace the page.

"So only the most important markets carried the pictures. Great. *Great!*" Shannon kicked the desk again. Why had he never thought of kicking his desk before? The metal side panel made a satisfying racket and deformed in a soothing way.

The pictures caused a ruckus, some bad publicity and a few hasty press conferences. The paper came up with its own press release, complete with its own sound bite. "We published the photos in limited markets, clearly stating that they were unverified. Our goal was to raise public awareness. If we were simply trying to sell papers, we would have run it in all our editions, across the country."

One of the *Today in the U.S.A.'s* own reporters tried to get to the bottom of the fiasco. Shannon explained the subject was forbidden.

"You can't stifle the free-speech rights of the press, even your own press," his too nosy reporter insisted. "It's against the laws of journalistic integrity—and it's illegal."

"So's murder."

"Don't humor me."

Oscar Shannon said quietly, "I've had my worst day ever in a career that's been almost entirely bad days. You think there's anything humorous about any of this?" His eyes flitted to the decorative carved onyx sacrificial dagger that he'd bought in Mexico.

"I use it as a letter opener," he explained, apropos of nothing. "But in the old days, the pre-Columbian residents of Mexico cut out hearts with daggers like that, according to unverified reports from souvenir sellers at the scene. You think I'm joking about that, too?"

The reporter departed.

Leaving Shannon almost disappointed.

24

Today in the U.S.A. put its news stories online. It also sold an electronic subscription service that gave the reader even more news, mostly regional filler. The only subscribers were transplants. A man who relocated from the Midwest to Phoenix could still keep up with all the daily reports of petty-corruption indictments back home in Chicago. There was a surprisingly large base of people who would pay good money to stay up-to-date on the daily indictments in Chicago, or Boston or New York or wherever they came from.

Harold Smith got the service, too, but he didn't pay for it. He had hacked a permanently open gateway into the servers, and every news story posted to the site was dumped a millisecond later into the Folcroft Four, the big mainframe computers that hummed away in their private basement operating center.

The paper purged the story, but not before Folcroft had it, and Smith's curiosity was piqued.

"The digital image wasn't manipulated," Mark Howard exclaimed finally. "I'm sure of it. Something else made them change their mind midstream about publishing it."

Harold Smith was working on that. They could have been hit with some sort of a breach-of-intelligence order from the federal government, but he quickly ruled that out. Very little went on in the federal Government that Smith didn't see.

So some other entity could have called for the photo to be pulled. Terrorists, threatening violent reprisals. The paper in question wasn't a bastion of journalistic integrity and it would bow to many kinds of pressures.

The answer was in the e-mails—it just took Smith a little while to find the right one. After all, the offices received something on the order of ten thousand messages per hour.

When he found what was looking for, he was stymied. "The *snowmannen*," he mused. "This picture was obviously staged—too obviously."

"*Snowmannen* sounds made-up," Mark observed. "What do you know—it's real. The legend, I mean. The wild man of Lapland. But the photo is so bad it's a joke. But if the dog photos were staged, it's a masterpiece. The clearest shot shows at least ninety-seven individual animals."

Smith had already crunched that data. He wasn't getting a good answer.

"The captions seem to bear it out," Mark added. "These animals all match the description of the Swedish elkhounds. There's a known large population of

Swedish elkhounds in Sweden—no surprise there. There are several large-scale breeding kennels in the country's northern and central coastal regions, which is to be expected. Not much of value here."

"Tell me about the breed."

Mark Howard had those facts at his fingertips. "Swedish elkhounds are an old breed used for centuries to hunt elk in the cold climate. They're powerful dogs. Have to be to take down elk, I would think. They know how to cooperate as a pack when they're hunting. They're good at selecting the best meat-bearing elk from a herd."

"How do they do that?" Smith queried.

"Not sure." Mark scanned his research. "That's not explained so far. It's not even mentioned in the other documentation. Wait. It's a Laplander myth—the dogs protect the people by keeping them from eating the meat of the diseased elk." Mark's voice rose in excitement. "There are Lapland folktales in which the men kill a diseased animal and their own dogs drag the carcass away. The dogs were punished, but the people later realize the elk was infected with a fever and the people would have contracted it if they had eaten the contaminated flesh. If there's a grain of truth to that story, it's a red flag, Dr. Smith."

Smith agreed, but he only nodded silently. He wouldn't allow himself to get enthused about the lead.

"Is there confirmation of the stories?"

"I'm looking." Mark Howard tried to stay as cool as Harold Smith, but he was caught up in the discovery. "Not much available on Scandinavian folktales anywhere."

Mark Howard's personally programmed search routines were assessing networks and databases around the world, public and private. The CURE systems were hacked into governmental intelligence and defense systems around the world, as well as huge government research nets and the higher-education document-storage libraries in every nation on earth. It was a university that gave them a hint of the truth—and it wasn't locked in a private network at all. The search results came from an open Internet archive of historical documents.

"This might help," Mark Howard announced, "if I only read Icelandic."

Dr. Smith looked at the screen. Only the About Us page was translated into non-Scandinavian languages. The automatic translation routines choked on the words.

"It's here," Mark fretted. "Stories about the dogs. But I can't get it into English." His voice rose in frustration.

Harold Smith wordlessly picked up his phone and, to Mark's surprise, summoned someone to the office who could read and comprehend written Icelandic.

"I'M SORRY for disturbing you just as you arrive home from Utah, Master Chiun," Smith said. "We have need of someone with your rare skills. I know of no one whose understanding of the written word is more vast."

Chiun, who arrived looking somber, was clearly pleased by the buttering up. "It is never a time for rest when the needs of the Emperor are unfulfilled."

"You're both laying it on a little thick, aren't you?" Remo said. If Chiun was in a sober mood, Remo was agitated and out of sorts. There must have been an argument in Utah, Smith thought.

Chiun was as dapper and neat as if he had spent an hour fixing himself up. Remo, on the other hand, could use a comb.

Remo glowered and tried to pat down the erect locks of dark hair over one ear. He was ignored by Smith and Chiun. The old Master was handling a stack of white pages printed from the Web site on Howard's screen. Remo studied it.

"Dogs. Soup. Snow. Snow. Ice. Snow. Soup. I guess I know what they were eating in the arctic in the old days."

"*You* can read that?" Mark said.

Remo said, "I can read four words on the whole page—*Dog, soup, snow, ice*."

"I'm astonished that you know any of it."

"You pick up stuff," Remo said. "Although I have no idea where I would have got the Icelandic word for *soup* stuck in my head."

"He is ignorant, not even knowing that he reads about the Swedes," Chiun said. "If he would only attend to what he learns, then he would learn so much more."

"It's not about the Laplanders?" Howard said, disappointed.

"It is written as a Swedish legend, which was recorded by the isolated people of Iceland," Chiun said. "The Icelanders spent their long winter months either starving or freezing to death. During the rare winters in which they had planned ahead and had enough food, they found themselves with no entertainment for month upon month. They turned in desperation to the written word, and thus became the chroniclers of all the lands from which they emigrated. Finland, Denmark, Sweden, Norway. The mash of cultures from the British Isles and the European mainland."

Smith nodded hurriedly. "We're looking for information about a specific breed of dog from Sweden. The Swedish elkhound."

"These are all tales that refer to dogs in some form," Chiun agreed. "And simply because a tale is placed in Sweden, it means only that the version of the tale that was documented by this so-called library was from Sweden. There could have been other tellings of the same story set in another country of the cold north— or in some principality of those lands. The Scandinavian countries of today didn't exist in these times."

Smith was nodding impatiently. "Yes, but can you establish if any of these stories do refer to the Swedish elkhound, specifically."

Chiun pursed his lips. "Of course," he said. "I will be pleased to answer." Clearly, he wasn't pleased. He flipped through the stack of pages, then released them. The stack plopped on the vast glass top of Smith's desk. "No."

Smith waited. "Just no?"

"It is what you requested. Yes or no. The answer is no."

Remo was getting intrigued by the subject matter, but this pair of amateurs didn't know how to get the best information out of an aged and cranky Master of Sinanju. Remo's skills were slightly better, and he knew Chiun was going to go into a state of silent sulking if he endured any more tactless treatment from Smitty. Remo broke in. "Okay, why don't you tell us what this is all about? You have a line on the dogs? Are they Swedish wolfhounds?"

"Elkhounds," Smith said. "We have a possible lead." He presented the photos from the morning newspaper.

"Crap, it's them," Remo announced, suddenly on his feet. "Where are they? Let's go."

"Hold on, Remo. We're not sure of anything yet. The photo could have been staged to extort money from the media." Smith explained the circumstances briefly.

Remo shook his head. "But we saw the dogs, Smitty, and this is them."

"Hundreds of eyewitnesses have seen the dogs by this time," Mark said. "At least half the accounts describe a dog like this. Somebody with a big kennel could have taken the pictures just for the payoff."

Remo glared at the images on the screen. "Computer pictures are always lousy," he said. "But these sure look like the exact same breed of dogs. Can you sharpen these up?"

"We've done what we can," Mark said. "You can't sharpen photographic details that don't exist."

Remo stared at the images. "I'm sure that's the

breed." He glanced at the silent and introverted Korean. "Chiun, don't you think?"

"I think the breed strongly resembles the animals from the Mormon Territories."

Patiently, Mark Howard explained the hint from the Laplander folktale. "If we could find more evidence that this breed was known to identify diseased elk, then maybe they can sense diseased people."

"I get it!" Remo snapped, pacing. "Why don't we just go to where the picture was taken and do some Guantanamo-style interrogating?"

"Slow down, Remo," Smith said, "That may be our only choice, but Sweden's an inconvenient day trip unless you have a good reason."

Remo snatched up the printouts of text. He scanned the pages.

"Dog. Dog. Dog. Every page has the word *dog*."

"We know that. That's why we printed them out. We need a full translation."

Remo spun around, short of patience. "Come on, Little Father, just read the frickin' fairy tales."

Mark Howard looked at Smith. Smith looked at Mark. They said nothing. Chiun waved the pages away with the back of his frail hand, the blue veins standing out beneath the pale, parchment-thin flesh. "There is nothing on those pages that will help."

"There's a lot more. Tons of it." Mark Howard waved at his screen. Chiun didn't move. "I'll just print it out for you."

The pages began spitting out of the silent little printer, which was almost never used for CURE business. Smith wasn't inclined to create incriminating documents. These would have to be carefully shredded and incinerated when their use was finished. Remo grabbed them and handed them to Chiun. More were coming.

Chiun flitted through the pages in seconds.

"Are you really trying?" Remo asked.

Chiun extracted one page and discarded the rest over his shoulder. Remo snatched them out of the air and handed them to Mark.

"This is the tale you wish to hear," Chiun said, resigned to his onerous, unappreciated responsibility. "It is the tale of the *jamthund*, the dense-coated dogs who endured the cold without the bearlike fur that was worn in the coats of the people—and the other breeds of dogs. They became known as the elk-hunters, then the elkhounds, and some strain of them are the Swedish elkhounds. The first of the *jamthund* joined the people on their migration, an unknown breed then, but tolerant of the people. They crossed the land together. There were two of them, the female and the male.

"When the people embarked on the elk hunt, the strange dogs accompanied them. The men killed an elk, then were filled with anger when the two strange dogs snatched the young, tender buck and dragged it away over the thickening ice. The men gave chase, and even attempted to slay the dogs, but the dogs were too fast, even with the carcass of an adult elk being dragged with them.

"The men were in despair, for the herd was nervous and took flight and there were no more kills. The dogs had stolen their food—and now the people would starve.

"The dogs reappeared in the coming days. The people chased them. 'Let us eat of these nice meaty mongrels that have fattened themselves on our sustenance,' the people said." Chiun looked up and was pleased to find all eyes were attentive to his translation. "The dogs were too agile and quick to be slain by the people, and yet they could not be scared off. The people were in fear. The dogs, they believed, had the wisdom of evil spirits. They took the people's food to weaken them, and then they would feast on the flesh of the people themselves when their strength ebbed from starvation. Their worst fears were realized when a young man who was on watch in the darkest hours was taken in a lax moment and dragged away by the dense-coated *jamthund*.

"The people gave chase, and came upon the young man sitting on the ice, unhurt but amazed. Nearby was a large herd of elk. The dogs brought one of the animals down, then dragged it still kicking to the confused men. The dogs and men together killed three more elk, and the people had all the food they could eat.

"It was days later when the people came upon the first herd of elk—their herd, which they had been following. The herd was decimated by sickness—a fever, which the people knew well enough.

"Finally, they understood all. The dogs were agents of benevolence, sent to protect the people. They stole the carcass so that the people would be spared the fevers, then brought the people, in their own way, to a source of good meat. The descendants of those dogs were forever after held as honorable friends of the people, who almost never ate them."

Remo nodded. "Not a bad story. For a non-Sinanju-type story, I mean."

"It is one more example," Smith said cautiously. "Two folktales don't make it a fact."

"Fact enough for me. I'm going to Sweden." Remo tapped the newspaper photo of the pack of elkhounds. "What's the address?"

25

Guirdag was sitting on a wad of cash. The icing on the cake: no more Rjuven Ystad hanging around the place all the time, looking for handouts of food and displays of appreciation. Oh, he had been fun for a while, but she wasn't exactly missing that needy little loser.

"My luck just gets better and better," she said to the man with the thick wrists and the nice shoes who appeared unexpectedly on her doorstep. "I think I'd actually enjoy showing my appreciation to a guy like you."

Guirdag was still giddy from her windfall, and she was saying whatever happened to come to mind.

The dark-haired, dark-eyed man didn't answer, just turned to his friend, who was an Asian man so elderly it was a surprise he had survived the climb to Guirdag's third-floor flat.

"What'd she say?" the young one asked in English.

"Foolish flirtations."

"I can flirt in English, too," Guirdag said, leaning her chest into the door frame.

Remo's preconceived idea of a Swedish woman

came from adolescent jokes learned in the orphanage—blond and strong and sexually outgoing. He tended to revert to the stereotype, despite having known Swedish women who were nothing like the stereotype.

Somehow, Guirdag fit the description perfectly while managing to be utterly unattractive.

"I'm looking for Gird Gag Fluffy-Hung?"

She smiled and enunciated, "Guirdag Freufelung."

"*This* Gird-Gag Fruh-Feh-Lung?" He displayed a printout of Rjuv's best photo of the dogs.

The Swedish eco-activist lost all her charming ways. "Who wants to know?"

"Passivested. Remo Passivested. My partner, Sir Chiun Wilhelm the Fourth. We're with UNAC. Animal Control."

"The United Nations does animal control?"

"Yes." Remo nodded seriously. "Yes, it does."

"He's a knight?" Guirdag scowled at the old Korean.

"Yes," Remo said.

"No," the old man said at the same time.

"Not in Sweden," Remo explained. "In one principality only."

The woman cocked her head. "Which one?"

"Crete."

"That's not a principality."

"I'm asking the questions here," the young one said. "Where was this picture taken?"

Guirdag folded her arms. "What's it worth to you?"

Remo Passivested made a smile that was not a happy

smile. His knighted Cretan partner was stoic but clearly impatient.

"May we come in?" Remo Passivested asked pleasantly, then he reached for her neck. The move was so fast she couldn't hope to dodge it, and when he touched her, her body was no longer in her control. His hold on her vertebrae turned her into a stiff puppet, and she was dangling on the strings he held.

He walked her into her flat and sat her down on her Hrúüåb kitchen chair—a sleek, contemporary, reinterpretation of the traditional kitchen chair—and proceeded to ask her questions. Guirdag tried to lie, but they knew when she was lying. She was the best liar she knew, but the UN inspectors saw right through her. And when she lied, Remo Passivested adjusted her spine. She felt as if her spine, and everything attached to it, were roasting in the fires of a blazing sun.

When she told the truth, the roasting ended, leaving no sign of damage.

It took little time for her lies to be dismantled, leaving only the naked truth.

"But you never actually called for the coast guard to go and help him," Remo prodded.

"He was just moments from drowning in water that was cold as ice. No one could have saved him."

"You could have made a phone call. It wouldn't have killed you."

"I suppose so."

"But you knew he'd be killed when you sent him to the island in the first place," Remo said sternly.

Guirdag said nothing.

"You knew it would be dangerous, but you wanted the photos. You gave him the camera phone."

She stared at nothing.

"Right?" Remo asked.

"Yes! So? What will you be doing about it?"

Remo did it, then called Rye, New York, and spoke to the answering service for the Atlantic City Mucking Specialists, a computer-generated front. When his voice was sufficiently analyzed, Harold W. Smith said, "What have you learned?"

"Guirdag didn't take the pictures. She fetched her boyfriend to take them, knowing he'd probably get wasted in the doing. He sent her the pics before he died. Instead of phoning for a rescue effort for her boyfriend, she called the papers and auctioned off the photos."

"I see. And the photos of the wildman?"

"She never sent those. That whole business was engineered by somebody else. Looks like it was meant to discredit her and keep the dog photos from getting printed. Guirdag thought it was a real laugh riot, because she already had her payoff. So the dog pictures are legitimate. Can you hail us some transportation?"

"What is the name of the man who owns the island?" Smith asked.

"I told you already. Peter. Whirly."

"Ohly," Chiun corrected.

"Ohly. Can we go now?"

"Peter Ohly. One of the world's most prodigious breeders of Swedish elkhounds. His puppies are considered some of the finest in the world, coming from an especially pure breed line. Wealthy buyers pay a premium for his puppies."

"Apparently he's breeding more than anybody ever guessed. Guirdag said her boyfriend saw hundreds of them. I'd love to talk about this all day, but I'd rather go do my job. Get us a good boat and we'll be on our way."

"Stord Island is more than two hundred miles from where you are now," Smith said. "It would take hours by water."

"Whatever. Give us *something*."

Smith said, sour as sucked lemons, "Hold on." He clicked off. He clicked back.

"Go to the roof."

To his surprise, Remo could already hear the approaching throb of helicopter rotors. "Nice work, Smitty." He banged down the phone.

In a moment, the unblinking Ms. Guirdag was alone staring at the empty walls of her lifeless apartment.

THE CHARTERED HELICOPTER followed the rugged coastline along the Gulf of Bothnia. Below them flashed hundreds of offshore islands, most just uninhabitable, lifeless rocks. The copilot finally pointed at the horizon. "That's it. We be there soon."

"Put us down on the shore," Remo instructed. "Here. Now."

The copilot heard him but didn't understand.

"Land. Now. No closer."

"Yes. What you want." The pilots brought the helicopter onto a few hundred yards of exposed shoreline rock that had all the natural beauty of a quarry. Marching away from the aircraft, Remo turned to Chiun. "It's a long hike."

Chiun looked at the dot of the island, then turned sternly to Remo. "It is not far."

"To walk, it is."

"It is but a few miles. Any man could walk it."

"It's you I'm worried about."

Chiun's face turned bright red and he walked in silence.

"I said I'm worried."

"Do not be."

"I am. Are you feeling okay?"

"Of course I feel okay. Only my patience is tested."

"The dogs zeroed in on you."

"Meaningless."

"They thought you were sick."

"Sick only of this discussion. Let it fall."

"Drop it?"

"Exactly."

"So you're up for a little run?" Remo asked when they had strolled around some rocks that blocked the view of the helicopter pilots.

Chiun answered by slipping across the rocks at inhuman speeds. Remo broke into a run, pushing himself to catch up to the incredibly swift Master Emeritus.

"I guess this answers my question," he said, although there was no need to say it and, in fact, he was more worried than ever.

Chiun kept the lightning pace all the way to the mouth of the fjordlike outlet, which was the nearest mainland point to the island. Then Chiun, and Remo, veered off the irregular shore and onto the water.

They walked on the surface of the ice-cold bay water, which bulged around their feet but didn't open.

Walking on the surface of the water was a Sinanju skill—one of the tricks that Remo could never quite believe was possible until he found himself actually doing it. That was years ago, during his early training. Long before he was a Master of Sinanju he had mastered walking on water, although explaining it was beyond him. It had to do with the surface tension of water. A small leaf could rest on the water's surface and not break the surface tension. Somehow a Master of Sinanju could step on the water with quick, controlled steps and, like the leaf, not break the surface tension.

The air was brisk and the gulf was heaving and swelling under them, but they soon found themselves at Peter Ohly's island.

They were assaulted by the smells. It was the smell of dogs—and other things. Chiun wrinkled his nose in distaste, then stepped lightly up a zigzag of carved steps and gazed at an opening at his feet. Chiun made out human remains, some days old and some weeks old. One of the newer cadavers was still holding a cell phone.

Remo glanced into the hole and they continued up the hillside. At the top, they could see into a rough-sided depression that filled most of the island.

Chiun's sandaled feet scarcely touched the rough rock on the way down to the bottom, where he toed the little disturbances in the shallow soil.

"Kennels," he pointed out.

"Smells that way," Remo agreed. "But they're gone now." In fact, the smell could have been a lot worse, considering how many holes were in the ground. Chiun was walking among the outlines of enclosures that the holes traced.

"That's a lot of dog runs."

"There were many dogs," Chiun said. "Hundreds. And hundreds more before them."

"But now they're gone," Remo said. "Not so much as a plastic squeaky steak."

"Or a cured pig's ear," Chiun added. But his attention was drawn to muffled sounds from the far side of the island. Up he went, finding a gleaming structure of polished steel and mirrored glass.

"Inviting," Remo said.

"It is the Swedish sensibility of aesthetics," Chiun said. "They call it a modernist sensibility when it is simplistic and dull."

"I guess when you grow up looking at architecture

from the Dark Ages, your tastes swing 180 degrees in the other direction."

"That does not excuse this," Chiun replied. "It is hideous. Will you bring such eyesores into the village of the Sinanju one day, Remo?"

"'Course not, Little Father. This is like the Jetsons, only real and without the laugh track."

"You admire the work of these Jets' Sons?"

"Not at all."

Chiun would have pursued it, but they were alerted to the sounds of animals, and a group of remaining kennels huddled together on one of the gleaming oblong houses. Remo and Chiun spoke too quietly for the dogs to hear as they circled the gates.

"He could keep lots of dogs right here. So where are they all?"

Chiun did not answer because, of course, he didn't know.

Each gated run included a wooden enclosure at one end, with stiff rubber flaps that fell in place over the entrance. They would help keep out the frigid cold of Scandinavian winters. He picked up no sounds from most of the enclosures. Only in the last half dozen runs did he hear sounds of activity.

A puppy poked its head through the rubber flaps and bounded to one end of the run. There was an adult yip from within, and the puppy headed back inside— then brought it to a skidding halt when it realized that two strange humans were standing just outside his fence, watching him. The pup recoiled into the corner, yammering plaintively.

In an instant, an adult female shot out of the enclosure and stood over its puppy, looking for the danger, and the other mothers emerged from their own dens. They twisted their heads wildly, seeing nothing.

Chiun leaped soundlessly and settled to the earth alongside the startled mother, who saw the apparition but heard almost no sound from it. The female brought its powerful jaws together on the nearest limb.

Its teeth locked, wide open. Chiun had two fingers spread wide inside the dog's gaping fangs. It was trapped like a hooked fish and it thrashed its head—but the hook would not give.

Chiun lifted his parted fingers in front of him, carrying the poor bitch off the ground.

"It is the same dogs," Chiun announced.

"I knew that before we even got here."

THE CAGED MOTHER Elkhounds raised a racket, but the house stayed silent. It had the same uninhabited feel as the rest of the place. Chiun was patient as Remo scoured the inside of the home, looking for anything that would help. He was distracted by the sound of watercraft approaching the island. Remo barged out the front door a moment later.

"Think Ohly's coming home?"

Chiun didn't answer the question. Sometimes Remo said things just to hear his own voice. Of course Chiun had no idea who was in the white boat. It headed for an empty dock below the house and the pilot tied up. When he turned off the engine, he finally heard the baying of the mother dogs and he grabbed for a firearm that was stowed conveniently close in the cabin of the boat.

"Afternoon." Chiun waited as Remo strolled up the wooden walkway with a foolish grin on his disproportionately large head. It was his way of putting people off their guard. It rarely succeeded. It did not succeed this time.

"Get on the ground, hands behind your head," the boat pilot ordered in Swedish. Remo didn't know Swedish, but it would have made little difference. Remo wasn't one to assume the position.

"*Hable inglés?*" he asked. Ludicrous. Still, Chiun sometimes, almost, admired Remo's persistent slack and flippant state of being.

The boat pilot shot Remo right in the chest.

Remo's chest got out of the way. The volley of buckshot rattled off the wooden surface and the nearby rocks. The pilot craned his neck, looking for his target. He seemed to think Remo had toppled into the shallow water.

In fact, Remo had slithered under the dock, as lithe as a salamander in a deep cave—and just as unhealthily pale, come to think of it, Chiun thought.

"Hey, watch it." Remo slipped out from under the dock and rose up just inches from the smoking barrels of the ungraceful weapon, then relieved the pilot of it.

The weapon made a plopping noise and vanished into the slate-gray waters.

The pilot dropped his jaw to his chest, then his eyes were drawn to Chiun, who came out of nowhere. The crude mariner was appropriately dazzled by the poise and stature of the beautifully attired Master of Sinanju, but he reserved his horror for the swollen-wristed, swollen-headed, underwear-garbed Caucasian.

"Sea troll," the pilot moaned.

"He thinks you are a sea creature," Chiun explained. "A merman."

"That's right. Came to get my vengeance for putting smelly dead bodies in my favorite cave."

The Swede gaped at him, apparently grasping some of the English nonsense that Remo spewed with an amazing lack of effort.

"Cave?"

"The cave. With smelly dead guys. Yuk."

"You are not a sea troll!"

"I'm worse," Remo told him. "I'm Sinanju."

The man waved him away, suddenly getting his nerves under control, and he took a swing at the Reigning Master, who stopped the anvil-like fist in midstroke and used the arms like a leash to lift the whimpering pilot off the dock. The pilot struggled, but he was helpless. Remo carried him easily off the dock. And up to the house. Across the yard where the barking bitches were spurred into a frenzy of new barking. Down into the bowl that filled the middle of the island.

"Always you play games," Chiun complained. He knew where Remo was taking his captive. The victim had figured it out, too, and now he was moaning and pleading for release.

"I have instructed you in a hundred methods of quickly dispatching your enemies, but you ignore the traditional techniques. You dally for your own amusement."

"Why not? And you can't say my methods don't work. I bet he's already telling us what we want to know."

The victim was telling them everything he could think to tell them. How he helped ensnare the poor devils in the cave. How he protected the island from intruders. How he watched over the farming of hundreds of litters.

Remo stood over the hole and let the dancing, dangling boat pilot flop around for a while. When the man was convinced he was trapped, Remo said, "Where's Ohly?"

"Ohly is at the Kivik Yearly Hunting event—a contest."

"With how many dogs?"

"Twenty-three."

"Not many," Remo said, shaking his head sadly. "There were lots of dogs here a couple days ago. Where are they now?"

The pilot struggled to understand. "More dogs?

Many more dogs, all shipped out. To America. The last packs."

"Where to?" Remo grumbled.

"America."

"America is big," Remo snapped, shaking the dangling pilot viciously. It was enough to dislocate the man's shoulder.

"Just America is all I know!"

"You sure?"

"They never tell me where. I don't know anything. I just keep security."

"And kill trespassers."

"Yes, kill trespassers, that's all. Oops."

"Bye-bye." Remo dropped him through the opening. "Come on, Chiun."

"Always playing little games," Chiun chided.

26

"Hey, boys, time to fly."

The helicopter pilots choked on their mineral water and sandwiches. Their passengers had materialized out of nowhere.

"No time for gawking. We got places to be."

The pilots stowed the leftover lunch and took the aircraft up to a few hundred feet. "Ready to go to Stord Island now?"

"We just came from there," Remo said. "Now we need to go to a hunting competition. You know where Kivik is?"

"Yes, we fly there before."

"Fly there again. Now."

The pilots were on the clock, all fuel expenses paid. What did they care where the Americans wanted them to go? They headed back southwest.

"What is this hunting contest all about anyway?" Remo asked.

"It is a hunt," the copilot said.

"What do they hunt?"

"Elk. What else?"

"How should I know? It's your country."

PETER OHLY WAS ENJOYING himself. The hard part was over. The dogs were shipped. Ohly was no longer involved. Anything bad that happened now, happened outside of his world. If the dogs had belonged to him once, if the dogs had been trained by him to detect the diseased and kill them without mercy, it had been in a different part of his life. It was before today.

Today, Ohly was back to being the man he had once been—but with an extremely large addition to his bank account.

He had been wealthy before. Now he was *extremely* wealthy. He intended to enjoy his wealth, to live the life he always dreamed of living. Never mind that he had actually been living that life before he became involved with the American insurance company president.

As a symbol of his new life of freedom and leisure, Peter Ohly intended to win this year's elk-hunting competition. He had won the competition in past years—so many times, in fact, that he was asked to refrain from competing to give others a chance at the trophy. This was okay, because he was starting his new project with the Americans at that time.

Now that project was over and his voluntary banishment from the Kivik competition was ended. He was hunting with his best dogs. Included in his pack were veterans of past contests—past their prime now but still exceedingly skilled animals. The pack he hunted with also included the descendants of the older champions. The younger dogs were also skilled animals, well trained, genetically superior to any animals he had fielded before. It was a perfect balance of experience and young blood.

The competition was simple. Each team of man and his dogs was given a plot of acreage to hunt, with elk placed on-site. Elk were run to ground and the quickest time won the contest.

Ohly had himself been instrumental in organizing the original competition years ago. The rules had changed little since then.

He wished he had had time to work out himself in preparation for the hunt. The competition required that he run with his dogs, and he felt himself getting tired already. He was slower than he had been once. He would be sure to get on the treadmill more this year, so that he would be perfectly fit for next year. Meanwhile, a shortness of breath wouldn't keep him from claiming the cup today.

Ohly had laughed at some of the Britons that were on hand. As foxhunting continued to be frustratingly illegal in the U.K., the Britons were turning to Swedish elk-hunting as an alternative. The Swedish hunts had some of the same elements. It didn't have the same ritualistic overtones. And no horses. Most Brits enjoyed their foxhunting simply for the chance to ride their horses in the countryside with their snooty friends and their baying dogs and their coughing rifles. Only the Britons who really enjoyed the hunt could make the transition to Swedish elk-hunting, and they still insisted on using their own dogs. They always showed up at the bottom of the list when the scores were tallied.

Ohly was getting concerned about his stamina and he had lost touch with his own dogs. They were far ahead. He did hear them when they bayed, but they were too far off to hear him. The chain of command was being fractured. He couldn't let his dogs, as well trained as they were, get out of his control.

With a groan he realized he was being watched—the orange fluorescent shape in the trees was an automatic camera, used to record and broadcast the event. A satellite network was sponsoring the event and broadcasting it across Europe. Viewers would see him in this state of near exhaustion. Shameful. He summoned his reserves of energy and ran after his dogs.

His legs were screaming by the time he caught up to the position where he had last heard the dogs, and now he could hear them barking excitedly. The sound was the cry of dogs on the trail of prey. He was delighted that they had tracked the elk so quickly, and horrified that they were going to run the animal down without him even there to guide them.

This was what they were trained to do, in fact, and yet the cameras would be recording every minute of it. They'd see the dogs doing the work, with Ohly nowhere to be found. He'd be a laughingstock even as he accepted the trophy.

He called for the animals, trying to sound calm and assured when he wasn't.

He pushed through the sparse forest and grasses and reached the scene of the kill at last.

But it was not the elk that was dead. The elk was standing tall, surrounded by the bodies of Peter Ohly's valuable hunting dogs scattered all around it.

Ohly decided that the sport had changed more in the past few years than he had realized.

The elk lowered its antler rack and lined up Ohly. Ohly didn't know what was more terrifying—a murderous elk or the fact that the whole humiliation was being watched by one of the fluorescent orange cameras up in the trees.

The elk charged.

Ohly ran, ears filled with the pounding of his heart, which was pushed far past its comfort level already. Ohly scrambled into the nearest tree, which was a poor, scraggly thing. This close to the Arctic Circle there weren't many trees big enough for climbing, but this one would support him. He hoped.

Then he saw the orange box. It was on a metal mount that was bracketed to the tree, near the top of the trunk. It filmed his frantic climb to freedom. His hunting reputation was instantly trashed.

He was bleeding, his arms ripped by the bark. He didn't care. The elk did a dance of fury just below his dangling feet, then it rose up on its rear legs in a strange, menacing ballet. Ohly withdrew his feet.

He didn't understand this. He had never heard of an elk becoming so aggressive. One elk didn't kill an entire dog pack. The loss was tremendous. So many dogs, with so many thousands of hours devoted to their training. All lost.

"That looked pretty damn stupid, you running away from Bubba the pissed-off reindeer."

Peter Ohly cranked his head around, too fast, and he had to grab the branch to keep from tumbling off.

It didn't seem possible that there could be anyone else in the tree with him. He should have been able to see that person before he climbed into the tree himself, and he surely had not. And yet, when he got his balance back, he found that there were, in fact, two human beings perched in the tree with him, and one was in a brightly colored kimono.

What was more strange was that these men were sitting on branches that couldn't possibly support their weight. They were on thin sapling branches that should have snapped off or bent to the ground. And yet they seemed comfortably settled, and enjoying Ohly's performance.

The one in the kimono was small and so incredibly old it seemed impossible that he could have muscled himself into this tree. He looked frail, a tiny Asian man whom time had desiccated.

The other one was a white man, thin, but there was nothing small about him. Dark hair, deadly looking eyes and strangely thick wrists.

"Who are you people?"

"Remo. That's Chiun." The white man nodded at the

small Asian man, who seemed absorbed in his own thoughts. "You know, I've personally attended some very stupid sporting events in my life, and I can tell you, this ranks with the stupidest."

"But who are you?"

"I answered that. Didn't I answer that, Little Father?" Remo said. The old Asian man didn't seem to be aware that he had spoken. "See? I did say that. Everybody heard me say that. Now, you have used up all your questions and it's my turn."

Ohly didn't know what to say.

"Now, about the dead bodies on your island."

Ohly felt his heart start slamming again, reaching far up into his throat. He pressed on his chest and felt it bounce out of control like a rubber ball.

"We are not even sure who all of them are. I know one of them is this guy named Runs. Something like that. An environmental green guy from your country. He's the one who got out the pictures of the last pack of the assassin dogs. He happened to know those dogs are no longer on your island. Where did those dogs happen to go?"

Ohly found himself breathing too fast and wondered how he could possibly respond to that question.

"It will make it easier on everyone if you just answer," Remo said. "Cooperate? Please? Okay, have it your way."

Before Ohly could respond, Remo had stepped light as a squirrel monkey across the flimsy branch, hooked himself to the branch on the crook of his legs and swung down like a circus performer. He snatched Ohly up and flipped him upside down.

Ohly found himself descending into the anxious antlers of the enraged elk.

"Wait," Ohly pleaded.

Remo didn't hear or did not care. The elk inserted an antler-tip into Ohly's back flesh, but before the next strike he found himself being lifted out of elk range.

"I think you better cough up some information," Remo said. "That elk means business."

"What do you want?" Ohly was still hanging upside down and his head was full of blood.

"The dogs were on your island when those pictures were taken a few days ago, and now they're gone. Where did they all go?"

"America."

"We know that much. Anywhere in particular in America?"

"The Americans will assign the offloading point. I don't have anything to do with it."

"Very helpful."

Ohly heard the old Asian man speak for the first time. "Remo, we do not need to know where the dogs will be. The only things we need to know are the name and location of the man who will use the dogs. My patience grows short at your games."

"Okay, you're right, Chiun."

Revolve was holding Ohly by the heel. Ohly had no

idea that a human being could hold another human being by the heel with just one hand. Remo's grip was good enough that he could give Ohly a good shake, rattling the bones inside his body.

"Who is the guy behind the dog attacks in the United States?"

"How should I know that? I'm only the dog breeder. Somebody asks me for dogs, and I sell them. Somebody asks me for a hundred dogs, and I sell them"

"I think you sold alot more than a hundred dogs," Remo said. "I think all the puppies that are being used in the United States to off the old, sick people were trained by you. I think they all come from your island. I think you are guilty of participating in mass murder."

"I just bred the dogs."

"Well, you trained the dogs, too. You trained them to ID people who might get sick and then murder them. Stop me if I've got it wrong."

"It was not exactly like that," Ohly stammered.

"What part, exactly, is it not exactly like?"

Ohly tried to compose himself. It was difficult to compose oneself when dangling upside down, from a tree, with a mad caribou stomping below you and hoping you'll fall to its clutches. Still he managed to say, "The facts as you speak them may be true, but the meaning is misconstrued."

"Whatever. Here, boy. Here, Comet. Have a nice treat."

Ohly descended into the range of the reindeer, then,

just as quickly, was raised back up. He was amazed to find that he was no longer in the hands of Remo, the white man. Now it was the tiny Asian who had him by the foot. The Asian man seemed to have lost his temper.

"Remo, for once, just do what needs to be done without the theatrics."

The tiny Asian man pulled Ohly high and snatched Ohly's wrists. The little old fingers squeezed his wrists, and Ohly was filled with pain beyond all pain. All the determination he had left vanished in the face of that all-consuming pain.

And then the pain stopped and he focused on the face of the Asian man just inches from his own. The Asian man spoke in his surprisingly high-pitched voice, almost a singsong, but a song full of merciless rage.

"You will tell us now. The name of the one in America, the name of the one who is making all this happen."

"MacMayor," Ohly cried.

"He's lying," Remo said.

"Lou MacMayor," Ohly insisted tearfully.

"He's a guy in a suit on hamburger commercials."

"He's the president of the Institute of Nationalized Humane Health Care—it's a health insurance company."

"Oh," Remo said.

"Then I suppose we are done with you," Chiun announced.

"Thank God," Ohly breathed. "Then put me down, please."

Ohly realized too late what he had said. Surely the old Asian wouldn't take him seriously.

The old Asian fully intended to take him seriously. He dropped Ohly as the stomping elk snorted and raised its head.

The elk turned in circles, with Peter Ohly impaled on him. Then the reindeer lowered its head and let Ohly slide off, still moving weakly.

Ohly crawled a few feet, propped himself up against the tree trunk and let his head drop onto his chest. He watched the rivers of blood flowing from the holes in his body.

The reindeer snorted unpleasantly and shook in an attempt to fling off the blood.

"Poor Comet," Remo said.

27

"Smitty," Remo asked from the helicopter, "didn't you mention once that this all might be a big insurance scam?"

"Yes," Smith said. "The nature of the attacks indicate that the insurance companies would be the obvious beneficiaries of the scheme. Pardon my pun."

Remo had no idea what the pun was. "You're pardoned."

"The difficulty is in the victims. They're from a cross section of insurance companies. None of them were covered by any one insurance company. Tell me what you've learned, Remo."

"Peter Ohly spilled his guts," Remo said. "He named Burger MacMayor as the guy who masterminded this whole dog-and-pony show."

Chiun snatched the receiver from Remo and stretched the long cord from the inside cabin wall. "Remo is quite addled, Emperor," Chiun apologized. "The name of the man is Lou MacMayor, and the plot involves only dogs. No ponies."

"MacMayor is president of the Institute of Nationalized Humane Health Care. It's not an institute at all, but the nation's biggest HMO insurance provider," Smith said. "This makes sense."

"It does?" Remo asked as the phone was deposited back in his hand. "I thought you just said insurance didn't make sense and you ruled it out."

Mark Howard, he of the instant information, came on the line.

"When we did an analysis of the insurance coverage of the victims, half of them were covered by INHHC."

"Well, wait," Remo said, "that makes it a very good reason to suspect them in the first place."

"No. Because half the population is covered by INHHC anyway. A random killing would come up with a fifty percent coverage ration. The second-biggest player is Lunar Health Care Systems, a rival health-care conglomerate. They have eighteen percent of the market, and that roughly correlates to the coverage of the ration of victims."

"Uh-huh," Remo said.

"Dr. Smith," Mark added, "INHHC has been negotiating behind the scenes to purchase Lunar. The fact is, the purchase transaction is ready to go. The papers are signed."

"It would never be approved," Smith replied. "It would give INHHC too much of the market."

"Not if they go through an offshore parent corporation," Mark said. "INHHC is actually a subsidiary of a company in Nassau—and that's the company buying

Lunar. The Nassau company is just a front for INHHC. Doesn't even have employees."

Remo said, "Smitty, Mark, I think this is the first time we have ever talked about a corporate buyout. Sort of a new phase in our relationship. I'd be thrilled except I'm about to swoon from lack of interest."

"This is relevant, Remo."

"I believe you. Please don't explain it to me."

"Roughly half the attacks targeted people insured by INHHC," Mark Howard said. "The other half had insurance coverage from various companies—but mostly from Lunar Health Care. Now, seventy percent of those cost savings will be realized by one company. We're talking tens of billions of dollars in the long term."

"I'm amazed how much you get into this crap, Junior."

"The thrill of the hunt, Remo," Mark said. "It's exciting, even from behind a desk. Don't knock it until you've tried it."

"I never will."

Smith broke in, "The point is, Remo, the rationale for the attacks is clarifying. Half the victimizations benefit INHHC directly. A quarter of the attacks benefit INHHC by driving down the value of Lunar Health Care and by culling the Lunar rosters of expensive enrollees."

"So why didn't we figure all this out from the start?"

"They baited us off the trail," Mark Howard said with chagrin. "The other victims were red herrings."

"So we go visit MacMayor and ask him to please stop killing people. How fast can you have us on his front door?"

"Fast, considering his front door is in Upstate New York and you're still in northcentral Sweden," Smith said. "Approximately nine hours."

"A lot more people are gonna get dog bit in the next nine hours," Remo said.

"Remo," Smith said, "we're quite aware of that."

28

The Foreman was alerted by the vibration of his phone. He read the text message without understanding it at first. It said, "Trouble out here. Team lost. Carts in jail. Do what? Jay."

The Foreman snapped back to reality. Jay was his field supervisor in Utah. Jack Cartfeld was one of his handlers. Cartfeld was a good man, but he must have screwed up big-time.

The first dog pack had been neutralized.

The Foreman dialed Jay Lettering.

"Foreman?"

"Yeah."

Jay Lettering knew better than to wait to be asked for his report. "Okay, so, Cartfeld made a mess of things out here. He handled the culling last night. Supposed to be at Nineveh Retirement City, and he gets there and off-loads the team, but then he hears about some drunk and disorderly going on inside the retirement home itself. Sheriff's gonna come and settle things down.

Naturally, Cart loads the team and moves on to other targets."

"Good."

"Yeah, that's all fine and everything. He calls and reports and says he'll wait a couple hours, then make a go at McCullan Oaks Center. He goes, waits, off-loads, everything's fine until the very moment the dogs start getting their strike commands. Then all hell breaks loose. Dogs start getting Xed out."

Dogs killed. That was bad news.

"How many?"

"In the end, all of them. Hundred percent losses."

The Foreman didn't like it at all. "How?"

"Unknown. I assume they were getting shot, but none of the audio pickups on the dogs picked up gunshots. I been going over the data myself. It's weird. No sound. Just some spooky voices. Making fun of the dogs and saying really strange things."

The Foreman shook his head. "Then?"

"Cartfeld watched them get Xed and he called them back, but something kept them from coming back. A whole bunch of them gathered a couple miles from the truck and they were still alive, and then there was more strange talking, and then bam—they all got Xed at one time. No gunfire. Just a bunch of fast-moving sounds and they're dead."

The Foreman felt a chill pass through him.

"Cartfeld took off. There were no more dogs alive, so he left in a hurry. The cops were coming by then.

Somebody called them, like, called them before the strikes even started. Cartfeld couldn't get past them."

The Foreman said, "I'll handle it."

"But what should I do here?"

"Business as usual. We'll raise security protocols to level two."

"What about Cartfeld?"

"I'll handle Cartfeld," the Foreman said.

THE FOREMAN SEARCHED his mental database for his contacts in the vicinity of Salt Lake City. There were none. He'd never done business in Utah before now. He extended his search to Las Vegas.

Naturally, there were plenty of good service agents in Vegas. Still, he needed someone who was known to be especially trustworthy and tight-lipped.

Philip Schwartzchild picked up the phone on the first ring. "Yeah."

"It's me."

"You. Been a long time since I talked to you, Foreman. So long that you don't know I'm out of the business."

"I did know. Otherwise I would have called you in on my current job. However, I need you now. I think I can get you out of retirement."

"Look, it's nice to talk to you, but I'm definitely retired, Foreman. Don't call me anymore."

"I will pay well."

"Must be a cleanup job. You're in a mess out here

and you can't get here on your own. I get the picture, and I ain't interested."

"Listen to my offer."

"Well, I guess I ain't hung up yet."

The Foreman named his price.

"Christ Almighty. For that much money, you must want me to plug a man who's already in jail."

"Maybe. I'll give you the details when you say yes."

"Aw, hell."

MARK HOWARD rolled out of bed at two in the morning, not knowing where he was until he stared down at the bed. Sarah Slate felt the disturbance and sat up.

"Mark? What is it?"

"I don't know. Something is closing in on me."

"It was just a dream."

Mark Howard shook his head. "It was not just a dream. I feel it still. I have to get back to Folcroft."

"You just left a couple hours ago."

Mark grabbed jeans out of a small dresser that crowded the master bedroom of their little Rye apartment.

"But what is it, Mark?" Sarah asked.

"I can't explain it, Sarah. It's there, right now. I feel it getting closer to us."

"To us?"

"To me, I mean. It's closing in on me. It might not have anything to do with the dogs. I don't know what it is. I just know it is getting closer."

"If it is the dogs coming to Folcroft, then we have

to be ready for it," Sarah said. "You have to convince Dr. Smith to call in Remo and Chiun."

Mark didn't want to try to talk Dr. Smith into doing anything. It was against his nature to speak against a well-thought-out Smith decision. On the other hand, Sarah had a point. It would be inhumane to allow the patients of Folcroft to be sacrificed to the brutality of the dogs simply to protect CURE's cover. All it took was a summons to the Masters of Sinanju and the Folcroft victims would be spared. The dogs were nothing to the skills of Remo and Chiun.

But Remo and Chiun were in Scandinavia. Hours away.

And whatever was closing in on him, Mark thought it was closer than that.

He had another problem. Mark couldn't escape the feeling that the imminent danger waited out there for him alone, not Folcroft. But that didn't make sense for many reasons—not the least of which was the very nature of Mark's extrasensory perception. It had not been much good at protecting him personally in the past. How many times had he faced dangers for which he had no premonition?

Sarah flung back the covers and yanked on her own clothes. When Mark made to speak, she beat him to it. "Whatever it is, Mark, I'm coming with you."

HAROLD SMITH greeted them with a quick update. "I ran a full security survey of the grounds when you called,

Mark. There's been no sign of any abnormal activity. Is there any change to what you're sensing?"

"No." Mark sat behind his desk, placed his hands on the keyboard as his screen appeared, then lifted his hands again as if he didn't know what to do with them.

"I have called in our extra security," Smith added.

Sarah perched on the couch, at a loss for something to do. She had trouble finding a role for herself in CURE. CURE hadn't needed her when she joined up, and now there was no natural task for her to perform. She was a third wheel.

But they all felt helpless, she realized. Smith scanned fretfully through screen after screen of information that served as his window to the world.

Nothing happened until fifteen minutes later, when the extra staff of hired security guards passed through the front gate and took up positions around the grounds of the sanitarium.

After that, they sat there, waiting.

29

The Foreman felt his skin crawling, felt pressure building in his brain, yet still he drove on. The terrain was confusing him, he decided, and he wasted hours driving out onto Long Island, searching for the source of danger. He was all the way to Riverhead before he was convinced that he was moving away from the danger. It took all his willpower to turn the car around and drive back in the direction of New York City.

It was like an idiot game of Warmer/Colder and he was the idiot, because he was driving right back into the warm danger.

Throughout his life, he had obeyed the instincts that told him to avoid the danger that he sensed. Only in the past few weeks had he found himself defying that instinct, fighting his own common sense, rebelling against his own self-preservation impulse. How had his life caromed out of control so completely, so quickly, that he was deliberately seeking out the danger, time and again?

He missed Maureen. He hated her, too, for what she had done to his life. She introduced something he did not know he had lacked. It took a freakish, beguiling woman to reveal the gaping chasm of want in his life.

He had trouble blaming her. She hadn't meant to do it. She wasn't a trickster. In fact, she had probably loved him, in her way. There was no doubt she paid for the crime, too. Poor Maur.

Maur was dead and gone. He couldn't afford to let her be a distraction now. The real problem was facing him now—a greater threat than the Irish lass ever represented. It was so big, so potent, it seemed to cover the East Coast. He couldn't get a lock on it yet, and trying to find it was agony. The sense of danger was an abrasive presence. It gave him a throbbing headache that a handful of ibuprofens failed to blunt.

He crept through New York, congested with traffic even at this time of the night. Then north.

The problem was that he had never in his life tried to move upstream, into the danger, and he didn't have the skills to do it to well. Moving closer to that danger made the mental warning even more shrill, but it didn't give him an easier tracer signal. He drove miles in one direction with the screeching in his head and still couldn't sense whether or not he was actually moving closer to the danger or just across its range of influence.

But going north out of New York City, he was suddenly aware that he was on the right track. The searing iron poker in his head became noticeably hotter. He glanced at his atlas, which was speckled with red dots. Each signified a possible target for the dog packs. The

Foreman was only assuming that one of those targets was the source of the danger.

But this was New York, with millions of people and hundreds of hospitals offering potential targets. The very nature of the dog-attack campaign called for flexibility, so none of the targets was a sure thing. There always had to be an option to pick alternate targets, if the danger at the original target was too high.

There were a number of small New York towns ahead, each with hospitals and nursing homes or other facilities ripe for the picking by his dogs. Beyond New York, Connecticut offered even more targets.

The Foreman dialed Trevor Sharp. Sharp was not a happy man under the best of circumstances.

"What's going on, Foreman? Why ain't you being up front with me? I feel like I'm getting jerked around."

"Trevor, I don't jerk people around. Can the attitude. You're getting paid by the hour, right?"

"Yeah."

"You are still parked near John F. Kennedy, correct?"

"Yeah. I've been sitting here for hours listening to the mutts getting their snouts in a snit every time a plane goes over."

"You'll be happy to know it's time to move out. Drive up the coast, out of the city."

"Where to, exactly?"

"When I know, I'll call you back."

"Ah, Christ."

THE FOREMAN hung up. Let Trevor complain. So long as the man did his job, he could be as much of a belly-acher as he wanted to be.

Still, it was almost satisfying to realize that Trevor Sharp might not survive to collect his paycheck from the Foreman.

The Foreman followed the coast, and the pain hit him hard. The sense of danger escalated almost by the mile. It was torture, but it meant he was definitely on the right track.

When he glanced at the map he had to blink away the white optical artifacts, as if he were looking away from a pair of blindingly bright headlights. There were trails in his vision from just the dim glow of his dashboard lights.

He was being physically weakened, but he was getting so close. He had to know for sure—he had to find the source of this danger. Knowing it was the first step to eliminating it.

On the map were six or eight facilities in the next fifteen miles. Any of them might be the source of the danger—assuming that one of his targets was in fact the source of the danger.

But it *had* to be. A place wouldn't endanger him if he didn't have business with it. Right? His mind reeled. He couldn't think clearly. His head pounded and he couldn't concentrate on his driving. He rolled through one small town, without even knowing which town it was. Then came a road sign for another town: 2 Miles Ahead. Rye, New York.

The thing in his head whistled like a train bearing down on him. It shrieked like a projectile cutting through the air as it zeroed in on him.

He was close, but his will was eroded by the constant cry of danger in his head, and somehow he forced himself to drive on. There was the howl of a car horn and he swerved out of the way, only then realizing he had drifted into the oncoming traffic lane. He was driving like a drunk, and that was no good. He couldn't afford to be picked up by the police.

He pulled into the parking lot of an all-night grocery store, grabbed his pack and started off on foot.

Even walking was difficult. He kept to the darkness, fighting against the warning, and he felt like a man forcing himself to walk through fire. How long he walked, he didn't know, but now he was in some trees and the darkness was all around him. There was a rush of surf a few miles away.

When the flashing lights came up the road, he saw them coming and he stumbled into the dark trees, leaning against the trunk as the squad car drove by.

Were they looking for him? Did they sense him coming like he sensed them? That seemed unreasonable, but everything about this was unreasonable.

Which made it all the more vital that he understand what he was up against. He marched through the trees, holding his arms in front of his head, but still the slashing bushes and branches cut into him. He kept the road in sight as a point of reference.

There was a sign alongside the road. The Foreman gripped his temples from the pain. The sign was striking at him like a hot laser piercing his brain. Every step was a heroic effort, and after ten steps he grabbed a tree trunk to hold on, as if a force like gravity would push him back. He squinted and read the sign.

Folcroft Sanitarium.

He recognized the name. It was one of the hospitals on his list.

Folcroft. That's where the danger was. He knew it. It made sense. It had to be right.

"MAKE A FULL SWEEP of the grounds," Smith ordered. "Send patrols outside the property to look for potential break-ins. I recommend using night-vision goggles."

"You're the boss," Captain Koln said.

Good private security forces were hard to find. He knew from experience that most of the men in the field were there because they failed their military or law-enforcement careers. Such men were not trustworthy.

The Koln Security Company, which he brought in very occasionally from Philadelphia, had proved itself to be professional and discreet—just what a private hospital needed. Still, there were times when Smith felt that Captain Koln didn't always take seriously the level of defense required for a rich man's convalescence center.

The recent spate of attacks on hospitals and nursing homes made it easy for Smith to justify bringing in this level of personnel and firepower. Tonight he had called in the entire Koln staff. They had night-vision goggles and they were all armed. He tried to give Koln the impression that there was a specific threat to Folcroft. Of course, that was true—if he trusted Mark's predictions.

"Can you tell how close, Mark?"

"Close."

"How many of them?"

Mark gave him a pained look. Of course, Mark couldn't answer that question. As it was, it was amazing and unprecedented that the young man could sense the danger so specifically. This wasn't the way Mark's abilities tended to work.

"Mark," Sarah said from the couch, "come sit down."

Mark strode across the office, sat on the old couch leather and bounced his legs. He grabbed his shins in his hands to hold them still, then bounded to his feet again and resumed pacing.

"What's happening with the security guards?" he asked.

"Nothing to report," Smith said. He was watching a pair of the security guards moving with commendable caution over the grounds outside the sanitarium property. They showed up on the security cameras Smith had long ago positioned throughout the facility.

"No sign of intruders," Smith added needlessly. "It's just Koln's men out there."

Mark nodded.

"Is it getting worse?" Sarah asked.

"No better, no worse. It's just sitting there."

Smith couldn't pull his eyes way from the display. He felt as if some invisible presence waited out there, about to tear into the security guards. He had to remind himself that they were talking about dogs. There was nothing supernatural about these animals. They were flesh and blood, and they had body heat. They would show up on the night-vision goggles of the guards and on Smith's night-vision video cameras. There would be no surprise attack at Folcroft.

Mark slowed his pacing.

"Is something happening?" Smith asked.

"It's retreating."

"You don't sound certain."

"I am sure. It's moving away. The danger is getting less."

"Do you have a direction, Mark?"

"Sorry. All I can feel is it going away. Not *where* it's going."

"Is Folcroft safe?" Sarah asked.

"I don't know because I don't know if the danger was to the sanitarium in the first place. I don't know what it was." He added gloomily, "I don't even know that was *real*."

THE FOREMAN FOUND his car. He wasn't sure how, but he was back in the town of Rye at the twenty-four hour grocery store. He fell into his car, and attempted to dial out. The phone wouldn't dial. Rather, his fingers wouldn't work the buttons.

As he drove out of Rye he struggled to keep his eyes focused on the road. He was still disoriented. He found himself going too fast or too slow. Wouldn't that be a laugh, after all he had done, to be arrested for speeding in the little burg of Rye, New York?

The mental noise dissipated with every mile he put between himself and Rye, and finally he felt stable enough to dial the phone. He rang Trevor Sharp.

"Now what?" Sharp snapped.

"I have the target for you, Trevor."

"It is about time. What and where?"

"Folcroft Sanitarium in Rye, New York."

"Fine. I know where Rye is. I'll be there in half an hour."

"They'll be waiting for you," the Foreman said.

The Foreman didn't really think Trevor Sharp would be able to neutralize the danger in Folcroft. Whatever the place was, its defenses had to be substantial. Sending in Sharp was simply a method of evaluating the enemy. Sharp would probably be destroyed. The dogs would be lost. But this was no longer about Lou MacMayor or his dogs. This was all about the Foreman's survival.

"WAS IT THE DOGS?" Smith said.

"I don't believe it was," Mark replied.

"Why not?"

"Don't know." Mark's vision seemed shrouded. He had trouble thinking. Why was Smith intent on labeling whatever it was that had come to Folcroft?

"The dogs are the logical explanation, and I don't trust the idea of some new and supernatural or technologically advanced foe tracking us down in the midst of this crisis."

"Whatever the enemy was, it was invisible on the security system," Sarah pointed out.

"It could have been the dogs closing in, then sensing a dangerous level of security. That would have scared them off," Smith said. "The scenario fits the pattern. Time and again, the dogs bypassed guarded facilities to hit facilities where the human security was insufficient."

"Yes," Mark said. He couldn't think of a good argument, but somehow he thought the reasoning was wrong.

But even his own senses insisted that the danger was decreasing. It was almost gone. It was slipping away like a song he was forgetting.

Mark Howard needed sleep. He hunched in the corner of the couch, lulled by the tapping of Smith's keys. Sarah was at Mark's desk, with nothing better to do than keep an eye on the video monitors.

He stirred awake again and again, listening for a break in the cadence of Smith's typing or a hint of alarm from Sarah. There was nothing.

No more danger.

He was safe.

30

Sarah sighed and gave Smith a wave, then pointed at the screen. Smith checked it out. The security patrol was taking liberties with its assigned route again. When the guards wandered far enough off the Folcroft grounds, the video monitoring was incomplete. The guards didn't know that, and Smith wasn't going to let them know that he was watching almost every move they made.

Smith turned up the audio feed from the patrol radios.

"Gary's spotted another wolverine," said one of the men in the field. It was their running joke. Apparently, the man named Gary had once shot at a wolverine breaking into a remote Upstate New York chemical storage yard, only to find he had blasted the head clean off an invading opossum. Smith didn't see the humor in it. It was well known that there were no active wild wolverines in New York State.

It was a long night already, but at least the end was in sight. Remo and Chiun would be back on the ground in the United States soon. They were headed directly to Albany, then to the home of Lou MacMayor. They would cut the head off the snake. They would learn what they could first about the dog teams.

They must be able to find and stop the dog teams. Under MacMayor's control, they were deadly, but without his control, the handlers would probably keep the dog packs operational, to their own ends.

The killing and mayhem could get much worse before it got better.

Would MacMayor be able to provide the intelligence needed to find the dog packs? Smith didn't think so.

MacMayor probably had an underling running the dog show, and whoever it was had done a first-rate job of choreographed mass executions.

Sarah Slate didn't seem to know that the Masters were back home in New York. Just as well. She would want them brought back to Folcroft to defend it against the dogs.

Should they ever come.

THE ONE NAMED Gary Tomoe thought he saw a flicker of heat through the thermal goggles, but it could have been anything. Squirrel. Rabbit. Wolverine. He was never gonna live down that wolverine.

Too small to be a dog. They had the glasses set high, just so they could watch for dogs. The setting made the whole woods look on fire.

He took the opportunity to take a leak, and halfway through it he imagined he heard something moving in the trees. It sounded small again.

He could swear it sounded bigger that a possum, and it did seem close. Still, he couldn't tell what direction it was coming from. He strained his ears as he finished his bathroom break, then pulled the thermal goggles back in place.

At once, the blackness was alive with hot creatures, and they were moving around him, so close he could probably reach out and touch one. He knew what they were. He could quite clearly make out their shapes. Canine bodies. Sure enough, they had the same collars that all the eyewitnesses reported from all the murder scenes.

Gary Tomoe pulled out his radio and it vanished from his hand. His hand was mauled. He felt the torn flesh.

His partner was only twenty paces away, waiting for Gary to report on his latest wolverine sighting. Gary tried to shout to the man, but his throat was clamped shut. A big dog had buried its fangs in his neck. It pierced his flesh even as it crushed his windpipe.

Tomoe need to produce a sound of some kind. He snatched out the knife on his belt and sank it into the dog's chest, scraping over the bones, then he forced it through the rib cage. It was a perfect strike. The dog expired and became a deadweight on top of Tomoe. The grip on his throat relaxed. Gary tried to shout, but he felt air bubbles forming up on his neck. He knew his shouting days were over.

When Harold Smith saw something warm on the screen where Gary the wolverine chaser was known to have gone, he thought nothing of it. He was simultaneously watching the other patrol, which seemed to have stopped to examine something of interest. But then the patrol moved on.

Over by the wolverine chaser, Smith saw the shape of the guard, also on the ground. There was another shape, on top of the guard. Neither of the shapes seemed to be moving.

Smith colored. Was the guard doing what it looked like he was doing? Did he have a young woman meeting him in the woods? That would explain his absence.

But there were still more shapes, many of them, coming together. Even the blur of the thermal images couldn't hide the fact that they were four-legged animals.

"It's them," Sarah Slate said just as Smith was about to.

"Alert Koln," Smith said.

Mark Howard was on his feet as if he had never been asleep. He grabbed a lower drawer of his desk, extracted his CIA handgun and met Smith at the door. Smith was holding his own handgun from earlier days. They closed the door behind them, leaving Sarah Slate alone.

It was as they had planned. Sarah was unskilled with firearms. Mark Howard had CIA weapons training.

Still, Sarah Slate could not believe that she was left alone in this ancient, intimidating sanctuary to simply watch it all happen.

31

Koln's job was to keep the dogs from getting in.

Smith and Howard were there to protect the patients, just in case the dogs did get inside anyway.

Sarah's job was to keep an eye on things.

The animals were gathering in the blackness where the patrol had been. The man who chased wolverines was clearly dead. What of his partner? The man couldn't be seen. The thermal images were blurry and disorienting. The video camera showed her nothing but blackness.

The animals had all gathered in a bright swarm of green waiting for something to happen. Then one of the beasts bolted across the patches of light on the hospital grounds.

The animal had a purpose. Sarah understood the method when she saw it was at a high-voltage shed, which brought power lines into Folcroft. The animal left behind a small package and bolted away. The electrical junction box disintegrated. Folcroft's power supply turned off.

HAROLD SMITH HEARD the blast and checked a nearby window. He could see the damage and had to admire the strategy. The detonation destroyed the electrical power coming into the buildings, as well as the junction boxes that distributed all electricity throughout the facility. So much for the emergency generators. Although the generators were churning to life, their power had nowhere to go.

Self-charging batteries in the emergency lighting system popped on. They would have enough charge to get the hospital through to morning, but it was limited. Only the surgery center had its own source of full-power battery backup.

And, of course, CURE would be unaffected. The battery systems for the computers and other CURE operations were designed to give them full power for weeks.

Another thought occurred to Smith—there was a service door at the electrical junction shed. The dogs were even smarter than he had given them credit for. They had not only turned off the power; they had also opened a locked entrance to Folcroft.

The black shapes were already slinking across the grounds to the smoldering corner of the building.

Smith went to meet them.

He reached the animals too late. Pairs of the powerful-looking animals were loping off in all directions.

Smith felt his hopes sink. Those pairs would be assigned to opening fire doors all around the building.

There was no way they were keeping the whole pack out now, unless Koln could stop them.

Where was Captain Koln?

Smith marched boldly into their presence. When he saw the first four-legged shape approach him, Smith began firing.

The dogs were caught off guard and three of the beasts tumbled to the ground after three bullets had been fired. The others pushed and shoved back outside—and in all directions inside. They went up three hallways.

Smith triggered his weapon into the knot of animals at the broken door, until his weapon was empty and there were no animals left alive. Smith reloaded and went in search of strays.

"Sarah?" he said into the phone walkie-talkie.

"They're in every patient wing," Sarah said despairingly. "They're acting irrationally. I think whoever was controlling them isn't controlling them anymore."

MARK HOWARD wasn't too concerned by the power outage. The emergency lights were more than enough to navigate inside the hospital.

But then he heard the opening of doors and the clatter of animal feet.

Mark Howard had never counted on facing a dog pack with his handgun. The CIA didn't train him for that kind of thing. He didn't even have enough rounds to respond.

All he could do was the best he could do. He strode into the front lobby and began blowing the mutts away.

They were just animals, and he felt bad to do it—but they were there to kill human beings. Folcroft human beings. Mark Howard's human beings.

Several animals turned as one and charged into the gunfire. Mark blasted them, taking them down, until one lucky survivor reached him and leaped onto his chest.

Mark had failed to keep tabs on his bullets. They had to be almost used up. He waited until the dog was on top of him, bearing him to the ground, before he squeezed the trigger one last time.

The weapon fired.

The dog's insides fountained above them as Mark Howard slammed to the linoleum floor.

"MARK!" Sarah shouted, then she grabbed her walkie-talkie.

"Mark! Mark Howard, you get to your feet this instant."

Nothing moved for what seemed like a long time, then the big dog rolled like a log off of Mark Howard and he got to his feet, already reloading. He looked around, spotted the security camera and nodded to Sarah. When he finished loading, he radioed.

"Where are the dogs?"

"Mark," Sarah said miserably, "they're in every patient ward."

In fact, Sarah felt numb staring at the screens. It was a horrible television show, staring at people she knew—being murdered before her eyes.

Then she saw the dogs get into the small wing for long-term residents. Sarah couldn't look and she couldn't look away.

One of the dogs was driven out of a room by an old man in boxer shorts. It was Larry the Lecher Leebok, armed with a cane. All he could do was infuriate the animal. It leaped at him, driving him back into the room.

The dog had a bloody snout when it emerged.

Then came old Mrs. Thorn-Mullet from the next room, hurrying to get to Leebok's aid. They were sweet on each other. And it was Mrs. Thorn-Mullet who had come to Sarah offering the help of all the long-term residents. They wanted to help convince Mark Howard to pop the question to Sarah Slate. It was very sweet.

But now Sarah watched Mrs. Thorn-Mullet risk her life to help Larry Leebok.

The dogs came to get her.

It did occur to Sarah that she was no longer useful to Mark or Harold Smith. She couldn't tell them where the dogs were if the dogs were everywhere.

So why was she just sitting here like a bump on a log?

THERE WERE DEAD PEOPLE in the halls of Folcroft. Their throats ripped open. Their eyes wide in death.

Smith ignored the bodies and concentrated on the living animals. They were everywhere in this wing, and Smith began the grisly work of killing them all.

MARK HOWARD heard the gunshots one floor beneath him, then the tumult on the stairs. He knew what it would be. Smith was driving the animals up.

Mark would drive them right back down again.

He stepped over poor dead Mrs. Gippsland and dragged the stairs doors open. The dogs coming up were in chaos. They never expected Mark.

He laid waste to them.

SARAH SLATE could tell where the others were by their gunfire. She knew the third-floor wing had no one to protect it.

She went there, swinging the fire ax pulled from a wall box. The ax was heavier than she had imagined.

And the dogs were faster.

She cleaved one of the beasts through the head, but the second animal sidestepped the blow and leaped at her. Sarah brought the ax down on its back. The creature staggered away and collapsed.

She spotted a beast nudging its way into one of the hospital rooms, and she followed it. It was sniffing around a woman who was covered in plastic devices. She was chained to the bed by tubes and wires, and she didn't seem strong enough to be afraid.

She was diseased. Of course she was diseased. The dog leaped onto the bed, and Sarah buried her ax head in its flank. It howled and crashed to the floor, then gnashed at Sarah's legs.

She grabbed the ax and tore it out, dragging the

snarling brute behind her, and swung him through the door. The ax head tore free of the wound.

Another dog watched its wounded comrade slide to a halt and decided to have his own go at Sarah. She put her weight behind the door and slammed it on the thing when its front half was inside the room. The door was a heavy piece of work.

The animal was creased up the middle, bones crackling.

Now Sarah heard gunshots coming close. The dogs were fleeing one way and another.

Soon enough, Folcroft was silent again, and at peace.

THE FLIGHT from Scandinavia to New York was one of the longest Remo could remember since his career as a globe-trotting assassin had began. Chiun was locked in himself in a way that made Remo uneasy. He preferred the complaining Chiun who never shut up to the quiet, morose Chiun.

Remo was left alone with his own miserable thoughts. They were selfish, and that made him feel guilty, but he couldn't shake them off. How would he go on without Chiun? How would he survive? How in the world would he keep the Sinanju machine running?

He didn't want to feel this way. He should be talking to Chiun, learning how Chiun felt about this, planning what they would do to fight this disease—whatever disease it was. But how could he reach out to someone who wouldn't respond to anything he said? Everything he said was disregarded.

Chiun simply sat and stared at the wing, and didn't look away for hours at a time. Remo stared ahead, half seeing the mindless, unstoppable stream of commercials displayed silently on the back of the next seat.

Remo thought about how much he hated the mobile telephone service with the dancing tree. He hated tropical vacation destinations. He hated male-impotency medicines and laser eye surgery.

He remembered he knew how to disable the screen and he did, then read the in-flight magazine. There was an article about hot-air ballooning and Remo mulled over how much he hated hot-air balloons. He loathed their careless bright colors and their festive shapes and their idiot baskets. He couldn't stand hot-air ballooners and, above all, he despised, with all his being, the photos of playful hot-air balloons floating about the Eiffel Tower on a sunny spring morning.

He read an article about how carpets were made in Turkey by skilled weavers, and it reminded Remo how much he hated Turkey and their carpets. He read an article about melon farming, which made him angry.

It was a long flight.

And it was a blessed relief to step onto the tarmac in Albany. A car was waiting for them at the rental desk, and Remo drove to a private community that had spectacular views of the foothills of the Catskill Mountains.

"I may not have ever told you this before, but I hate the Catskill Mountains. And I hate gated communities. What's the point? Do they think gang bangers from New York City will drive out into the Albany boondocks to spray-paint their four-car garages?"

Chiun had no opinion to offer.

They left the car, leaped the gate without effort, then strolled through the dark community. It was the darkest hour, too early even for newspaper delivery or for the arrival of the house staff at the huge homes.

The MacMayor house was some sort of European throwback, to a time when mansions were really just castles without the moat. It must have had forty rooms, and the light was on in one of them.

Remo didn't bother to knock or even to use the front door. He followed Chiun up the side of the building.

To one who has trained in the ways of Sinanju, the tiny crevices in a brick wall were like chiseled foot holes. Their fingers clung to the surface and they slipped up the building side. It was virtually effortless, and they stepped onto the balcony of a dark bedroom. The glass doors weren't locked. When they walked through the bedroom they were silent enough to not disturb the middle-aged woman sleeping in the vast bed with her hair ensconced in a protective rubber bag. Also undisturbed was the little dog sleeping next to her. To Remo, it looked like nothing more than a well-coiffed rodent—or three foam balls on wooden sticks.

"Can you believe," he said quietly, "that that thing is even in the same species as the dogs we met, Chiun?"

"I suppose you hate such little dogs?" Chiun asked, speaking for the first time in hours.

"Yeah, I do."

The next room was outfitted like a study for a man of leisure, circa 1900. It was all highly polished wood shelves and furniture, which probably dated back a century. The desk was vast, covered with a dark leather surface. It had award plaques with tasteful messages and small but expensive prize cups from charity golf tournaments.

The man at the desk was making good use of an old-fashioned electric adding machine. He jabbed harshly at the keys, adding to several yards of white tape already curling up on the carpet.

The man was talking to himself, using words like *forecast* and *fiscal* and *accrual*, *P and L*, and *hidden assets*. Remo's mind refused to try to make sense of such babble.

Chiun knew of such things, although he never discussed them with Remo. Chiun understood accounting and fiscal planning. When Remo thought about it, Chiun *should* understand such things. He controlled a fortune in jewels and gold and cash. A Master of Sinanju should have an understanding of what to do with that much money.

How could Remo, an uneducated orphan from the streets of Jersey, deal with the Sinanju legacy of wealth? He couldn't. Not without Chiun. Never without Chiun.

While Remo fretted, Chiun acted upon Mr. Lou MacMayor, drifting behind the desk and peering over his shoulder, as if the computations somehow made sense to him.

MacMayor didn't know Chiun was there until Chiun chose for him to know. He shifted his position, putting a shadow across MacMayor. MacMayor got to his feet and backed into the desk.

"Who the hell are you?"

Chiun would suffer no questions. The ancient Master lifted his hand, so the kimono sleeves fluttered briefly, and then he touched MacMayor on the side of the head. MacMayor was hoisted off the ground and held dangling by his neck, so that the segments of the spine began to strain in their sockets, and MacMayor made a huffing, terrified sound. Just before his brain stem snapped, Chiun moved his hands to the man's shirtfront and drew the corporate giant close.

"Now you face a man such as you do not know," Chiun said. "A man who is entirely outside of your world, where gold is measured in manipulation and intimidation. I will suffer none of your pomposity. Best for you if you will understand this now."

"Don't touch me," MacMayor shouted, trying to get his hands on the desk, on anything.

Chiun pushed MacMayor higher, then let him go, and as he fell Chiun placed his fingers around the man's face.

MacMayor should have been able to run, but he was stiffened by the force of Chiun's finger on the nerves near his temple and ear. MacMayor tried to shove Chiun away, and Chiun exerted more pressure with his probing fingers.

MacMayor opened his mouth, his eyes losing their focus.

"Your horror will go on and you will suffer as only an enemy of Sinanju can suffer. Your only relief or hope comes from he who delivers this pain to you. I tell you again, you will cast away your pomposity and bluster."

MacMayor nodded. Chiun threw him away and the insurance man flopped into his leather chair, which rumbled across the carpet until it banged into the wall. MacMayor was limp in the chair.

"So, talk," Remo said.

MacMayor was startled. He hadn't even known Remo was there. "I'll talk. Whatever you want to know. Please don't kill me."

"Sorry. Your time is up, MacMayor. We know that you're the one behind the dog attacks. You paid for the breeding and training. Peter Oglee told us all about it."

"Ohly," Chiun corrected.

"Ohly," Remo said. "He told us everything he knew. He named you."

"He'll pay," MacMayor snarled.

"Too late, " Remo said.

"I see. Now you'll kill me, too. Why should I tell you anything?"

"Not a wise plan."

"As long as I don't tell you what you need to know, you won't kill me," MacMayor said. "Why should I say a word?"

Before Remo could respond, Chiun stepped up onto the leather arms of MacMayor's chair, inserting his fingernails into the flesh on either side of MacMayor's throat.

It was a Sinanju pain technique—and it was quite extreme, like putting hot nails directly in the human nerves, but in two places simultaneously. It could erase a man's mind, that kind of anguish.

Chiun was apparently in no mood to dicker around. He extracted his fingernails and MacMayor rolled his head onto one shoulder, then the other, eyes blank and empty, and Remo thought Chiun had pushed the man too far.

"You underestimate my state of mind," Chiun informed MacMayor in a singsong that was almost childlike—and that made it all the more chilling. "Do you wish to extend a life that is capable of sustaining pain such as you had just known? Have mercy upon yourself."

"Have mercy." MacMayor burbled.

"Tell us the names of who runs your scheme. Where can we find these men? Where are the dogs?"

Remo was surprised when MacMayor laughed harshly. "I will tell you everything, and then you can kill me, and you will find the dogs and end it all. But you will never find the one who runs the operation. It is the Foreman. The Foreman can never be caught."

"Let us worry about that, " Remo said. "Just tell us where to find him."

"I do not know where to find him. I have never known where he is. I only met him personally one time. He organizes attacks from coast to coast, he puts in place handlers for the dogs, and it is always done anonymously. I don't even know his name."

MacMayor was rambling.

"Maybe he is in New York," MacMayor suggested. "He has handled some of the New York attacks personally."

Remo looked at Chiun. Chiun, for the first time in hours, acknowledged Remo.

"What are the targets in New York?" Remo asked.

"We have five hundred targets. That's part of the Foreman's genius. He plans multiple targets, and then strikes at the target that is most vulnerable at the moment he strikes. I'm telling you, he never gets caught."

"Give me the list of targets," Remo insisted.

"You think I would keep a list here?"

"Mind if I use your phone?" Remo said.

REMO DIALED the old-fashioned phone on the desk, and asked for information for Ocracoke, North Carolina. He demanded to be connected to Will Takers T-Shirt Emporium. The operator connected him and for the first time, Remo was hoping that he would be engaged in an idiot conversation with the artificially created William Taker, proprietor of the fictional Fourth-Largest T-Shirt Shop in Ocracoke.

But a mechanical voice told him that the number he was calling was no longer in service.

"I must have been connected to the wrong T-shirt shop," Remo said.

"That is likely," Chiun agreed.

"Smitty always answers the phone," Remo said.

"Of course," Chiun said.

Remo called information again and had himself connected directly to the switchboard at Folcroft. If Smith found out he was calling the place directly, he'd shit a brick.

The switchboard didn't answer.

It was as if the whole Sanitarium was closed for business.

"It is early in the morning, Remo. It is likely that the Emperor keeps no operator on staff overnight to field calls."

"Probably." Remo said. He called information again and asked for the police station in Rye, New York.

"Officer Magio," answered a harried woman.

"I'm calling about Folcroft. I've got an uncle who's a patient there."

She should have said, "Yeah? And?"

Instead she said, "Look, I'm sorry, but we don't have any information here. We're still trying to figure out what happened. All I can tell you is we got ambulances going to at least three hospitals in the vicinity. Your uncle could be at any one of them. Or he might be perfectly fine. Not everybody was killed."

Not everybody was killed?

Remo put the phone in its cradle and impulsively whacked the adding machine. It turned to junk and sailed off the desk.

As Chiun stepped down, the adding machine embedded itself deep in Lou MacMayor's front, crushing his skull and sending bone splinters into his gray matter.

32

It didn't take long to clean up the mess. Repair the power junction box. Bleach away the bloodstains. Haul away the carcasses.

Folcroft was a little emptier than it had been, but it was just one hospital. How many dog attacks had there been? A hundred? And how many dead? Nobody seemed to know for sure, but they knew that Folcroft Sanitarium, with just thirty-four casualties, wasn't worth headline coverage.

Because on the same day, the biggest attack so far occurred in a seaside retirement village in Port Wroclaw, Florida. It was a perfect siege that lasted hours, with casualties four times that of Folcroft.

At his mansion outside Albany, New York, the president of the Institute of Nationalized Humane Health Care was found murdered in his home.

Anonymous tips to the nationwide newspaper *Today in the U.S.A.* claimed Lou MacMayor, the INHHC man, was the mastermind behind the dog attacks. There was a plot that involved insurance profits and the acquisition of a second insurance company, Lunar. It all got complicated from there, so the newspaper buried the details at the bottom of the story.

Remo Williams found himself returning, alone, to Utah.

He hated Utah.

PHILIP SCHWARTZCHILD could still be a lawyer if he wanted to. He had all the identification and he had a nice briefcase.

He signed in to see Jack Cartfeld. He gave Cartfeld the paperwork. "Message from the Foreman," he told Cartfeld. "Read it carefully."

The ink on the middle pages was toxic. Cartfeld would be dead before dinner.

He drove away from the Salt Lake City lockup and loosened his tie, tossing it over his shoulder.

"Hey, do you mind?"

He almost steered off the road. As the intruder slipped into the front seat, Schwartzchild grabbed the gun he kept under the seat for emergencies. He pointed it at his intruder—who took it away.

"Who the fuck are you?"

"Remo Brominated. Here's your gun."

Remo Brominated handed him his gun in several pieces.

"You can't take it on an airplane anyway," Remo said. "We're going to New York, you and me. Along the way, we'll talk about somebody named the Foreman. I assume he is a friend of yours."

A GUARD with rubber gloves snatched the paperwork from Jack Cartfeld before he even put his manacles back on.

"That's from my lawyer. You can't take that!"

The guard slipped it into a heavy plastic envelope. "Believe me, Jack, you don't want it."

THERE WERE NO further dog attacks. The dogs were dead. The dog handlers were dead as well.

In Arizona, in Florida, in California, across the country, packs of slain Swedish elkhounds were found, along with their handlers. Whoever was cleaning up the mess was cleaning it thoroughly.

Covering their tracks.

THERE WAS ONLY ONE puzzle piece missing, and it was Philip Schwartzchild. The man had literally vanished minutes after his attempted poisoning of Jack Cartfeld. Cartfeld had the poisoned papers taken away before they could harm him. The law knew about the assassination attempt. The law, it stood to reason, had Schwartzchild, and they would use him to get to the Foreman.

The Foreman decided to let them.

It was time for another identity. This one had become too well known and too dangerous. The Foreman must die so that this new identity could be born.

The Foreman knew how it would begin. It would begin with Philip Schwartzchild. Schwartzchild could contact him. Schwartzchild was the only man alive who still knew how to contact the Foreman directly.

Let Schwartzchild come.

"HEY, FOREMAN, it's me," Schwartzchild said when he finally did call. "I need your help. I need to get broken out of here."

"Where is here?"

"Here" was Pangeville, Utah. Schwartzchild was in lockup for thirty days for DUI. He said. "Any day they're going to link me to everything you been doing. It is in your interest and mine that I get the fuck out of here, now."

The Foreman was quiet, then said, "Agreed. I'll handle it personally."

Then the pain began.

It was the pain he had known in New Zealand. It was the Folcroft pain.

The setup wasn't just a federal sting—it was them. They knew about him and they wanted him.

PANGEVILLE, UTAH was on fire to the Foreman. The danger was everywhere, but it radiated from a hotel a half mile outside town. They were waiting for him there. The Foreman spent an hour driving up and down the main street, trying to make sense of the danger.

It was everywhere, pockets of it, but the real danger still came from the hotel.

He was confused. His senses were addled. But he had to see this through. Especially now that they knew about him, they would never stop trying to find him. The Foreman must die, so that he could live.

He had his patsy with him, a stupid man who would do anything for a hundred dollars.

Drive a car around for a hundred bucks? Sure.

The Foreman parked at the courthouse and went inside.

The danger from the hotel seemed to wash out everything, but it looked like any other sleepy small-town police station. When he asked to see Philip Schwartzchild, nobody thought anything of it. They took him in back.

Whatever the trap was, it hadn't sprung yet. Were the cops going to alert the ones in the hotel? Would he start to feel their danger coming closer?

He briefed Schwartzchild on the timing. It was a tiny jail, definitely low-tech. The breakout would be a piece of cake. The breakout didn't even matter. It was just a part of the game.

The Foreman left and came back with his shotgun. No danger. The cops ran out the back entrance like idiots. No danger. Schwartzchild was removed from his cage and led out the back. Not much danger, but the cops were getting in their cars to set up a roadblock.

The Foreman's patsy was blissfully ignorant, and was surprised when Schwartzchild was shoved in the rear seat. The Foreman knocked Schwartzchild on the head. Schwartzchild was out cold. The Foreman buckled him in.

"Is that the groom?" the patsy asked.

The Foreman told the patsy this was all a bachelor-party prank, and he apparently believed it. "That's him. Remember, drive slow out of town. Slow."

"Whatever."

The pseudo-Foreman drove slowly out of town.

The shriek of danger from the hotel increased. The cops had finally got the word out.

The cops surrounded the Foreman's car. The patsy did an admirable job. He thought the cops were part of the gag.

The danger escalated and the Foreman watched, terrified, as a human being became visible on the road. He was running like a cheetah, impossibly fast, and he was going to be upon the Foreman's car in a matter of seconds.

Time to end it. The Foreman hit the remote. A bunch of handgun blanks fired from the trunk of the Foreman's car. The cops didn't know they were blanks.

They returned fire.

They nailed Schwartzchild.

The patsy tried to surrender, but the Foreman triggered a volley of blank rounds and the cops thought they were being ambushed. They lost their cool and emptied their weapons at the Foreman's car.

The patsy Foreman took two rounds in the head.

Then the danger diminished. The cops closed in on the car. The stranger examined the aftermath. He seemed annoyed.

The Foreman studied him from afar, until the man seemed to sense it. He looked up at the Foreman.

The danger alarm shrilled.

The Foreman strolled in the crowd of interested onlookers, acting casual but trembling. When he looked at the scene again, the stranger was walking away. The virulent danger he represented leveled off.

The stranger strolled up the street, then entered the hotel.

It was over.

THE FOREMEN, and anyone who might recognize him, was dead. Even the stranger who had terrified him in New Zealand, who inhabited the terrible Folcroft Sanitarium, had ceased to be a potent danger to him.

It was time to move on.

"SMITTY. It's me."

"Yes, Remo?"

"The cops killed the Foreman."

"How did it all go down?"

"Just like we planned, at first. He tried busting out Philip Schwartzchild, but he did a piss-poor job of it. Got the cops all riled up. Started shooting at them. They started shooting at him. He missed, they didn't. I have to tell you, the Foreman wasn't as impressive as I had come to expect."

"It seems not," Smith agreed.

"I'm out of this state. Forever, I hope."

"Fine." Smith hung up. It was as warm a goodbye as you were likely to get from Harold Smith.

Remo checked out and drove back to Salt Lake City, eager to get home to Chiun.

THROUGH BINOCULARS, Mark Howard watched Remo's rental car leave town in the opposite direction.

"All clear."

"Good," said Harold Smith on the phone. "Proceed."

Mark Howard hit the gas and drove through town like a maniac, then floored the gas pedal on the state highway.

"How are you, Mark?" Smith asked.

"A little tense."

"A little."

"Very tense!"

"You getting close?"

"I'm getting closer."

"Keep it together, Mark." It was the most encouraging thing Smith knew how to say.

THE FOREMAN looked back over both shoulders. What now? He took the car to eighty, then ninety. Whatever the danger was, it was closing in fast. It was strange and familiar at once. Christ, *what now?*

The sedan appeared in his rearview mirror, going like a drag racer. Dust billowed behind it. His rental car was maxing out at 120 miles per hour and the other car was still gaining on him. It was the middle of nowhere and there were no other roads. Driving his rental into the hard-packed dirt was suicide. He was trapped.

Son of a bitch, they were going to get him!

But they didn't have him yet. He kept the gas floored and tried not to shout when the shrill warning magnified. It was like the painful warning that had come from Maureen, the warning that went on and on until she was dead. But he couldn't kill whatever it was in the car behind him. Did that mean he had to kill himself? He had to do something because the alarm was unbearable.

His car died.

He couldn't believe it. The engine sputtered. The dashboard went blank. The steering stopped working. The brakes would only operate if he stood on them with all his weight. He decelerated into the rutted shoulder and the car jostled and bounced before skidding to a halt. *They* had done did this—an electrostatic discharge on the road or an electromagnetic pulse or whatever.

The pursuit car slowed on the empty highway and closed in on him, having no trouble bounding on the rocky earth. The Foreman knew what it was like to have rusty barbs dragged through his flesh—the warning was just like that, but they kept dragging and dragging.

Oh God—another warning alarm from behind him. Another car coming. It was a fucking limousine that braked broadside on the highway with white smoke coming from the tires. The driver leaped out. Just a girl. A young, brown-haired girl in a chauffeur's visor and formal jacket.

"Get in!"

"Who are you?"

"What does it matter? Just get in!"

The fast car came barreling down on the Foreman. He tried to dive out of its path, but the warning was so intense it practically inebriated him and all he managed was to tumble limply to one side. He could barely stand. He couldn't think and more than anything he needed to *think!*

The car skidded to a halt, the window rolled down and the driver aimed a black shotgun at the Foreman.

The man's face was red, as if he was in extreme distress. The man made a ghastly sound in his throat, then squeezed the shotgun trigger. The Foreman fell flat, but the twin buckshot blasts ripped at his back, tearing his shirt and flaying his skin.

"Get in the car, asshole!" the limo driver shouted.

The Foreman had two bad choices. Stay out here and be killed by the shotgunner, or get in the limo with the young girl.

Whatever she was, she was dangerous—but less dangerous than the shotgunner.

He cracked the weapon and thumbed in two fresh shells, then snapped the barrel into place.

The Foreman scrambled for the limo, yanked on the door, threw himself inside. He slammed the door behind him just as buckshot rained on the windows.

The shotgunner slammed his weapon down and grabbed his head, staggering into to the side of his sedan, then clambered inside and swerved away.

The old dangers were gone.

It was replaced by a steady drone of something that was strange and new and worse.

The girl slid behind the wheel and took the radio.

"How you feeling?"

"Awful," answered a strained male voice. "But it's getting better every second."

"You dropped your shotgun."

"Mind getting it for me?"

"Sure, sweetie."

The Foreman started yanking on the handles and banging on the windows. He laid on the seat and kicked on the driver's glass divider. The glass didn't break. It didn't even rattle.

"The Foreman's getting nervous," Sarah Slate said to Mark. "I'll call Smith."

"Who are you? Let me go!"

"I take it your prisoner is secure," Harold W. Smith said sourly.

"I've got him," Sarah said. "But what am I going to do with him?"

"I have a place," Smith said.

"Not Folcroft, I hope,'" she said. "Mark can't stand being near the guy."

"Folcroft?" the Foreman cried. "You're from Folcroft? Who are you?"

Sarah closed the audio connection. The Foreman became totally silent, like a television show with the volume turned down.

It was silent on the other side of the glass, as well.

The Foreman was utterly isolated. He couldn't hear Sarah Slate, and he couldn't touch anything in the outside world.

"No, let me go. You don't understand. I can't stand this."

It was true. He couldn't stand it. It was torture, this new buzzing warning, unlike anything he had ever experienced, that went on and on. The sensation maddened him.

It was the sensation of imprisonment.

33

Remo found Chiun in their rooms at Folcroft.

Never had the place seemed so depressing. He felt surrounded by the ghosts of all the Folcroft victims—and he was here, now, with the ill Chiun.

The old Master was sitting with a fresh sprig of Sinanju chrysanthemums and the neatly rolled newspaper clipping.

Remo sat across from Chiun and unrolled the paper.

"'An Ancient Tradition Is The Latest Thing In Self-Defense. Lincoln High School Students Go One Step Beyond Karate To Learn The Way Of The Ultimate Fast Wrestling Fist. Wearing their distinctive *gis*—karate robes—and standing tall with a new sense of pride, it's easy to spot a practitioner of the latest martial art. Called t'ai shou jiao ch'uan or The Way Of The Ultimate Fast Wrestling Fist, this ancient art has taken off at Lincoln High School and throughout Baltimore…'"

"I was pretty proud of myself for this," Remo said. "I thought we were really gonna be able to rub Smitty's nose in it. We could point to this article and tell him you and your kimonos were just as part of the latest fashion trend. No way he can tell you to lose the robes."

Remo nodded. Chiun was actually smiling as he stroked the threads of his beard.

"I guess it seems sort of trivial at this point."

"Not at all, my son. I appreciate this more than you know. It was clever."

"Clever?" The old man was facing some sort of a terminal illness, and he was in a superhappy mood, buoyant as a schoolboy. Remo knew Chiun wasn't mocking him, but he was at a loss to explain it.

"I think now would be the perfect time to present our good news to the emperor," Chiun added happily.

Remo was astonished. "What?"

Chiun shook his head and held up the clipping. "*This* news."

"Oh. Okay."

They stood up and walked to the door.

"And," Chiun said, "we shall rub his face in it together."

A long-lost sword.

A willing heroine.

A quest to protect humanity's
sacred secrets from falling
into the wrong hands.

ROGUE ANGEL™

Her destiny will be revealed.

July 2006.

GOLD
EAGLE®